OTHER MEN'S HORSES

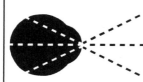

This Large Print Book carries the
Seal of Approval of N.A.V.H.

OTHER MEN'S HORSES

ELMER KELTON

THORNDIKE PRESS
A part of Gale, Cengage Learning

GALE
CENGAGE Learning™

Detroit • New York • San Francisco • New Haven, Conn • Waterville, Maine • London

GALE
CENGAGE Learning

LIBRARY OF CONGRESS CATALOGING-IN-PUBLICATION DATA

Kelton, Elmer.
   Other men's horses / by Elmer Kelton.
     p. cm. — (Thorndike Press large print western)
   ISBN-13: 978-1-4104-2235-4 (alk. paper)
   ISBN-10: 1-4104-2235-6 (alk. paper)
   1. Texas Rangers—Fiction. 2. Large type books. I. Title.
PS3561.E3975O87 2010
813'.54—dc22   2009048785

Published in 2010 by arrangement with Tom Doherty Associates, LLC.

For Glenn Dromgoole
and Ron Anderson

CHAPTER 1

Cletus Slocum stole Donley Bannister's best horse and crippled it. Now Slocum lay facedown in the dirt, as dead as he would ever be.

Bannister was known locally as a horse trader, finding them in faraway places and bringing them to the West Texas hill country for sale. He could recognize a good horse as far as he could see it, and spot a blemish from fifty yards. He loved horses as other men might love a woman. The blue roan, he thought, was one of the best he had ever owned.

The four Slocum brothers — three now that Cletus was gone — also had a reputation for knowing good horses, stealing them when and where they could. They had gone unpunished because law officers had not been able to bring a strong case to court. It was difficult to persuade a witness to testify against one of them, knowing that to do so was to invite an unfriendly visit by the other three.

Bannister did not wait for the law to act. He pursued Cletus across the rockiest ground along the South Llano River. He caught up with him when the roan stumbled and went down, breaking a foreleg. While witness Willy Pegg trembled and begged for his own life, Bannister put an end to Cletus's dubious career. He felt no remorse over the man, but his heart was heavy with pain when he shot the crippled roan.

Riding back to Junction, he stopped at a modest frame house he shared with his wife Geneva. While he hastily gathered a few necessities for travel, he told her, "I just killed Cletus Slocum. It was a fair fight. You stay put here till I come back. Don't try to follow me."

Thoughtfully, he left her some money. Not so thoughtfully, he neglected to kiss her good-bye before he rode away. Afterward, though she often thought about that oversight, he never did.

Andy Pickard stood in the open boxcar door, feeling through his boots the rumble of steel wheels against the rails. Wisps of coal smoke burned his eyes as he watched West Texas hills roll by at more than thirty miles an hour. He wished he were heading home. Instead, the train was carrying him farther and farther from his new wife.

He sometimes wondered why he had decided to rejoin the Texas Rangers. There were less stressful ways to make a living. He had had more than enough of farming, walking all day behind a plow and a mule, taking verbal abuse from a cranky brother-in-law. He wanted to raise livestock, for that was something he could do on horseback, but a decent start in ranching required money. He did not yet have enough. Rangering seemed his best option for now. He regretted that it often took him too far and kept him too long away from Bethel.

He turned to a stall where his black horse stood tied, feet braced against the pull of the train's forward motion. He said, "At least you're gettin' to ride most of the way. Bannister's horse had to take it all on foot."

The Ranger office in Fort Worth had received a wire saying that Donley Bannister was seen in the West Texas railroad town of Colorado City. Andy happened to be in Fort Worth to deliver a prisoner. He had been dispatched to apprehend Bannister and bring him back to stand trial for shooting Cletus Slocum.

At least the disagreement had been about

something worthwhile, Andy thought. Too many men had been killed quarreling over such trivial matters as whiskey, cards, or dance hall girls. A horse was a different matter. A good horse might well justify a righteous killing.

Extension of rails across the state had given Ranger efficiency a strong boost in these early 1880s. No matter how fast he traveled, a fugitive could not outrun the telegraph, and now he had to contend with the railroad as well. Rangers could put their horses on a train and cover distances in hours that would otherwise keep them in the saddle for days. They could move ahead of a fleeing suspect and cut him off or at least rush to wherever he had last been seen and shorten his lead. That was Andy's mission on this trip.

To the best of his knowledge, he had never seen Bannister. He had a physical description of the man, however, in the handwritten fugitive book he carried in his pocket: tall, husky, with pale gray eyes and a small scar on his left cheekbone where a mule had once kicked him. Probably a bit crazy too. A kick in the head could do that to a man, and nothing could kick harder than a mule.

The train chugged to a stop at a siding beside a tower upon which stood a large wooden water tank. Andy climbed down to stretch his aching legs and beheld the largest windmill he had ever seen. He judged its wheel to be twenty feet across, maybe twenty-five. Locomotive boilers required a lot of water to produce steam. The windmill, vital to the railroads, had also done much to open up large areas of West Texas for settlement by farmers and ranchers. They provided water where nature had neglected to do so.

He had recently placed a smaller mill over a hand-dug well on acreage he had bought in the hill country west of San Antonio. Someday, when he had saved enough, he planned to resign from the Rangers again, build a house beside the windmill and move there with Bethel. It was a good grass country for cattle, and several people had brought in sheep. Andy had no prejudice against woolies. They seemed to thrive so long as their owner could fight off the wolves and coyotes and bobcats. These had a strong taste for lambs.

The thought of Bethel brought both warmth and pain. Stationed in a Ranger camp near a former army post town, Fort McKavett, he had rented a small house at the edge of the settlement. There she was able to grow a garden and raise chickens.

He had spent nights with her when he was not away on duty. He realized this was not the customary way for a young couple to begin married life. Too often he had to kiss her good-bye and ride away without knowing when he might return. Looking back, which he always did, he would see her small figure standing there, waving, watching him until he was beyond sight.

He had warned her at the beginning that as a Ranger's wife she would spend many days and nights alone, waiting, wishing. But he wondered if she had fully understood how often she would have only a flock of chickens and a brown dog for company. He even wondered if he should have put off marriage until he could provide her with a more stable home. But both had waited a long time already, almost beyond endurance.

He hoped he could capture the fugitive quickly and get back to her. A dispatch had indicated that Bannister could probably make a strong case for self-defense if he had stayed in Junction and faced trial. But he had chosen to run, so he was playing hell with Andy's married life.

The train's black-uniformed conductor walked down the line after seeing that the boiler was properly filled. Pulling out his

12

pocket watch and checking the time, he said, "We'll be pullin' out in a couple of minutes, Ranger. Ought to be in Colorado City in an hour."

"Good," Andy said. "The sooner there, the sooner I can get my business done and go home."

The conductor gave him a quizzical smile. "I'll bet you've got a young wife waitin' for you. That'd account for your constipated look."

Andy's face warmed. "I didn't know it showed."

"I know the signs from personal experience. Seems like I've been married since I was six years old."

Andy asked, "How do you handle it, bein' away from home so much?"

"Home these days is whatever train I happen to be on."

"You don't miss bein' with your wife?"

Thoughtfully the conductor said, "Son, the fire burns hot when you first get married, but then it cools down. There's times you start feelin' crowded. You look for a reason to get away for a while, and she's just as anxious to be shed of you."

"It won't be that way for me and Bethel."

"It will. Nature works it out like that to keep married couples from killin' one another." The conductor frowned. "You ain't told me, but I suspect you're after a man. Is he dangerous?"

"I just know that he's charged with murder."

"Then he's dangerous. And you're fixin' to tackle him by yourself?"

"He's just one man."

"If I was you, and I had a young wife waitin' for me, I'd find a safer way to make a livin'."

Bethel had not said much directly, but Andy had sensed that she felt as the conductor did. One of these days, when he could afford to buy more land and the livestock to put on it . . .

The train slowly picked up speed. Andy watched the telephone poles going by. A line had been strung alongside the tracks all the way from Fort Worth. It didn't seem logical to him that progress could advance much farther. Just about everything conceivable had already been invented.

Colorado City was mostly new, an offspring of the railroad as it had advanced westward. When the boxcar was centered in front of a loading chute, Andy led the black horse down the ramp to a water trough. A little Mexican packmule followed like a faithful dog. After both animals had drunk their fill, Andy rode up the street toward the courthouse. It was customary for a Ranger to call upon local peace officers unless there was a reason not to, such as a suspicion that they were in league with the lawbreakers. That was not the case here.

Andy introduced himself to the sheriff, a middle-aged man with graying hair and an expanding waistline. The sheriff said, "I got a call that you'd be on the train. I thought they'd send an older, more experienced man."

"I'm old enough. What's the latest about Donley Bannister?"

"Nothin' much more than what I wired your captain. I got wind that he'd spent time here playin' poker and puttin' away whiskey. Me and my deputy found his tracks and trailed him to the county line. That's as far as we had jurisdiction. I can take you to where we turned back."

"I'd be much obliged."

"I hope you're a good tracker."

"Not especially."

"Bannister don't seem to be tryin' hard to cover his trail. He likely figures he's already outrun whoever may be after him. I doubt he considered how hard it is to outrun a train."

Standing at a window, Andy let his gaze

drift wishfully to a sign that said *Restaurant. Where the elite eat.*

He was not sure what *elite* meant. Schooling had been limited by a tendency toward fighting more than studying when other boys offered offense, which they often did. He had been taken by Indians when he was small and lived with them several years before being thrown back into the white world. Fellow students made fun of his Indian ways and his awkward attempt to relearn the language of his people.

Even yet, a Comanche word occasionally popped out of his mouth. Moreover, he sometimes had a flash of sixth sense about situations and events beyond his sight. To the Indians, these were visions; to Andy, they were a mystery. He had no control over them. They came unbidden. Often when he would have welcomed one, it would not come at all.

He had such a hunch now about Bannister. He felt it likely that the man was no longer in a hurry, probably assuming he had traveled far enough to be safe. Otherwise he would not have tarried in this town to seek after pleasure.

The sheriff said, "Why don't you walk over yonder and grab you some breakfast while I go saddle my horse?"

16

Andy said, "Suits me fine. There wasn't anything to eat on the train."

The sheriff started to turn away, then stopped. "See that dispeptic-lookin' gent goin' into the café? That's Luther Fleet. He's a tinhorn gambler. I heard that Bannister and him have done business together. He might tell you somethin'."

Andy said, "Thanks. I'll go talk to him."

Fleet sat at a table alone. Andy sized him up at a glance. Restless eyes and slick, long-fingered hands told him this was not a man to whom he would trust his horse or even his dog.

Andy said, "Mind if I sit down with you?"

The answer was a growl. "There's other tables."

"But you're sittin' at this one, and I want to talk with you."

"If you're lookin' for a game, it's a little early in the day."

"I'm a Ranger." Andy touched the badge on his shirt, handmade from a Mexican silver five-peso coin. "I'm lookin' for a man named Donley Bannister. I hear you and him are friends."

The gambler's eyes flashed a negative reaction. He said, "Friend? Not hardly. Him and me have done a little business together. I always came out on the short end."

17

"Do you know where he went when he left here?"

"He didn't share his plans with me, and I didn't watch him leave town. He could've gone north, south, east, or west. Maybe even straight up. Why don't you try straight up?"

Andy moved in closer and noticed a small bruise on Fleet's left cheek. It looked fresh. He asked, "By any chance, was that blue spot a gift from Bannister?"

The gambler involuntarily brought his hand up to the bruise and flinched. "He claimed I've been owin' him money."

"Do you?"

"Go to hell."

The man's attitude was enough to sour Andy's appetite, strong though it was. He moved to another table and sat with his back to Fleet.

As Andy and the sheriff rode out from town, the lawman asked, "Did you have any luck?"

"I'd've learned more talkin' to a fence post."

"Fleet's pretty good at fleecin' cowboys and railroad hands, but he's not good enough to go up against the real professionals. He'll welsh on the wrong one someday and get his lights blown out. I'd volunteer to sing at his funeral."

"I might be inclined to join you, if I could sing."

The tracks led north. The sheriff said, "Ain't a lot in that direction, not for a long ways. Ranches and maybe a mustanger's camp or two. Hunters killed out the buffalo. Indians stay pretty much to the reservations anymore, where they belong. There's no way of mixin' the white race with the red. Too many differences."

Andy knew the differences all too well, for he had lived in both camps. He said, "The Indians were just fightin' for their land."

"But before it was theirs, they took it away from somebody else. This land has been fought over by first one and then another since God finished it and took the seventh day to rest."

Andy knew the futility of arguing the Indians' point of view. He understood the white view as well. The dilemma was too much for a man in his late twenties to reconcile. Old men had difficulty with it, too.

After a time the sheriff reined up and made a sweeping motion with his hand. He said, "This is the county line, as near as I can figure it. From here it's for you to catch up or to give up."

"Rangers don't give up easy."

"I've seen some that wished they had. Don't take it for granted that your outlaw will surrender peaceably. Been many a good rider thrown off by a gentle horse."

Andy was unsure about his ability to stay on Bannister's trail to its end. He had known Indians who could follow anything that walked, but the tracking trait had eluded him despite his best intentions. Perhaps the fugitive would become complacent and stop somewhere long enough for Andy to catch up.

Toward dusk he smelled wood smoke and spotted a chuck wagon camp a short distance ahead. He judged that it was about the time for a cowboy crew to be eating supper. He rode warily toward the fire, knowing the cook would object to dust being stirred up near his wagon. The men were scattered about, squatting on their heels or sitting on bedrolls, plates in their hands. They paused in their meal to stare at him with curiosity.

A little man in a frazzled old derby hat walked toward him, a grease-stained sack tied around his soft belly. He gave Andy's badge a quick study, then gestured toward a line of pots and Dutch ovens near the fire. He said, "Tie up your animals and come get yourself some supper. What's left, I'll have to throw out anyhow."

"Thanks." Walking in, Andy gave each upturned face a glance. He tried to picture Bannister from the brief description that had been given him. He had been told more about the dun horse than about the man who rode it. He saw no one who unmistakably fitted his preconception, but he remained uneasy. A couple of men quietly arose and walked away from camp.

"You're in luck," the cook said. "Boss brought us some dried apples. Got cobbler pie for you to finish off with. Help yourself."

Andy held the tin plate in his left hand, leaving his right hand free in case of a challenge. None came, and he loosened up. He said, "That coffee sure smells good." The cook poured a cupful for him. Andy seated himself on a tarp-covered bedroll and attacked the supper. Rangers on a trail missed many meals. They seldom passed up an opportunity to eat.

He could feel the men's gaze fastened upon him, a few with suspicion, one with open hostility. Likely as not, some were wanted by the law for one thing or another. He decided the best course was to lay his cards on the table. He said, "I'm lookin' for a large man ridin' a big dun horse with a TR brand on its left hip."

21

No one spoke at first. The cook broke the silence. "May I make so bold as to ask what he's wanted for?"

"Seems like there was a disagreement over a horse. The other man lost the argument."

"Permanent?"

"Real permanent."

The cook shook his head. "I always said there's three things it's dangerous to argue over: politics, religion, and horses. Women would make four."

Andy asked, "Has anybody here seen such a man?" He looked from one face to another but saw no sign that anyone would answer. Cowboys as a rule were slow to give a man away unless outraged by what he had done. Especially if they had done the same thing themselves, or had been tempted to.

The cook ventured, "Maybe the other man was a son of a bitch that needed killin'."

Andy said, "Just the same, I've been assigned to bring Donley Bannister in. The rest is up to the court."

The cook frowned. "Last time I was in court, the judge gave me ten days just for singin' too loud on Sunday mornin'. He counted the money I had in my pocket and fined me all of it. Ain't trusted ary court since."

22

Andy recognized that he would not get help here, even if the men in camp *had* seen Bannister. He said, "I'm much obliged for the supper."

The cook said, "It'll soon be too dark to ride. You're welcome to stay all night. You can start off in the mornin' with a good breakfast in your belly."

Andy nodded his thanks. He wondered if the offer was made to allow Bannister more time to travel.

The cook said, "Look, Ranger, we've got nothin' against you. You seem like a nice young feller, but we've got nothin' against the man you're after, either. We don't poke our nose in when we've got no dog in the fight."

Andy understood the reticence. He said, "A man's got to follow his own leanin's."

He had no specific reason to distrust the cowboys, though it was possible that one wanted by the law might fear Andy had come for him and do something drastic.

He slept fitfully, hearing everything that moved. When the cook arose to begin preparing breakfast, Andy rolled up his blanket and packed the compliant little mule. He was waiting with a cup of water when the coffee began to boil. He poured the water in to sink the grounds, then dipped into the pot. He could barely see first light in the east.

Shortly the cook shouted, "Chuck!" and the cowboys began rolling out of their blankets. Andy took a plate from the chuck box and filled it with fried steak, water-and-flour gravy, and steaming high-rise sour-dough biscuits that burned his fingers. He still sensed the men watching him in silence, looking away if he glanced toward them. He could probably find one or two in his fugitive book, but he considered it an abuse of hospitality to eat at a man's wagon and then take him into custody.

He spent more than an hour finding what he thought were probably Bannister's tracks. The roundup crew and their horses had compromised everything within a mile or more of camp. But he finally came across the print of an iron shoe that seemed to be the same one he had followed yesterday. He lost it a while, then found it again. He wished he had Choctaw John with him. A half-breed, John seemed able to track a hawk in flight. But his home was far away. Besides, the state in its frugality disliked paying for outside help. It assumed the Rangers it hired should be able to do anything the situation called for. Sometimes they fell short, however. Andy had, several times. He had already found some of his limitations and knew there must be others yet undiscovered.

He almost overlooked the dugout. It appeared to be some ranch's line camp, cut into an embankment and roofed with cottonwood limbs covered by a deep layer of dirt. Only the chimney showed above the surface. He saw the smoke first, then several log pens, one with three horses in it. In the last glow of the late-afternoon sun he rode close enough to examine the animals. His nerves tightened as he saw that one was a big dun with a TR brand on its left hip. Exactly the description he had been given.

Dismounting, he drew his rifle from its scabbard and checked his pistol. He looked about but saw no one outside. Because the dugout was essentially a roofed-over hole in the ground, it was unlikely to have a back door through which a fugitive might escape. He saw one small window beside the wooden door. He circled around so he could approach the door without exposing himself to the window. The glass was so encrusted with smoke and dirt that he doubted anyone could see much through it anyway.

He gripped the rifle firmly, put his shoulder against the door, and pushed hard. He stepped through the opening and shouted, "Hands up!"

Two men sat at a small table, cards spread before them. Andy recognized Bannister from his description. The fugitive froze in surprise, his gray eyes wide. The other man made a grab for a pistol in its holster hanging from a peg in the earthen wall. Andrew tickled the back of the man's neck with the muzzle of the rifle. He said, "You heard me. Raise your hands."

The big man had not moved. He demanded, "What is this? If you've come to rob us, you've picked a damned poor place."

"I'm a Ranger. I've been trailin' you, Donley Bannister."

"Bannister? My name is Smith. John Smith."

"Half the men I ever arrested called themselves John Smith." Andy addressed the other man, who had a face full of brown freckles. "And what's your name?"

"It's John Smith too."

"I'll bet I can find your real name on my fugitive list, and it won't be Smith. I'm takin' you in on general principles till we find out for sure who you are."

"What am I bein' arrested for?"

"Playin' cards on Sunday will be enough

to hold you a while."

"This ain't Sunday."

"How do you know? I don't see a calendar in here."

Andy flinched as cold steel touched the back of his neck. He heard a pistol hammer cock back. A gruff voice said, "Ease that rifle to the floor real slow, or we'll be scrubbin' your brains off of the wall."

Andy felt a paralyzing chill. *What a damnfool thing to do,* he thought. *Stepped into a trap with my eyes wide open.*

The man behind him said, "Lucky thing I went out to pee. I kept low when I seen this feller snoopin' around. Now that we got him, what'll we do with him?"

The freckled one said, "Ain't but one safe thing, Ches. Shoot him and bury him deep enough that he won't even raise up on Judgment Day."

Bannister shook his head. "Now, boys, killin' a Ranger is about the worst thing you can do. The rest of them will trail you plumb to China, if they have to. They'll hang you or shoot you down like a yeller dog."

"Not if they never know what happened to him," the freckled one said.

Bannister argued, "I already got one killin' against me, Speck. He had it comin', but I don't want to answer for another one."

"You don't have to be a part of it. You can ride off and pretend you never seen us."

Bannister looked regretfully at Andy. "Sorry, young feller, but you ought to've rode on by."

Andy knew the other two were serious. He said, "The sheriff knows I came this way, lookin' for you."

Speck said, "But there's nothin' to connect us with this camp. It's been deserted for a while. We just decided to stop here and rest our horses."

Sweat broke out on Andy's forehead. He saw no help in Bannister's face and no mercy in the other two men. They were going to kill him if he didn't do something.

He grasped the edge of the table and quickly tipped it toward Speck, spilling the cards, sending a bottle of whiskey rolling off. In the confusion, he dropped to one knee and grabbed the rifle. He did not get to fire it. A pistol shot reverberated in the small confines of the dugout. His ears felt as if they had exploded. The bullet struck his shoulder and spun him around. The rifle fell to the dirt floor. The heavy smell of burned powder stung his nose.

His shoulder afire, he heard Speck say, "Shoot him again, Ches. You didn't kill him the first time."

Bannister stepped in front of the pair, holding a pistol. "I told you what happens when you kill a Ranger. Be damned if you're goin' to make me a party to it."

Red-faced, Speck glared at him with an air of defiance. Through a haze, however, Andy saw that the larger man had him cowed. Bannister said, "If I was you two, I'd gather up whatever belongs to me and scat. You can put a lot of miles behind you before daylight. I'll find you if I need you."

Ches argued, "He came here to take you in. He could still do it."

"I ain't doin' this for him, I'm doin' it for me. They'll follow me to hell and back if I let you kill him. I already shot one man. You-all don't want to make it three."

Speck grumbled, "That's what thanks we get for splittin' our grub with you." He started to pick up Andy's fallen rifle.

Bannister said, "That ain't yours, Speck. Leave it."

Ches said, "You're makin' a big fuss for nothin'. Look at the way he's bleedin'. He's fixin' to die anyway."

"Maybe, but it won't be none of my doin'."

When the two were gone, Bannister set a wooden bar into place to prevent them from coming back through the door. He hung a coat over the window. "I don't know why I have to deal with yahoos like that. I wouldn't put it past them to try to shoot you through the glass. Now let's take a look at what they done to you."

Unable to remain on his feet, Andy slumped into a chair. He had trouble holding his head up or focusing his eyes. Bannister unbuttoned his shirt and slipped it down from the shoulder. "You're bleedin' like a stuck hog. Serves you right, stumblin' in here, all guts and no brains." He pinched the shoulder. "I'll bet that hurts."

"Damn right it does," Andy wheezed, his teeth clenched. Sick at his stomach, he felt the tickling sensation of blood running down his arm.

Bannister said, "If you die, it'll be your own fault." He looked into a crude wooden cabinet near the small cast-iron stove and found a flour sack somebody had used to wipe dishes. He said, "You spilled most of the whiskey. Don't reckon you brought any more with you?"

Andy shook his aching head. He rarely drank whiskey. He wondered whether Bannister wanted it for the wound or for himself.

Bannister roughly felt around the wound, causing Andy to cry out in pain. "I don't think the bullet's still in there, but you need a doctor. Nearest one I know of is back in Colorado City. The way you've been bleedin', you might not get that far."

Andy struggled to keep his eyes open. "I'm not dyin', not if I can help it."

Bannister seemed torn by indecision. "You won't make it by yourself, but if I take you, the law is liable to grab me." His voice was angry. "I don't see why they won't leave me alone. The man I shot stole a good horse from me. Crippled him so that I had to shoot the horse too." He picked up the bottle from the floor and held it high. It was nearly empty.

Andy was too weak and nauseated to walk on his own. He clenched his teeth as Bannister helped him to a cot. Bannister said, "You ain't goin' to enjoy this, but try to hold still." He took a swig from the bottle and poured the rest of it into the wound.

Andy heard himself cry out just before he sank into a deep well of pain. Consciousness left him.

When he struggled back out of the darkness, the pain returned with a vengeance. Through a haze he saw Bannister tear the empty flour sack into three pieces. He used one to wipe away the blood. Another he folded and placed over the wound to stanch the bleeding. The third he used to bind Andy's shoulder as tightly as he could.

Bannister said, "I got shot in the leg once. Had to take care of it myself. They said I was lucky not to die of blood poisonin'. If you don't get to a doctor, you're liable to take blood poisonin' yourself."

Andy measured his words, for each required an effort. "It's a long way . . . back to town."

"You need to go, though. Otherwise you'll be startin' a brand-new cemetery here."

Andy tried to raise up, but vertigo gripped him. He dropped heavily onto the cot. His head felt as if it were being forcibly pushed through the thin cotton mattress.

Bannister grumbled, "You haven't got a chance in hell of reachin' there by yourself."

"Maybe after I've rested some."

"You ain't really started to feel that wound yet. Tomorrow you'll be runnin' a fever and beggin' the Lord to let you die. Someday some cow hunter'll find your bones layin' on the prairie along with them of the buffalo."

Andy thought of Bethel, and the pain this could cause her. She might always wonder what ever became of him.

Bannister said, "Dammit, Ranger, you came here hopin' to take me in. I don't owe you nothin', not a thing." His face flushed with frustration. "This day ain't brought me nothin' but bad luck."

"It hasn't been lucky for me either."

Bannister lifted the coat just enough that he could see through the window. "Dark outside. I think the boys are gone."

"Do you know who they are?"

"Sure, but I ain't tellin' you." Bannister frowned darkly, wrestling with a decision. He demanded, "Are you a married man?"

Andy nodded.

Bannister said, "I was hopin' you wasn't. I don't want a widow-woman on my conscience. You lay still while I fetch up the horses."

"We're fixin' to travel?"

"We have to. You're in bad shape now, but you'll be worse in the mornin'. Once I find somebody who can help you, you're on your own."

Andy said, "You're on the Rangers' list. There'll be others come lookin' for you."

"You could say you shot me. Then they'd quit huntin'."

"But one day you'd turn up alive, and I'd be on the list too."

Bannister grumbled, "Some people have got no gratitude."

CHAPTER 2

Andy's shoulder throbbed. He knew Bannister was right about one thing: if he intended to ride anytime soon, he had better get at it. The fever would come before long, and the hurting would be more intense.

He struggled but could not lift his right leg over the saddle's cantle. Bannister gave him a boost and said, "Do I need to tie you on?"

Andy could barely hear his own voice. "I'll do all right."

"You didn't do very good against Ches and Speck, and they're a pair of sorry specimens."

As the hours dragged on, Andy became disoriented. He was dimly aware that they were riding in a southerly direction. Daylight came, the sun rising on his left. He was leaning forward, holding to the saddle with both hands to keep from falling off.

Bannister had spoken little during the night except to ask periodically, "Think you can make it?"

Andy was not certain, but he mumbled, "I'll make it."

As the sun rose, Bannister was ill at ease. "I'm lookin' for that chuck wagon camp. It's got to be around here someplace."

Andy wondered if they might have passed it in the dark. The thought of having to ride horseback all the way into town left Andy in despair. He was barely holding on.

Bannister's voice turned hopeful. "Yonder comes the whole outfit."

Fever clouded Andy's vision, but he made out a dozen or so horsemen riding in a northerly direction. Bannister shouted and waved his hat. The riders altered their course. As they approached, Andy recognized some of the men he had seen at the chuck wagon.

The wagon boss rode up close and gave Andy a quick looking over. He asked Bannister, "What'd you do to the Ranger?"

"Nothin', except bring him here for help."

"As I remember the description, you're the one he was lookin' for."

"Unlucky for him, he ran into a couple of other old boys who suspicioned they might be on his list too."

The cowboys gathered around, curious.

Bannister said, "I'd like to turn him over to you-all. I've got places to go."

"We're busy with the roundup. What would we do with him?"

"Get him to town, to a doctor that can fix him up proper."

Impatiently the boss said, "I'm already shorthanded as it is." He glanced over the gathered cowboys. "Kid." He beckoned with one finger to a youth of perhaps sixteen. "You take the Ranger to camp. Get Cookie to look at that wound. Then you hitch up the hoodlum wagon and carry this man on to town." As an afterthought, he said, "Ask Cookie if he needs anything from the store. We don't want your trip to be a waste."

One of the cowboys said, "The kid ain't old enough for that much responsibility. I'll go instead."

"And wind up drunk for three days? No, the kid ain't lost all his innocence yet."

"He's liable to, if he goes to town by hisself."

The boss turned back to Bannister. "I won't ask you where you're headed."

"I'd just lie to you if you did." Bannister said, "Ranger, I've done all I can do for you. More than I should've. From now on you'd better have eyes in the back of your head, or somebody may put a bullet there."

Andy murmured, "Obliged. But you're still on the list."

Bannister had already turned away. Andy doubted that he heard.

Andy rode as if in a painful trance, his mind roaming aimlessly from Bethel to Bannister and to the pair who had wounded him. The kid finally broke into Andy's consciousness by saying, "Yonder's the wagon."

The cook helped the kid lift Andy down from the saddle. They eased him onto a bedroll. Cookie unwrapped the crude bandage and swore. "Was this the cleanest thing he could find? It's a wonder you ain't got blood poisonin' already."

Andy could barely remember Bannister working on him in the spartan dugout. "I expect he did his best with what he had," he murmured. He did not feel like talking.

The cook maintained a one-sided conversation. He fetched a bottle from deep within the chuck box. He said, "This ain't goin' to feel near as good as if it was goin' down your throat." He poured whiskey into and over the wound. He and the kid had to push hard to keep Andy down. He said, "It wouldn't do you no good if it didn't burn a little."

"A little?" Andy wheezed, struggling to get his breath.

"You need a sure-enough doctor. It's your good luck that there's one in town."

Andy thought he would be glad to have a little good luck for a change.

The kid unloaded supplies from the camp's second wagon to make room, then took Andy's roll from the packmule and spread the blankets in the wagon. He said, "It ain't no feather bed." He and the cook helped Andy up into the wagon. He lay on his back, his felt hat a poor substitute for a pillow.

The cook admonished the kid, "Don't you tarry no longer than you have to. And don't you forget that barrel of flour if you want any biscuits tomorrow." He turned his attention to Andy. "While you're healin' up, Ranger, you might give some thought to another line of work. Yours can get a man hurt."

Andy nodded. "Maybe I can do somethin' for you sometime."

"The best thing you can do for me is to forget everybody you've seen here. This outfit is already shorthanded. A Ranger raid would just about finish us off."

The cook tied Andy's horse and mule on behind. The kid clucked at the team, and the wagon lurched forward. Andy gritted his teeth against the pain.

He was dimly conscious of their arrival in town. He heard the kid ask someone how to locate Dr. Coleman. Shortly he found himself being half supported, half carried into a frame house. A strong voice said, "We'll lay him down on that cot."

A man in his thirties leaned over him with a stethoscope and listened to his heartbeat. Andy heard the kid say, "The feller that brought him to us said he didn't think the bullet is still in there."

The doctor said, "I'll have to find out." He poured ether into a wad of cotton and held it to Andy's nose. Andy fought it for a moment, then drifted off. He was only vaguely aware of the probing, though he continued to feel pain. When it was over, he peered up through a misty veil at the man who had operated on him.

The doctor said, "I found no bullet, but I took out a tiny chip of bone. You'll feel better now that I've cleaned the wound."

Andy did not feel better. He tried to lift his hand. It weighed a hundred pounds.

"Easy, young fellow," the doctor said gently. "You won't be going anywhere for a while."

"How long?" Andy managed.

The doctor shrugged. "Hard to say. I'll keep you here a day or two, then move you over to a boarding house where I can look in on you till you're ready to travel. Is there anybody we should notify?"

"My captain. And my wife Bethel, down at Fort McKavett."

"I'll see that it's done."

The kid gave Andy a look of concern and said, "I always thought I'd like to be a Ranger myself someday. After this, bein' a cowboy looks pretty good."

Andy hurt too much to smile. He said, "Most Rangers hardly ever get shot."

"Cookie is liable to shoot *me* if I don't show up before dark. Good luck, Ranger."

"I'll put in a word for you if you ever decide to join."

"Don't expect me any time soon."

When his head was clear and the fever had subsided, Andy started reading through his fugitive book, staying with it until his eyes went blurry from trying to decipher the penciled notations. He thought he probably found a match for the two who had shot him. One appeared to be a cow and horse thief named Chester Lamplin, charged with murder. The one with the freckles was probably Francis Fuller, better known as Speck.

He had half a page of charges against him, chiefly horse theft.

Andy was in his third day in the widow Kelly's boarding house when he heard a woman's voice from down the hall. Bethel burst into the room and threw her arms around him.

His heart jumped. He hugged her though it set off a sharp throbbing in his shoulder. "How did you get here?"

"In a fast buggy."

"By yourself?"

"Almost." She turned and nodded toward a tall, skinny man with a homemade silver star on his vest. "Len Tanner rode along with me on horseback."

Len's lopsided grin reached from one ear across to the other. Though his hair was graying, and he was missing a tooth, under present circumstances Andy considered him handsome. Len had been a Ranger before the Civil War and had rejoined when the force was reorganized after the reconstruction years.

Andy said, "Len, you oughtn't to've drug Bethel halfway across Texas."

"But ain't you glad I did?"

"Seein' her is better medicine than anything the doctor has given me." Andy warmed to Bethel's smile. Her dress

41

wrinkled and her long brown hair in a tangle from the long trip, she had never looked so beautiful.

Len said, "Sergeant Ryker sent me to make sure you wasn't just layin' down on the job. I tried to tell Bethel it was too hard a trip for her, but you've tied yourself to a stubborn woman."

Andy squeezed her hand. "I've found that out."

Len's face went serious. "I'm supposed to try and pick up Bannister's trail."

"It'll be cold by now. Anyway, if it wasn't for him, I'd be layin' dead somewhere out yonder."

"But he shot you, didn't he?"

"It wasn't him." Andy explained about Ches and Speck. "Bannister stopped them from finishin' the job. Then he took me to a cow camp for help."

"You may be givin' him too much credit. He did that for hisself. He knew that if you died, he'd be blamed for it. He'd be charged with two killin's instead of one."

"Whatever his reasons, he did it. I don't feel right about huntin' him down."

"That choice ain't up to me or you. Maybe a judge'll see fit to give him some slack."

Andy knew Len was right. And if any

Ranger could find Bannister, Len was the one. He was like a grassburr that refused to be shaken off.

Bethel said, "It won't be your worry, Andy. As soon as the doctor says you can travel, I'm putting you in the buggy and taking you home."

"We can't go off and leave my horse and packmule."

"We can tie them on behind."

Len said, "It's better this way. The sergeant had rather you was home. Doctors and boardin' houses cost money."

Andy was not surprised. He was not even certain the state would pay him for the days his wound had kept him off duty. The money dispensers in Austin could be arbitrary, especially when expenditures did not bring them some political benefit.

Len said, "I brought my own horse, but I'll take your packmule. Tell me where Bannister was the last time you seen him."

They made the trip home in slow and easy stages, camping before sundown each day to allow Andy more time to rest. Bethel seemed to enjoy cooking in camp, and Andy enjoyed lying on a blanket, watching her. However, he felt wrung out by the time they reached the little frame house at the edge of

Fort McKavett, near the banks of the San Saba River. Bethel had to help him unharness the buggy horse. His shoulder was board-stiff and painful. He had limited use of his arm. "I'd better report in," he said as Bethel supported him to the door.

Sternly she said, "You'll do no such thing. I'll send one of the town boys to camp with a message. If the sergeant wants to see you, he can come here. The state of Texas doesn't own you. I do."

At another time he might have argued, and might even have won, but he was too tired and weak to put up much of a case. He said, "You could get me fired."

"We might be better off." Tears glistened in her eyes. "Look at you, all shot up. Next time, instead of bringing you home to get well, I might be bringing you home to bury."

"This kind of thing doesn't happen often."

"Once more may be enough. Tell me the thought of facing another gun doesn't make you feel cold."

It did, but he would not admit it. He could see they were dangerously close to an argument. "We'll talk about it tomorrow. We're both tired now."

"I'll feel the same tomorrow, and the day after that. You don't have to be a Ranger. We could get by somehow."

He would not promise what he could not deliver. "When it's time."

Sergeant Ryker knocked on the door as Andy was finishing his after-supper coffee. Bethel invited him in, giving him no chance to speak before she declared, "He's only been home two weeks. He's a long way from being well."

Removing his hat, Ryker gave Andy a quick and critical study. "You've got your color back. Think you can sit on a horse?"

Andy said, "I already have, a little, just to see if I could."

Bethel protested, "He needs more time."

Ryker said, "Austin is ridin' us about expenses. If you stay off duty much longer they'll make us discharge you."

Andy nodded. "Been expectin' that. I guess I'm strong enough to stand horse guard." Most Rangers disliked being assigned to loose-herd company horses on grass. They considered it monotonous, even demeaning. A day on horse guard could feel like a week. From Andy's viewpoint, however, it was preferable to losing his job.

Ryker said, "Maybe someday a gang of outlaws will stage a raid on Austin, and the money changers will realize how much they need the Rangers." One difficulty was that most incidents requiring Ranger attention occurred far away from the state capitol, so the lawmakers were only dimly aware of them, if at all.

Andy asked, "Heard anything from Len Tanner?"

"Got a couple of wires. He lost Bannister's trail."

"If Len can't find Bannister, nobody can." Andy could not say he was sorry. Bannister could have left him to die but had risked capture to help him. Such a man deserved to be forgiven for killing a horse thief.

The sergeant said, "We're not givin' up. There's more than one way to sack a cat."

"How?"

"Bannister's been livin' in Junction with his wife. It stands to reason that he'll sooner or later come back, or at least try to let her know where he's at."

Andy glanced at Bethel. "I sure would, if I was him."

"The sheriff down there has been watchin' her mail. He hasn't reported anything so far. Of course, Bannister might be cagy enough to send word by somebody instead of writin' a letter."

Andy was thinking faster than Ryker was talking. He said, "She might try to join up with him."

The sergeant nodded. "I'd like for you to go down to Junction and keep an eye on her. If she leaves, you follow her."

Bethel frowned.

The sergeant said, "You might be there a while. It'd give you a chance to be useful while you finish healin' up."

Bethel cried, "Andy, no."

Andy touched her hand. "I want to keep my job."

"Then let me go with you."

Andy glanced at Ryker. The sergeant said, "That'd be contrary to regulations. If Bannister's woman made a move, you might have to go without takin' time to say goodbye."

Bethel's shoulders drooped.

Ryker spoke softly. "I know how you feel, girl. Many's the time I've had to ride away and leave my wife. Andy can wait till tomorrow before he goes off."

Andy said, "Thanks, Sergeant." He watched through the open door as Ryker rode away. Then he turned back into Bethel's arms.

"We've got tonight," he said.

Before arriving in Junction, Andy took off his badge to make himself less conspicuous. The sheriff guided him toward a modest frame house with peeling paint once white but now a soft shade of gray. He said, "She putters around with the flowers by the porch and goes to the store most mornin's. Otherwise, she doesn't show herself much. I've got the postmaster watchin' to see if she gets any mail. She hasn't had a letter since Bannister left."

Andy frowned, thinking of Bethel. "Seems like a man would want to let his wife know somethin'."

The sheriff shrugged. "I would, and you would, but everybody ain't like us. There's some men that don't know how to appreciate a good woman."

"How do you know she's a good woman?"

"People around here like her, other than some of the womenfolks. You know how women can be about judgin' other women, especially one that's good-lookin'."

Andy said, "And this one is good-lookin'?"

The sheriff continued, "She is, but she doesn't go in for paint and powder and such. She's pretty much of a mystery."

"Did you know Bannister?"

"Some. Makes his livin' handlin' horses. He'll be gone for weeks at a time, then come in with a big string to sell. We never know where they come from, but he's appeared to be honest enough, considerin' his occupation. An honest horse trader is one who never cheats his neighbors. He goes somewhere else to do that."

"You don't suppose he deals in stolen horses?"

"Possible, but I never got notices on any of them. I've had no cause to suspicion him."

Andy studied the house, wishing the woman would come outside so he could get a look at her. "How did he come to shoot a man?"

"Somebody stole a roan horse from him. One day Cletus Slocum rode into town on that roan, bold as all get-out. Bannister challenged him, and Cletus took out a-runnin'. Bannister ran him down. Willy Pegg swore that he saw Bannister kill Cletus in cold blood."

"Do you believe him?"

"That lyin' weasel? No, everybody knows he's a lackey of the Slocum family. But it don't matter what I believe. On his testimony I had to swear out a warrant."

"What do you know about the Slocums?"

"They're a hard lot. They come out of the brush down on the South Llano. Folks around there have lost cattle, sheep, even goats and hogs. There ain't nothin' too low for the Slocums to steal. But knowin' it and provin' it are two different things."

Andy said, "Sounds like Bannister might've done the community a service."

"There's plenty that think so, but if anybody besides Pegg saw the shootin', they haven't come forward. Afraid to, I guess. The Slocums are a bad bunch to get on the wrong side of. They was raised on catclaw brush, alkali water, and rotgut whiskey."

Andy frowned. "Are *you* scared of them?"

The sheriff considered. "A little, to tell you the truth, but that don't keep me from tryin' to do my job. Ordinarily Junction is a decent town, as towns go. That Slocum bunch dances to different music than most of us."

Andy knew he might stand here the rest of the day without a glimpse of Mrs. Bannister. He said, "I need a place where I can watch without bein' noticeable."

The sheriff pointed with his chin. "I've got a shed yonder. Side door faces this way. You can sit in there out of sight but have a good view of the Bannister house."

"Good."

"I don't think you need to watch her all day. She keeps a horse and buggy at the wagon yard. I doubt she'd go anywhere without them. And the postmaster will alert us if she gets any mail."

50

Andy saw the sheriff's logic. He recognized a slim chance that Bannister himself would come back. If he did, he would almost surely use the cover of darkness. And if his wife left town, she would also likely do so in the dark. He said, "I'll rest in the daytime and keep watch durin' the night." His shoulder remained stiff and more than a little sore, though not enough to keep him from his assignment.

The sheriff said, "Good idea. Come with me and I'll buy you a drink. I need it whether you do or not."

"Just one. I'm on duty."

"Rangers are always on duty. The beauty of bein' a sheriff is that nobody can fire me except the voters."

The saloon was built of square-cut stones, the walls double thick. A painting of a Longhorn steer graced a slab of wood over the door. "Nothin' much fancy in here," the sheriff said, "but the beer is good honest German brew. What the world needs is more honest beer. And more honest men, German and otherwise."

He stepped inside and stopped abruptly, gazing at four men who sat at a table near the back of the room. He elbowed Andy and said, "There's the three Slocum brothers, Vince and Judd and Finis. The other, with

51

the chubby face, is Willy Pegg. Around here they call him Never-Sweat."

"What does he do for a livin'?"

"Hangs around people like the Slocums, pickin' up whatever drops off of their table. Got a wife who takes in washin'."

Andy was conscious that the four men were staring at him. He took a place at the bar alongside the sheriff, waiting to see if the Slocums made any sort of move.

One did, after a time. He pushed away from the table and approached the sheriff, limping a little. He was a large man with dark stubble that needed shaving, and black eyes that cut like a sharp blade. He declared, "Hey, Sheriff, you ain't goin' to find Bannister in here."

The lawman shook his head. "Nor anywhere else, looks like. It seems he just plain evaporated."

"You ought to be out lookin' for him instead of wastin' time in town."

"Finis, you know my jurisdiction stops at the county line."

Slocum turned toward Andy. The intensity of his eyes raised a tingle along Andy's spine, the kind that came when he heard a snake's rattle. Slocum demanded, "Who the hell are you?" as if he had every right to know.

The sheriff said quickly, "He's a cousin of mine, lookin' for a ranch job. Not often I get to see my kin anymore."

Slocum made no effort to hide his disbelief. "You're a liar. He looks like the law to me. I can smell them every time."

The sheriff said, "He's just a cowboy out of work."

Andy admitted nothing. It usually paid to keep one or two cards up his sleeve.

Slocum pointed a thick finger in the sheriff's face. "You'd better find Bannister before we do, or there won't be enough left of him to feed a buzzard. I'll bet that woman of his could tell us where he's at."

The sheriff's voice reflected a flash of anger. "Don't you even think about botherin' Mrs. Bannister. Folks around here would cut you into little pieces and feed you to the catfish."

Slocum did not yield. "You better find him."

"Nice feller," Andy muttered when Slocum had retreated to his table.

The sheriff replied, "Every word he says, you can write in your Bible. He means it. Those Slocums remember every slight and insult that was ever sent their way, and they've evened the score for most of them."

Andy stabled his horse at the wagon yard with a lean and hungry-looking man who introduced himself only as Spence and who reminded him of Len Tanner. At the sheriff's suggestion, he began taking his meals at a nearby small boarding house. The proprietress was a middle-aged German woman who spoke limited English and showed no curiosity about Andy's business. Her eyes brightened with interest only when she counted the coins Andy placed in her hand. Her silence suited Andy better than her cooking, but he could not expect everyone to cook as well as Bethel.

His first full day, he saw Mrs. Bannister leave her house with a basket in her hand and walk up the street to a store. When she returned, she carried groceries. Andy checked his pocket watch. A little after nine in the morning. A slat bonnet covered most of her features. He noted, however, that she was slender — some would say skinny — and walked proud and straight as if she had a ramrod tied to her back. He considered her attitude defiant, as if she silently dared anyone to call her husband a murderer.

He admired loyalty, whether misplaced or

not. He felt guilty as a burglar for spying on her.

He dozed through the day, waking occasionally to look toward the Bannister house. He saw no activity there. At dark he set a chair just inside the door and settled down for the night watch. Lamplight shone in her windows until nine o'clock, then winked out. The night passed without incident. He suspected he was wasting his and the Rangers' time here, but at least his shoulder was having a chance to heal, and he was still on the payroll. His main concern was that this assignment kept him away from Bethel.

Next morning, hoping for a closer look at the woman, he walked to the store before nine o'clock and sat on a bench near the front. He began whittling a stick, hoping she would pay little attention to an idler. Every town seemed to have a few of the spit-and-whittle persuasion.

She was later than yesterday. He began to think she might not appear. Finally she did, carrying the basket. He managed a quick glance at her face. It startled him. She was beautiful. His male reaction brought a rush of self-recrimination. A married man had no business letting his mind drift in that direction.

Presently she came out of the store, the basket on her arm. He concentrated his attention on his whittling, hoping she would not realize he was watching. His gaze followed her as she walked back down the dirt street.

He became conscious that the husky grocer had stepped outside and stood beside him. The sheriff had told Andy his name was Addison Giles. The grocer wiped his large hands on a canvas apron and said, "Fine-looking woman, don't you think?"

"I wasn't payin' much attention."

"I saw you watching her." Giles was a stout man of about forty who probably could toss flour barrels around without straining himself. His voice coarsened. "I hope you're not thinking about taking advantage of her situation."

Andy used his most innocent voice. "I'm a stranger here. I don't know the lady's situation."

"That's Donley Bannister's wife. He's on the run, accused of murder. Most people feel like he got a raw deal. He had to leave Geneva here by herself."

"I'm sorry to hear it."

The grocer's face was somber. "Don't get the notion that she's helpless, though. She's got friends who'd make short work of the

Slocum brothers or anybody else that tried to do her harm. Any stranger who drifts into town, we want to be sure the Slocums didn't send for him. Do you know them?"

"The sheriff pointed them out to me."

Mention of the lawman brought a grunt from the grocer. "What business have you got with the sheriff?"

"Kinfolks. He said he might find me a job."

The grocer grunted again. "Whatever Geneva Bannister does or doesn't do is nobody's business but her own. I hope I've made myself understood."

"You've made it mighty clear."

Giles left him and went back into the store. Andy arose, closing his knife and tossing away what remained of the stick. Geneva Bannister was no longer in sight. He returned to the sheriff's shed and lay down on the cot, hoping to sleep a while. He kept seeing the woman's face, the features fine, the eyes a dark brown, almost black.

He knew that if he were Donley Bannister, he would do whatever was necessary to get back with her. Even kill, if it came to that.

Andy had been in town a week without seeing anything that aroused his suspicion. More and more he felt he was wasting his time and the state's money. The sleep he managed during daytime did not make up for what he lost at night, watching the Bannister house. What he was doing made him feel like a spy. He took no pride in it. His only consolation was a letter from Bethel, sent to him at the sheriff's office. It had been written the day after he left. In it she told how much she already missed him.

He thought often about the time he would be able to leave the Ranger service and build a house for Bethel on his hill-country land. There they could dwell in peace without duty constantly interrupting their lives. But they would have to eat, and his place was not large enough to provide a living. He wondered how many more Donley Bannisters he would have to trail before he could make the break.

This assignment was made even more unpleasant by the nagging realization that Bannister had in all likelihood saved his life. It was not Andy's place to ask questions or pass judgment, however. Once he did his part, the matter was out of his hands. He could tell himself he was not responsible. That sounded simple, but he could not turn off his feelings as he would blow out a lamp.

He was at the livery barn, brushing his horse, when Finis Slocum appeared unexpectedly. He gave Andy a suspicious looking-over and declared, "You're the feller I saw with the sheriff a week ago. How come you're still around here?"

Andy made a guess at Slocum's weight and decided the man had him bested by thirty or forty pounds. Andy would probably be badly outmatched in a fistfight. *If it comes to that,* he thought, *I'd best just shoot him.*

He said, "Still tryin' to find me a ranch job."

"Jobs are scarce around here. You'd be better off in a bigger town, like San Antonio. Lots of ranchers go there to do business."

"I like these hills."

"People that hang around with sheriffs can get awful unpopular. I already don't like you very much."

"I'm sorry. I try to get along with everybody."

Slocum gave Andy a long frown, plainly trying to figure him out. He started to move away but turned back. "You been hearin' much talk while you been here?"

"Some. Mostly about how everybody needs a good rain."

Slocum shook his head and left, dissatisfied. Andy had a disturbing feeling that the man might figure him out sooner or later.

Even more bothersome was the possibility that Geneva Bannister might do so as well.

He sensed one morning that something had changed. The woman made her usual trip to the store, carrying her basket. When she emerged her face was flushed with excitement. Grocer Giles stepped out onto the porch to remind her that she had forgotten her basket. She quickly returned for it, then started toward her house, her step lighter than Andy had seen it before. Shortly afterward, the grocer walked down to the wagon yard. The liveryman Spence met him at the door, and they went inside together, out of sight and hearing.

Andy waited a while, then went to the wagon yard. His black horse was in an open corral with several others. The horse stood still while Andy brushed him.

The liveryman stepped out of the barn and observed Andy for a minute. He said, "You're shinin' him up like you're fixin' to leave us."

Andy said, "Can't leave till I find a job."

Spence let his suspicion show. "Some people around here say you may already have one. With the Rangers, maybe?"

Andy swallowed. Had everybody figured it out? "Why the Rangers?"

The liveryman glared. "Because you've

been spyin' on folks that deserve to be let alone."

Andy found it difficult to nap during the rest of the day. He had a strong premonition that something was about to happen. He had learned to trust his hunches. At dusk, though feeling a little sleepy, he began his steady watch on the Bannister house. About nine o'clock, as usual, the lamplight winked out. After a few hours he began to think he had let his imagination run away with him. He found himself dozing off.

He was brought suddenly awake by hoof-beats and the whispering sound of thin iron rims cutting tracks in the soft street. Blinking, he made out the form of a buggy stopped in front of the Bannister house. A portly man stepped down. Though Andy could not see him clearly, he guessed him to be the grocer Giles. He heard a muffled knock on the door and saw lamplight in the window. A woman came out onto the porch, bearing a bundle. The man took it from her and placed it in the buggy while she went back into the house to bring out something more.

That was all Andy needed to see. He trotted to the wagon yard to saddle his horse. He was tying his pack on a little mule when a man spoke behind him. "The middle of the night is an odd time to be goin' somewhere." Turning half around, he saw stable keeper Spence.

"I got a job," Andy said.

"After midnight? You owe me a board bill on that horse and mule."

Andy paid him. He noticed, with no surprise, that Geneva Bannister's buckboard was not in its accustomed place. Her buggy horse was gone, too. The stable keeper said, "You're fixin' to follow Miz Bannister, ain't you? I hope you ain't goin' to arrest her."

Andy had realized he had not fooled everybody in regard to his mission here. He said, "I've got no reason to. As far as I know, bein' married to a fugitive is not a crime."

"She's got a right to go anywhere she wants to, ain't she, without bein' bothered?"

"I don't intend to bother her."

"You figure she'll be goin' to Donley."

Andy had no argument against that. He did not attempt one.

Spence shrugged. "I can't stop you, but I ain't wishin' you no luck. Donley always gave me lots of business. He used to keep his horses in my pens till he got them sold."

"He ought to've been slower on the trigger."

"Cletus Slocum would've killed him."

62

Andy held the black horse to a walk as he moved into the street, the packmule following. A small cloud had drifted overhead, covering the moon. He could see little past the horse's ears except vague shapes. Stopping short of the Bannister house, he heard the faint sound of buggy wheels and the tread of a horse moving in a fast trot. The buggy was going northwestward. That fit with the direction of Donley Bannister's flight. Andy found the pace that would keep him within hearing and followed the sound. In a while the clouds drifted on. Moonlight allowed him to see the buggy moving along a well-traveled road that meandered around a rocky hill. He dropped back farther so Geneva Bannister would not see him.

He thought once he heard someone coming behind him. He stopped and listened, holding his breath. A deer burst out of a thicket and bounded away. Satisfied, Andy lightly touched spurs to the horse's ribs and moved on. The buggy maintained a steady pace except when it encountered rough ground. The dark hours dragged by. As color began to show in the east, Andy pulled back farther, knowing Mrs. Bannister would see him if she happened to look behind her.

A while after sunup the buggy stopped at a small creek. Andy pulled in amid some live-oak trees to hide. He watched the driver dismount, stretch, and remove a bundle from behind the seat. His jaw dropped. This was not Geneva Bannister. This was a man, short, heavyset, and he was alone. The grocer!

"I'll be damned!" Andy exclaimed. He felt a flush of anger, first at the people who had fooled him, then at himself for allowing them to do it. He realized that Addison Giles had been a decoy, luring him away so Geneva Bannister could make her escape in some other direction. Andy had never been close enough to see the difference.

When his initial anger was vented, he rode toward the buggy. He saw no reason to conceal himself.

The grocer smiled as Andy approached him. He said, "Welcome. I was just about to fix me some breakfast. Would you join me?"

"I'd rather jail you."

"For what? Can't a man take Sunday off and go fishing?"

Andy was not sure it was Sunday, but that made no difference anyway. "What're you doin' with Mrs. Bannister's buggy?"

"She was kind enough to lend it to me. I promised I'd bring her some fish."

Andy looked in the buggy. "Where's your fishin' pole?"

Giles feigned surprise. "By George, I forgot to bring it."

Andy gradually saw humor in the situation, though it was painful. "Looks to me like you caught the fish you were really after."

The grocer smiled again. "One of them. The others are coming behind you."

Turning, Andy saw three Slocum brothers and Willy Pegg pushing their horses into a long trot. Finis Slocum's face was contorted with anger as he reined up just short of the buggy. Glaring at Giles, he said, "Smart son of a bitch, ain't you?"

The grocer did not change expression. "Smarter than some."

Finis's gaze searched in all directions. "Where's she at?"

Giles said calmly, "There's just me and the Ranger here."

Finis jerked his thumb at Pegg. "Go look around."

Pegg made a wide circle and returned. "Ain't nobody else here."

Finis cast a smoldering gaze at Giles, then concentrated on Andy. He cursed until he was hoarse. "We'll find her yet, and then we'll find him. As for you sons of bitches, people that poke their noses into other people's business sometimes get their noses broke." Jerking his head, he said to his brothers, "Come on. We've been dealt one off of the bottom." The three and Pegg turned their horses around and started back toward town, quarreling, the brothers blaming one another. Pegg hung back a little, out of the line of fire.

Andy said, "They thought the same as me, that they were followin' Mrs. Bannister."

"No, I believe they were following you. They thought *you* were following Geneva. Help me get a fire started and we'll fix some breakfast. Unless you've lost your appetite."

Andy brought himself to grin. "Nothin' wrong with my appetite. Just lost a bit of my reputation."

He gathered wood while Giles sliced bacon from a slab and placed it in a skillet, then poured ground coffee into a pot. "I don't get to enjoy this outdoor life near often enough," he said. "Running a store sure ties a man down."

Andy had made many a meal on an outdoor fire, and missed many a meal for lack of the fixings. He saw no romance in it. "I like it better when I can put my legs under a table," he said. "Especially when my wife does the cookin'."

Giles pointed a fork toward the buggy. "You'll find some tin plates in yonder."

Andy lifted the edge of a tarp. He found a carpetbag and several boxes and bundles. The buggy was too well provisioned for a one-day fishing trip, but he decided against saying anything about it. He sensed that all was not as Giles claimed it to be. He saw a saddle, a blanket, and a bridle beneath the tarp. Surely Giles did not plan to ride off on the buggy horse.

Afraid his face might betray what he was thinking, he kept his back toward Giles for a long moment. When he turned, he said, "I'd like nothin' better than to stay with you for the day. I've never done much fishin'."

Giles blinked, and for just a moment Andy saw concern. Andy added, "But I'd better go back and send a report to my sergeant. I'm afraid I'll get dressed down for lettin' Mrs. Bannister slip through my fingers."

Giles's look of relief confirmed Andy's suspicion. The grocer said, "A man shouldn't feel disgraced just because a woman fools him. It happens all the time. My wife, for instance . . ."

Andy sipped coffee and ate bacon and cold biscuits, probably leftovers from last night's supper at the Giles house. The pudgy grocer talked on a wide range of subjects — business, the weather, politics —

but carefully avoided what was foremost on both men's minds. Finished, Andy pushed to his feet and said, "There's no use puttin' it off any longer. I'll go in and take my medicine."

Giles extended his hand. "I hope there aren't any hard feelings."

Andy accepted the handshake. "You did what you thought was right, and I did what I was told to."

Andy mounted the black and rode southward until a bend in the trail took him around a heavy live-oak thicket. He worked his way inside it and dismounted, tying the horse. The mule followed, as it had been trained to do. Andy moved afoot to the edge of the motte where he had a clear-enough view of the creek crossing and Giles's buggy. There he found a seat on a fallen dead limb and waited.

CHAPTER 3

Geneva Bannister stood beside her horse at the edge of a live-oak clump, watching Addison Giles and the buggy some three hundred yards up the creek. She asked stableman Spence, "Do you see a sign of anybody else?"

"Nope. Just Giles, waitin' where he's supposed to."

"We can't be too careful. It's not only the Slocums we have to worry about. There's that man you say is a Ranger."

"I accused him, and he didn't deny it."

"I've known for several days that he was watching me."

"But we fooled him — and the Slocums too."

Geneva was not so certain. "My husband is a horse trader. He says it's always the ones you underestimate that will beat you on a deal. Let's wait a while longer before we ride down there."

They had waited in the dark past midnight until both the Ranger and the Slocums left town, following the buggy. Then they saddled two horses from the stable and took a roundabout course to reach this rendezvous point. They had arrived in time to see first the Ranger, then the Slocums, ride up to the buggy. The Ranger had remained the longest but had finally turned back toward town.

Spence said, "I'll bet the Slocums were mad enough to bite theirselves when they found they'd followed Giles. By now they've probably figured out that he baited them to clear the way for you."

"I just hope the Slocums don't do him any harm. Addison is one of the kindest men I know."

"Don't you worry about him. Even with his gray hair, he can wrestle an ox to the ground. You could worry about *me,* though." Spence was spindly and would probably snap in two like a dry stick.

"I worry about both of you."

Her concern was genuine. She realized that Giles and Spence were putting themselves at risk by helping her get away. She suspected both were in love with her, or at least felt a physical attraction. Giles was married to a woman who complained a lot.

Spence was a bachelor. She suffered pangs of conscience about taking advantage of them, but both had offered of their own will. Her eagerness to rejoin Donley overrode her sense of guilt.

She said, "I think it's all right to ride down there now."

"Whatever you say."

She sensed reluctance. Spence had grabbed at this chance to enjoy her company, offering protection should anything go wrong. Shortly she would leave him and Giles and go on alone.

Giles had a cup of coffee and a broad smile waiting for her as they rode in. He said, "Looks like everything worked out. They all probably figured you lit out for Fort Worth and points east."

"I hope so," she said.

"Got some bacon here, and a few of last night's biscuits if you'd like to eat before you go on."

"I'll eat them while I travel."

Spence removed her sidesaddle from the horse she had been riding and stowed it in the buggy. He took out Giles's saddle and put it on the horse.

She felt like kissing both men out of gratitude but feared it might stir up futile feelings that were already too near the surface. Spence's eyes were as sad as if he had just buried one of his kin. "You're good friends," she said. "I can't thank you enough." She shook hands, and Giles helped her up onto the seat. She said, "I promise, Donley and I will be back when the time is right."

Spence said, "I might just shoot them Slocums myself."

She knew he was speaking rashly, in the spirit of the moment. Neither he nor Giles was likely to do anything that extreme, though she suspected the husky Giles would be the wrong man for the Slocums to hem up in a corner.

She saw a long stretch of gravel the creek had deposited during overflows. She put the buggy on it to minimize tracks. She stayed on the gravel as long as it lasted, a couple of hundred yards, then angled back on the trail northwestward toward Fort McKavett.

Looking behind her, she saw that both men were still watching. Ever since her teens, she had been aware that men were drawn to her, that she could manipulate them with a smile, a half promise not really meant. At times that invigorating power had served her well. Yet it could also bring troublesome consequences when men took it to mean more than she intended. She had taken pains not to misuse it here, but Giles and Spence had needed no persuasion. In fact, this ploy had been Giles's idea.

She thought about the Ranger and the embarrassment he must be feeling. He had been young and good-looking. For no good reason she could think of, she had caught herself wondering if he was married. She had quickly curbed the thought. She had a man already. Donley Bannister had remained heavy on her mind ever since he had left town ahead of the vengeful Slocums. She had waited for him to kiss her good-bye. It still stung her that he had not.

She remembered in the early days of their marriage that his passion had been strong, but with time it had ebbed while hers remained warm. With Donley, the horses came first. They were where his true passion lay.

The winding road was by turns rocky and rough, skirting rugged limestone hills, then smoothing awhile as it meandered around live-oak mottes and scattered cedars in the valleys. Now and then her passing set deer bounding away, their white tails flashing. She flushed a flock of wild turkeys, which soared off into a thicket and settled on the limbs.

She met an occasional traveler. She wished

she could avoid them, but she knew she would arouse more suspicion by attempting evasion than by simply meeting them head-on. It might strike them as unusual, seeing a woman traveling alone, but by the time they reported it in Junction she would be miles farther on. Her tracks would be obliterated by the many who would travel this way after her.

She saw three horsemen coming south along the wagon trail. As they approached she took them to be cowboys. They were singing, which told her they had probably spent too long in a Fort McKavett saloon. The singing stopped as the three pulled out of the road and stared. Geneva's heartbeat picked up a little. She looked quickly behind her, hoping some traveler might be coming from that direction to help her in case of trouble. She saw no one.

A rifle lay beneath the buggy seat. She resisted an urge to reach down for it. She had long recognized the necessity for guns but had almost rather pick up a snake than handle one. After Donley's shooting of Cletus Slocum, she had even less liking for them.

One of the cowboys removed his hat and made a broad gesture of welcome. He was young, with just a hint of soft whiskers.

"Ma'am," he said in a youthful voice much too loud, "why don't you get down and tarry a spell with us? Better yet, why don't I join you in the buggy? Me and you will go a ways up the trail together and leave these two drunks behind."

He reached out as if to touch her. One of his companions, suddenly sober, took his arm and pulled him back. He declared, "You damned idiot, can't you tell a lady when you see one? This could get you horsewhipped. Even shot."

"I was just funnin' with her."

"There ain't nobody laughin'." The sober one touched fingers to the brim of his hat. "Sorry, ma'am. He ain't usually like this. He's just a big old kid, and it's the whiskey talkin'. If you feel like he's insulted you, we'll take the double of a rope to him. He'll know better next time."

Though Geneva's heart still raced, she gathered composure enough to say, "Never mind. When he's sober, tell him he's lucky my husband didn't see this. You'd be picking him up in pieces."

"First waterhole we come to, we'll throw him in it. He'll sober up fast."

"Just don't drown him."

She set the horse into a trot to quickly put the cowboys behind her. Looking back, she could see that the older pair were giving the other a severe talking-to. He was taking it with his head down.

She realized she had been in no danger, at least not from the single cowboy. Had the other two been equally reckless, she might have had to take up the rifle. She could, even if she did not like it. She had reluctantly learned the use of it as a girl. She was a crack shot.

The incident pointed up the hazards faced by a woman traveling a long distance alone. To justify this risk, Donley had better be damned glad to see her, she thought. In point of fact, his letter — written in someone else's hand — had indicated where he had gone, but it had warned her not to follow after him. She had decided to do it anyway.

The third day, the trail led into the village of Fort McKavett on the San Saba River. Though she wished she could pass through without anyone seeing her, she needed supplies for the trip ahead. From here she would travel northwestward to Fort Concho and, finally, the rolling plains many days farther on.

McKavett had been a military post before the war. The original army structures had been converted to civilian use or cannibalized for newer buildings. She was aware that a Ranger camp existed near here. She wondered if the Ranger who had followed her buggy from Junction had come from this post.

She intended her visit to be short so she could avoid excessive scrutiny. She stopped in front of a stone building whose sign proclaimed *Groc. & Sundry Merch.* She deflected a curious merchant's questions with a story she had made up along the way about she and her husband breaking out a new farm. She bought enough goods to last several days, about all the buggy had room for, then crossed the river at a shallow ford. The San Saba was broad and clear, its banks shaded by towering native pecan trees. She resisted a temptation to stop there and rest.

Downriver, the merchant told her, Spanish padres long ago had built a mission but were slaughtered by hostile Indians, the buildings destroyed. The last Comanche raid had torn through this part of the hill country barely more than a decade ago. As a small girl in Erath County she had hidden beneath a bed while her mother held a rifle ready in case Indians prowling outside took a notion they wanted more than horses. The memory sent a chill along her back, though she knew she need not worry about Indians anymore, not here.

She had always marveled at her mother's courage and wondered if she could match it should the need arise.

She had never camped by herself before this trip, but she had no dread of it. Because the cowboys had been a reminder of her vulnerability, she pulled the buggy a hundred yards off the trail and stopped behind a live-oak motte that would hide her from anyone passing by. She hobbled the horse, then scooped out a small fire pit and lined its perimeter with limestone rocks. She prepared a small supper, washing it down with boiled black coffee that left grounds stuck in her teeth. She wished for a tent to shield her from the damp that carried a hint of rain.

She pulled up dry grass and made a crude mat on which to spread her blankets. She wrapped herself in them and listened to the sounds of the night. She wished Donley were lying with her. She had missed him. Though he presented a rough exterior to most people, she knew it was a defensive posture meant to gain advantage over those who might challenge him. He occasionally spoke roughly to her, too, but in the privacy of their bedroom he had sometimes been tender and loving. She wished he could have been that way more often.

She awakened at daylight, built a new fire and started the coffee. She fried bacon and two eggs she had bought in Fort McKavett. Traveling had given her a strong appetite. She put her belongings back in the buggy and poured leftover coffee on the flickering coals, then kicked sand over the pit to smother them.

Darkening clouds threatened rain, but none fell until late afternoon. The wind blew it in beneath the buggy's top. Wrapping a blanket around her shoulders in an effort to stay dry, she began looking for shelter. She saw a low goat shed, but a couple of dozen goats were huddled beneath it. She did not care to share the night with them.

She was about to despair of finding a dry place when about dusk she spotted a house two hundred yards from the trail. She found a dim wagon trace and turned onto it, winding past live-oak trees and junipers. The house was plain, the sort of nailed-together box-and-strip structure common to this developing land. It had once had a coat of paint but was in need of another. In back were a barn and an open shed and several pens built of upright live-oak branches. Seeing no sign of anyone outside, she pulled up in front of the house and shouted, "Anybody home?"

She thought for a minute that no one would answer, but the door opened slowly. A man peered out, showing only his face at first, then pulling the door all the way back. "Yes, ma'am," he said. "Let me help you down from there."

Friendly-eyed, he was approaching middle age. A bristly stubble darkened his face, for he had not shaved in two or three days.

She said, "I'd be obliged for a chance to get out of the rain."

"You've found it," he said, smiling, raising both hands to support her as she climbed down from the buggy. "You go right on inside. I'll put away the horse and buggy while you move up close to the cook stove and get dry."

Geneva had not seen a woman, though there were curtains on the two front windows. "Sure your wife won't mind?"

"I'm a widower," he said.

"I'm sorry." Geneva paused, considering the potential complications of being in the house with a man she never saw before.

He seemed to read her thoughts. "Don't you worry, ma'am. I can see that you're a lady, and I've always tried to be a gentleman. Even if I ain't had much trainin' for it." He lifted the tarp that covered her belongings. "Need me to bring any of this in?"

"Just the carpetbag," she said.

The dampness had given her a chill. She spread the wet blanket across the backs of two wooden chairs and stood in front of the stove, shivering a little, holding her hands near the source of the heat.

In a few minutes the man returned, casting off a woolen poncho from his shoulders. "Got your horse and buggy took care of," he said. "Are you gettin' dried out all right?"

"I'm fine, Mr. . . ." She had not heard his name.

"Nathan," he said. "Jess Nathan."

"I'm Geneva Bannister." She said it before she thought better. If Nathan had heard of Donley Bannister, he might put two and two together.

She looked around the spartan room, which had a cast-iron cookstove, a plain wooden table and four chairs, an open cabinet for kitchen utensils, and little else. A closed door indicated a bedroom, probably just large enough for a bed and perhaps a chest of drawers.

He apologized, "If I'd known a lady was comin', I'd've cleaned the place up a little." He felt his chin. "And shaved."

81

"Everything looks fine, Mr. Nathan. The main thing is that it is warm and dry."

"It's gettin' late for you to go any farther. You're welcome to spend the night here."

Geneva involuntarily glanced toward the bedroom door. "Thank you, but there's a problem."

"No problem at all. You'll have the bed. I'll sleep in the barn. I've got a cot out there for when company stops by."

"Just the same, don't you think people might talk?"

"I've been hurt by horses and run over by a wagon, and I've been in a couple of foolish fistfights that didn't do me any good. But talk has never hurt me. Besides, the only way anybody'll find out is if you tell them. I won't."

"You're a kind man, Mr. Nathan."

"Just tryin' to remember my upbringin'. I was about to start some supper when you came. I'll bet you're hungry."

"I am. Show me where everything is, and I'll fix the supper."

"It's a deal. I don't often get to eat a meal cooked by a woman."

She sensed that Nathan was a lonely man, living here by himself. The window curtains told her a woman had once lived here too, but they were faded and beginning to fray.

Trying to make conversation, she said, "I saw a field out yonder, and some cattle."

"I've got the startin' of a nice little ranch. It'll be bigger someday. Losin' my wife took the heart out of me for a while, but I've got myself back on the road now."

"You need to find a good woman."

"I suppose, but women like Martha don't come along often — women willin' to scrape by on a hardscrabble place like this and take it on faith that things'll get better."

"There may be more of them than you think. A lot of women would be glad to have a husband who's settled down, knowing every day where he is, knowing that come night he'll be home where he belongs."

Nathan was silent awhile, deep in thought, perhaps reviewing old memories. He said finally, "It always seems like the best ones have been taken already. I'll bet you're married."

"Yes, I am."

"Happy?"

"I suppose." She was not sure exactly what *happiness* meant. It had to be more than simply settling for occasional shining moments that never lasted long enough. She said, "The coffee has come to a boil, if you're ready for it."

After supper she washed the plates and

utensils in a large tin pan. Nathan dried them on a towel that once had been a flour sack and placed them on open shelves. It occurred to her that Donley had rarely helped her in the kitchen. Finished, they sat at the cleared table and talked. Actually, Nathan did most of the talking. He told of coming to Texas from Missouri after the war, bringing with him his childhood sweetheart, living on little more than beans and cornbread while he share-cropped cotton on worn-out ground. Gradually he had saved enough to buy a section of land here in the Concho River country. There had been two children, but neither had lived past the first year. Martha had gradually pined away and died just as their fortunes seemed at last to be on the rise.

He asked questions, but Geneva was wary about telling too much, especially regarding her life with Donley. It had had its high points, but it also had its lows. Donley was reckless, ever ready to gamble on the long chance. She never knew if he was going to bring home a bag of silver or simply an empty sack.

As sleepiness tugged at her eyelids, she looked toward the bedroom door, wondering if Nathan meant what he said about sleeping in the barn. True to his word,

Nathan lighted a lantern and gathered up a couple of blankets. He said, "There's a bar for the front door, if that'll ease your mind. But I promise you won't need it."

"I'm sure I'll be fine, Mr. Nathan."

She lighted a lamp and carried it into the bedroom, which was as small as she had expected. One window faced toward the barn. She blew out the lamp before she undressed.

She lay awake a long time, thinking about Donley, wondering if he would really be pleased to see her despite sending her a message to stay put. She found herself comparing him to Nathan. Her impression of the rancher was that a promise made was a promise kept. He had probably never had as much money in his hands at one time as Donley occasionally did when he made a good trade on a string of horses, or when the cards favored him in a high-stakes game. Donley's trouble was that he could never hold on to it. It came easily and went the same way.

Her last thoughts before sleep carried her away were of Nathan. She felt conflicted between gratification that he had not taken advantage of her, and disappointment that he had not even tried.

She had not barred the front door.

CHAPTER 4

Andy was pleased to see that Geneva Bannister's buggy remained on the trail toward Fort McKavett. He had half expected her to go around, avoiding the town and any report that might find its way back to the Slocums. She probably also knew of the nearby Ranger encampment. For whatever reason, though, she went into the little settlement. He saw her stop at a store.

That would occupy her a while, he thought, time enough for him to steal a few minutes with Bethel. He should also report in to Sergeant Ryker, but that would take away from the little time he could be with his wife. Instead, he would send Ryker a note.

Nearing the door of his and Bethel's house, he shouted. The dog came running, scattering chickens that were pecking around the yard. As Andy dismounted, Bethel rushed to him, her skirt flaring, spooking the horse and packmule. He had to make a quick grab for the reins. He said, "Don't you know not to scare a horse that way?"

She threw her arms around him. "Two weeks gone, and the first thing you do is fuss at me."

She smothered his attempt to answer by pressing her lips against his and saying from the corner of her mouth, "Hush up and kiss me." She was a little thing, the top of her head barely coming up to his top shirt button, but she had surprising strength when she embraced him.

Breaking free, he said, "I haven't got long. I'm trailin' a woman."

Her eyebrows went up. "A woman?"

"Not one you need to worry about. She must be over thirty years old."

"What do you want with an old woman?"

"We don't want her, we want her husband. If things work out, she'll lead me to him."

"If she's an old married woman, I guess it's all right." Bethel laughed. "Come in the house."

"I don't have much time."

She kissed him again and gave him a coquettish smile. "Then let's not waste it standing out here where all the neighbors can watch us." She stopped in the doorway and waited while he tied the horse. The mule would stay close.

Inside, she closed the door behind them and fell into his arms.

By the time he came back outside an hour or so later, the black horse stood hipshot and appeared to be half asleep. The mule had strayed off a little way, grazing. Andy said, "Mrs. Bannister could already be pretty far along on the trail to Fort Concho. I stayed some longer than I intended to."

Bethel clung to his arm as he walked toward the horse. Her face was flushed, her eyes shining. She squeezed his arm and smiled. "Do you wish you hadn't?"

"No, except that you keep makin' it harder and harder for me to leave."

"All part of the plan. Maybe someday I'll convince you not to leave at all."

"The way I feel right now, I could ride over to the Ranger camp and tell Sergeant Ryker that I'm quittin'."

"Why don't you?"

"Because despite what they say, newlyweds can't live on love alone."

She said, "I think we could, for a while."

Andy awakened at first light, wondering if he smelled like a goat. Unable to find another suitable shelter away from house and barn, he had made a cold camp beneath a low-roofed shed, sharing space with twenty or so spotted goats. He had followed Geneva Bannister at a respectful distance and saw her turn the buggy toward a plain little ranch house. Hunched up beneath a yellow slicker, rain running off the brim of his hat, he had watched her go inside. Shortly afterward a man came out and took the horse and buggy to a shed. It was obvious she intended to spend the night there.

He had little hope that the man was Donley Bannister. It seemed unlikely that he would come back so soon and be this near to the scene of the shooting, but Andy had learned that fugitives could be unpredictable. He remembered one who had robbed the same bank a second time within a week, dodging posses still out hunting him for the first offense.

He waited for darkness before riding closer. Leaving his horse and packmule tied, he walked to a side window and cautiously looked inside. Geneva sat at a table, in earnest conversation with a man wearing the plain clothes of a rancher or farmer. Andy did not recognize him, but he knew this was not Donley Bannister.

Perhaps he was kin of Geneva or Donley, or he might be simply a stranger with whom

Geneva had sought shelter on a rainy night. If that was the case, Andy thought, Donley had better be broad-minded about his wife. Even a tolerant man might scratch his head over this situation. There did not appear to be another woman in the house.

Somewhat later, from beneath the goat shed, Andy saw the man carry blankets to the barn. He did not return to the house. Though it was none of Andy's business one way or the other, he felt a measure of relief.

Damp, chilled, Andy did not sleep much. He kept thinking about Bethel. He had much rather have spent the night with her. Instead, he had to settle for the goats and the shed's accumulated odors.

Next morning the man milked a Jersey cow and carried the milk to the house. He sat the bucket on the porch and knocked on the door. Geneva opened it, smiling. The man touched the brim of his hat in response. Smoke rose from the chimney, reminding Andy that after spending the night in a cold camp, he was not going to have breakfast for a while, if at all. At least it was no longer raining.

After an hour or so, the man ventured out and hooked Geneva's horse to the buggy. Andy kept low. He watched the man help Geneva up onto the seat, then take off his hat as she extended her hand to him, holding for a long moment. She set off to rejoin the trail that would continue taking her toward the Conchos. Andy waited until she was three hundred yards along before he caught up his animals and rode down to the house. He knew she would move far ahead of him, but he could catch up.

The man was at the barn, saddling a horse. He looked up in surprise at Andy's approach. "Howdy," he said affably. "All of a sudden I'm gettin' a lot of company. Somethin' I can do for you?"

Andy said, "You can tell me about the lady who just left here."

"Mrs. Bannister? Ain't much to tell. I never met her before yesterday evenin'. How come you to ask?"

Andy showed his badge. "I'm a Ranger. Name's Andy Pickard."

"Mine's Jess Nathan." A worried look came into the man's eyes. "Is she in trouble?"

"She's not, but her husband is. Did she tell you about him?"

"She called herself Mrs., so I knew she was married. I didn't think it was my place to ask personal questions. I did get a feelin' that everything ain't just right."

"Did she say where she's goin'?"

"No. I figured if she wanted me to know she'd tell me, and she didn't." Nathan frowned. "Look, Ranger, she struck me as bein' a real nice lady. I wouldn't want to see her hurt."

"I'm afraid that's already happened. There's not much me and you can do about it. You're sure she didn't mention where she's headed?"

"She didn't. And to be truthful, I don't believe I'd tell you if she had. Like I said, she's a nice lady. I wouldn't want to add to whatever problems she's already got."

Andy sensed that Nathan had become mildly infatuated with Geneva Bannister. He had suspected she had the same effect on Addison Giles and the liveryman Spence. He would bet that Nathan had not slept well last night, lying in the barn and thinking about the woman sleeping in his bed.

He said, "Maybe you'll feel different if I tell you the whole of it."

Nathan appeared dubious, but he said, "Come on down to the house. I suspect you haven't had any breakfast."

"Nor much of a supper yesterday. I stayed all night under your goat shed."

"I slept in the barn. You could've joined me."

"I didn't want to tip my hand too early."

Nathan fried bacon and eggs and listened without comment while Andy told him what he knew about the trouble between Donley Bannister and the Slocums. While Andy wolfed down the breakfast, Nathan said, "I know about the Slocums, a little. They've made a couple of sashays up into this country, carryin' off cattle. Even stole sheep one time. A man has got to be low to steal sheep."

Andy said, "That's their reputation."

"But if you're followin' Mrs. Bannister to try and find her husband, who can say that the Slocums ain't doin' the same thing?"

"They tried at first. She got them decoyed away on a wild-goose chase."

"But she didn't shake you off."

"She almost did. She's a sharp lady."

"But like you say, a lady."

Andy finished his eggs. "It'd be better for her and her husband if I find him and bring him back to stand trial. The talk around town is that no jury there would convict him. The only thing the folks blame him for is that he didn't kill the other Slocums too. But if he doesn't come back and get cleared, he'll stay on the run and drag her along with him."

Nathan considered. "I didn't lie to you. All she said was that she still had a long

93

ways to go. She didn't tell me where."

"Clean out of Texas, maybe."

"Maybe. She was headed north. There's a lot of country between here and the Canada line."

Andy grimaced. "I doubt that the money counters in Austin would pay my expenses to go as far as Canada."

"I wish I could go along and help you. I can see where it'd be a favor to her in the long run. But I've got my livestock to take care of, and a crop that'll need weedin'."

"I started by myself. I'll go on by myself. But much obliged for the thought. I wish I could stay and get better acquainted."

"She's got an hour or so start on you."

"That buggy'll leave deep tracks in the mud."

Putting his horse into an easy lope, Andy caught up. He held back just out of sight, occasionally moving close enough to be sure she had not changed direction. A rider came along, heading south, leading four horses tied head-to-tail. Geneva stopped him. They talked for a minute, and he pointed northwestward.

As the horseman approached him, Andy raised his hand in greeting. "Howdy," he said. "I'm tryin' to catch up to a lady in a buggy."

The rider hesitated. Andy pulled his jacket open to reveal his badge.

The rider said, "I met her. She wanted to be sure she was still on the right trail to Fort Concho. I told her she was."

Andy started to ride on.

The rider asked, "Is the lady married?"

"I'm afraid she is."

"Seems like the best ones always are. I guess I'll have to keep lookin'."

"Good luck," Andy said, and put the black horse into a trot. The little packmule followed as if it were tied to the horse's tail.

Fort Concho had been built at the confluence of three rivers. Its original mission had been to protect travelers from Indians on the San Antonio-El Paso road. Now Indian hostilities had ended except for Apache raids far to the west. The fort seemed to be marking time, awaiting closure. It was still home to the Tenth Cavalry Buffalo Soldiers, however, and was a vital source of revenue for the fledgling town of Santa Angela on the north bank of the Concho River. Though the citizens by and large had a strong prejudice against black soldiers, that prejudice did not extend to the money they spent.

Because it was late afternoon, Andy felt it

likely that Geneva would spend the night in town before traveling on. He discounted the possibility that she might meet Donley here. This was only about a hundred miles from the scene of the shooting. Every sheriff within two hundred miles probably had his description.

Andy's first move was to visit the post and dispatch a wire to headquarters. He wrote it in longhand, wishing he had taken school more seriously when he had the chance.

I wish to report that I have arrivved at Fort Concho. Am keeping Mrs. Bannister in site. No sine yet of her husband. Will follo unless orderd otherwize.

He was surprised that the telegraph operator was black. He had heard that most buffalo soldiers were illiterate, a result of their upbringing in slavery. The trooper read the scribbling and smiled. He said, "Be all right with you if I correct the spelling?"

"Go ahead," Andy said. "I didn't know there was anything wrong with it."

The wire was sent. The operator asked, "Do you want to wait and see if there is any answer?"

"I'll be back and check with you before I leave town."

He crossed the river and presented himself to the sheriff, as was customary. He briefly explained his mission. The sheriff, a middle-aged man of solid build, removed a smoking cigar from his mouth and asked, "Need any help?"

"I believe I've got it under control. I expect I'll be movin' on in the mornin'."

"Where are you stayin', in case a message comes for you?"

"At the wagon yard. The only place cheaper is the riverbank. My horse and packmule have earned some grain."

He remembered the wagon yard from a previous visit. Looking over the animals in an outdoor pen, he recognized Geneva's buggy horse. He visited with the hostler while he unsaddled his black and removed the pack from the mule. He pointed toward the buggy horse. "Nice-lookin' animal," he said. "Reckon it's for sale?"

The hostler shrugged. "Not as I know of. It belongs to a lady who came in a while ago." He nodded toward Geneva's buggy, parked beside the barn.

"Reckon where she's stayin'? I might decide to ask her about the horse."

"I told her Mrs. Tankersley's hotel is a nice place."

"Are you sure that's where she went?"

"I watched her all the way. Pretty women like that don't come in bunches."

Andy would like to rent a hotel room too, but Ranger budgets did not provide for luxury. He would sleep on a cot in the wagon yard. At least that would be off the ground.

The hostler warned, "You may have a hard time sleepin' tonight. The soldiers got paid today, and they'll be noisy. It's a caution how quick they can drink up thirteen dollars."

"Even us Rangers get paid more than that." Andy immediately wished he had not spoken. He had put his badge in his pocket, not intending to noise it around that he was a Ranger.

The hostler quickly put things together. "Then you ain't really interested in that horse. You're interested in the woman. Did she kill somebody?"

"She didn't do anything except maybe marry the wrong man. I'm hopin' she'll lead me to him."

"If you shoot him, she'll make a fine-lookin' widow. Every bachelor in the country will be after her. And some that ain't bachelors."

"I don't figure to shoot him. I'm supposed to bring him in so a jury can find him innocent and turn him loose. Then he won't have to be on the run anymore."

"If he's innocent, I don't see no reason to try him in the first place. It's a waste of the taxpayers' money, and I'm a taxpayer."

"Naturally it's wasteful. It's the government."

Andy walked down Chadbourne Street and found a café. He splurged on a two-bit meal. While he sat finishing his last cup of coffee, two black soldiers paused at the door and looked in. The proprietor gave them a threatening frown, and they moved on.

The man said, "I'll be glad when they shut down the fort and all those dark-complected Ethiopians are gone."

Andy did not speak his thoughts, but it seemed likely that some of the town might shut down when that happened. He remembered something old Preacher Webb had told him years ago: the worst punishment God could inflict on the world would be to give people everything they wished for.

Returning to the wagon yard, he took his blanket roll and spread it on a steel cot. The hostler came and said, "I hope you're not a smoker. A careless cowboy come near burnin' this place down a while back."

"A man is entitled to only so many vices. I don't waste mine on tobacco."

Tired, Andy quickly dropped off to sleep. Sometime later he was awakened by boisterous shouting and celebratory gunshots. He raised up on one elbow but could see little in the darkness. A lantern burning near the open barn door showed him nothing. He tried to settle back down to sleep but kept being jarred by the noise. Occasional shots continued to be fired. After one, he sensed that the tenor of the shouting changed. It turned angry. Footsteps indicated that men were running. Somewhere a window was smashed, and another.

Hell of a place to get any sleep, he thought, and turned over for another try. He had managed to doze off when someone shook his shoulder. "Ranger, wake up. The sheriff says he needs you."

In the darkness he could not see the young man's face. He asked, "What's the trouble?"

"Somebody shot one of them darkey troopers, and now there's hell to pay. The soldiers are swarmin' across the river lookin' for the man that done it. If they don't find him, just about anybody else will do."

Pulling on his boots, Andy asked, "Where's the sheriff now?"

"At the jailhouse. He's locked up the man that pulled the trigger, but he may not be able to keep him. He needs all the help he can get."

Andy put on his holster belt. He said, "This sure isn't the way I intended to spend the night. I wasn't plannin' on havin' to shoot anybody."

"You never know what you may have to do around here come payday."

Andy did not count the soldiers who clustered in front of the jail. To do so would probably scare him. Many were armed with rifles and pistols. Others carried driftwood clubs picked up along the river. They shouted furiously at the sheriff and another man, evidently a deputy, standing in front of the door. The sheriff held a shotgun close to his chest. The deputy had a rifle.

Andy saw a pathway open up between the members of the mob. He rushed through it, the young man following. Someone grabbed at him, but he jerked loose and joined the sheriff and deputy at the door. Soldiers grappled with the young man and prevented him from getting that far. The sheriff raised one hand, calling for quiet. It was slow in coming, but most of the shouting died down.

"You soldiers," he said, "I'm callin' on you to go back across the river. There's been killin' done, but the man that did it is behind bars. He'll stand trial accordin' to

Texas law."

A soldier with sergeant's stripes shouted, "And get turned loose, like they always do?"

"That'll be up to a jury."

"A white jury," the sergeant declared. "You think they'd ever convict a white man for killin' one of us?"

The sheriff shouted, "I don't want to shoot anybody. But I would do it to protect my prisoner."

The crowd surged forward. The sheriff tried to swing the shotgun into line, but someone struck him on the head with a heavy club. He went down. Hard-hit, the deputy went to his knees too. Andy reached for the sergeant who had shouted loudest. He grabbed him by the collar and shoved the muzzle of his pistol against the man's neck. "Now you-all back away," he ordered. "I don't want to kill anybody, but I've got my finger on the trigger. If anybody jostles me, this pistol will go off."

The sergeant yelled, "Don't nobody jostle him."

The troopers moved back a little. Andy found himself looking into the muzzles of a dozen or more guns. His heart hammered. Any one of them could kill him in an instant. He tried to hold his voice steady, but it quavered. He said, "If anybody shoots me, I'll pull this trigger as I go down."

He had found over the years that the ones who shouted loudest were usually the first to cave in. The sergeant begged the others, "Back away. He'll blow my head clean off."

An angry buzz showed the troopers were still in a mood to fight, but their comrade's plea stayed their hands.

Andy seized the moment. "Everybody ease back. No use in anybody else gettin' bloodied up. Payday is supposed to be a time to celebrate, not to get yourselves killed."

A soldier demanded, "You guarantee that the prisoner will pay?"

Andy knew the realities. "I guarantee he'll be tried. I can't promise you anything beyond that."

"Then he'll go free. They always go free. A soldier's life ain't worth six bits in this town. Not if'n he's black."

Andy kept his grip on the sergeant's collar but lowered the muzzle an inch. It appeared to him that the mob's anger had peaked. The men had had their confrontation, and several had had their say. Gradually they began fading back into the darkness. A few loitered a short distance away, watching, muttering empty threats.

Andy told the sergeant, "I'm puttin' you in jail for the night."

"What for? All I done was talk."

"Sometimes talk can do more damage than a gun."

The rioters had released the young man who had summoned Andy. He knelt beside the sheriff and said, "Looks to me like he's out cold. The deputy don't look good either."

Andy said, "Help me get them inside, then you better run and fetch a doctor. I'll lock the door."

The sergeant voluntarily helped carry the two lawmen into the jail and place them on cell cots. He asked, "You really goin' to lock me up?"

Andy nodded. "That way your friends won't come back and burn the jailhouse down." He frowned. "You've got to realize that what you-all did here tonight was wrong."

"As wrong as shootin' a soldier in cold blood? We was just tryin' to get justice. There ain't no other way we'll see it around here."

Andy recognized the futility of arguing, for the sergeant was right. "I know. Maybe someday things will be different."

"Someday. That's what they always tell us when they want us to stand back and be quiet. It'll be better someday."

"I wish it was otherwise, but it isn't. Probably won't be till we've been dead and buried for a hundred years."

Two men were locked in separate cells. One appeared to be a cowboy overloaded on whiskey. Andy assumed the other was the man who killed the soldier. After taking a sidearm from the sergeant, he pointed him into an empty cell and asked, "For the record, what's your name?"

"Joshua Hamlin. *Sergeant* Joshua Hamlin. When you write it down in the book, don't forget the *sergeant.* I been a long time gettin' that far."

The sheriff was stirring a little. He mumbled incoherently, vigorously moving his hands as if he were fighting. Blood had trickled down the side of his head and into his collar. Andy found a water pitcher and wash pan. Using a wet towel, he wiped away as much blood as he could. It continued to ooze slowly.

The deputy had raised up. He sat on the edge of his cot, holding his head with both hands. He let out a sharp oath when Andy inspected his wound. He wheezed, "What did they hit me with, a sledgehammer?" He opened his eyes wide, evidently having trouble focusing. "They didn't get the prisoner, did they?"

"No, he's still safe in his cell. I'd like to go in there and stomp the clabber out of him for the trouble he's caused."

"I'll do it myself when I get my feet under me. How's the sheriff? I saw him go down before I did."

"He took a bad lick. I've sent for a doctor."

Andy heard a knock on the door, then the young man's voice. "Ranger? It's us — me and the doc."

He unlocked the door and pointed the doctor toward the sheriff. He said, "He took a mean blow to the head. Hasn't come around yet."

The doctor set his black bag on the floor beside the cot and bent over the mumbling lawman. "I'll see what I can do."

Andy wandered back for his first good look at the prisoner accused of the killing. The register showed his name to be Ephraim Burnsides. That seemed too high-sounding to be real. Probably made up, he thought. The culprit looked like a road tramp. Eyes defiant, he smelled of whiskey but appeared cold sober. A close call like tonight's should sober up anybody, Andy thought.

The prisoner regarded Andy with apprehension. He demanded, "Who the hell are you?"

"A man who's tryin' awful hard not to go in there and beat out what little brains you've got. Do you have any idea the hell you've stirred up?"

"I don't let no darkey get uppity with me. He sassed me, so I shot him, like any self-respectin' white man would do. I don't see anything wrong with that."

"You got the sheriff and his deputy both hurt tryin' to protect you."

"That's their job. It's what they get paid for." The prisoner stood up and gripped the bars. "How long they goin' to keep me in here?"

"I've got a good mind to turn you loose right now and set you on the street. I wonder how long it'd take for the soldiers to rip off both your arms and beat you to death with them."

Fear flickered in Burnsides's eyes, then evaporated quickly. He knew as well as Andy did that such a thing could not be allowed to happen. He said, "You're responsible for takin' care of me."

"Not me. I'm just passin' through. The local law is responsible, and it's layin' out yonder helpless on account of you." He placed a hand on the cell door. "Now, do you want me to turn you loose?"

The prisoner retreated to the back of his cell. "Go to hell," he said.

The doctor's face was grim. He told Andy, "Neither man will be able to do much for a while. I understand you are a Ranger."

"I am."

"Then you'll have to take over here, at least for now."

"But I've got another job to do."

The doctor shook his head. "Right now this town is sitting on a ton of black powder. It's just waiting for a spark. For the moment that is more important than your assignment, whatever it may be."

Andy saw his point, but he knew also that several roads led out of Santa Angela. He could only guess which Geneva Bannister might select while he was tied up here, guarding a prisoner who did not deserve all this attention. He nodded toward the young man. "What about him?"

"He is not an officer. He is the sheriff's nephew. I am sorry, Ranger, but you have inherited the responsibility, like it or not."

Andy swore in frustration. He was at a fork in the road. Both roads called to him, but it was painfully clear which was the most urgent.

"You're right," he said in regret. "I've got no choice but to stay."

From time to time during the night, he stepped outside to look and listen. The town had gone quiet, deceptively peaceful. He sensed that it slept fitfully at best. Sleepy-eyed, he watched the first bright rays of sunshine break in the east and hoped the long dark hours had cooled tempers on both sides of the river.

Andy unlocked the cowboy's cell. He asked, "You got someplace to go?"

"Back to the ranch. Done spent all my money."

"Then you'd better get started. If the trouble comes back, you don't want to be caught in the middle of it."

"Much obliged. I was in a cold sweat last night, thinkin' they might bust in here and not know which of us to lynch." The cowboy picked up his belongings but paused at the door. "I don't reckon you could lend me five?"

"Git before I change my mind."

"Next time I may take my business to a different town." The cowboy disappeared down the street.

The sheriff struggled to his feet to relieve himself. He seemed disoriented, lost. The deputy was more stable but said he had the worst headache of his life. He was seeing double. He said, "I hope you'll stay a while,

Ranger. I couldn't blow a hole in the wall with a double-barreled shotgun, and the sheriff is worse off than I am."

"I don't see where I've got a choice. I'll stay as long as I'm needed."

He badly wanted to go to the wagon yard and watch for Geneva to move, but he dared not leave the jail while the prisoner remained in it.

At mid-morning an attorney showed up, wearing a black swallowtail coat and an officious expression. He said, "I have here a court order for the release of Ephraim Burnsides."

Andy had expected this. His opinion about most criminal lawyers was that they were well-named. He answered that the sheriff was incapacitated and unable to acknowledge the order. "You'll have to wait till he's in better shape. That may be a couple of days."

The attorney argued, "What is your capacity here?"

"I'm a Texas Ranger, passin' through on an assignment. I've got no authority to let your man go."

"On the contrary, because you seem to be the only officer here in possession of his faculties, I contend that you do have the authority. I demand that you release Mr.

Burnsides. Otherwise I shall have no choice but to bring the judge and force you into compliance."

Andy's stomach soured at the prospect of releasing the prisoner. He said, "His life will be dirt cheap once he walks out into the street."

"It is the responsibility of the law to protect him."

"The *local* law. Look at them. They're in no shape to help anybody."

"There should be no problem from the soldiers. The commanding officer has ordered all military personnel restricted to the post."

"Let me see your warrant."

The paper showed that bail had been paid in the amount of one hundred dollars. Andy said, "That's not much of a price to place on a soldier's life."

"A *black* soldier," the attorney pointed out. "From time to time those people have to be reminded of their proper place."

Grudgingly Andy signed the release order. He fumbled through two rings of keys before he found one that fitted the lock. Burnsides showed no gratitude. He growled, "Good thing you didn't hit me last night, Ranger. You'd be takin' my place in that cell."

"Get out of here before I hit you anyway. I was in the middle of a job, and you've probably blown it to hell." To the lawyer Andy said, "You'd better collect your fee right now. If your client has got any sense, he'll clear out of town and never come back."

"But that would forfeit his bail."

"A hundred dollars? That's not much of a price to put on a life, white man or black." Andy reconsidered. "In his case, it may be too much. Half that would be about right."

Burnsides said, "I need a drink. A bunch of drinks." He jerked his head, and the lawyer followed him.

Andy felt an emptiness, seeing Burnsides walk out into the open sunshine. As the rioters had predicted, he was escaping justice. It was a foregone conclusion that even if he went to trial, a white jury would acquit him. It was the tenor of the times.

Andy approached the black sergeant's cell. "Do you think you've simmered down enough that I can afford to let you go?"

Hamlin looked toward Burnsides's cage. "You turned him aloose."

"I had to. His lawyer served me with a court order. But he'll stand trial."

"He'll go free, like they always do."

"I can't argue with that. But I'm offerin'

you a chance to leave if you want to take it. Or you can stay in here."

"That cot is way too hard for my achin' bones. I'll go."

The soldier picked up his belongings, which amounted mainly to eleven dollars, a large pocketknife, and the army pistol. Andy asked him, "Where did you come from, Sergeant?"

"Mississippi. I was born a slave, but we got emancipated when I was still too young to move cotton bales. By and by the army come along lookin' for some of us to be soldiers. Said it was our chance to be somebody." His face twisted. "Bein' somebody don't mean some lowdown white trash can't kill us any time they take the notion."

Andy said, "You'd best head straight to the post. I'd hate to see you back in here."

"I'd hate to *be* back in here." In a minute Hamlin was out of sight.

The sheriff was asleep again, his head wrapped in a white bandage. The deputy sat in a horsehide chair, eyes pinched in pain.

Andy said, "Since we don't have a prisoner to worry about, I need to walk over to the wagon yard and check up on things."

The deputy said, "Take your time. We ain't goin' nowhere."

As Andy had feared, Geneva had left town soon after daylight. The hostler offered no information about the direction she had taken. She could have chosen the west, which would take her to the Pecos River and beyond. But she might run into Apache trouble there. She could have gone east, toward Fort Worth, or she could have traveled northward, toward the cross timbers and the rolling plains. He decided to take his horse out a while and try to pick up her tracks. At least when he left here he might have some inkling about her direction.

He picked the western road, traveling it for a time without seeing tracks he could be sure were left by the buggy. He circled around to the north road. Again, if her tracks had been there, later travelers had obliterated them. He had no more success on the trail east. He started westward back toward town, frustrated. He would have to stop at Fort Concho and send a wire to headquarters. He hoped his superiors would understand that the situation had been taken out of his control.

At the edge of town he saw a horseman moving toward him at a steady lope. Andy discerned that he wore a soldier's uniform. Close up, he recognized the sergeant who had spent the night in jail. Hamlin rode a conventional stock saddle, not army issue. His brown horse had a brand, but it was not the army's U.S. Andy thought it likely that the mount was stolen.

He called, "Hold up a minute. I thought you were goin' back to the fort."

Without replying, Hamlin brushed past and galloped eastward. Andy started to follow and challenge him again but decided against it. If the sergeant was deserting, that was the army's business. Andy had trouble enough on his hands trying to keep up with Geneva Bannister.

He rode first to the post to send the wire. The same black soldier read Andy's message with a quizzical look in his eyes. "Still want me to fix the spelling?"

"Suit yourself. They pay me for ridin', not writin'."

The telegrapher tapped out the message on his key. He looked up and said, "Aren't you ever going to let Sergeant Hamlin out of jail?"

"I turned him loose several hours ago."

"He's never reported back in. Some of the boys are afraid he's in trouble in that hog wallow across the river. Come dark, they may go looking for him."

"They'll have to look farther than Santa Angela," Andy said. "I saw him a while ago, ridin' like the devil was on his tail."

The telegrapher registered surprise. "It's not like Sarge to desert. You sure there wasn't somebody after him?"

"Nothin' was chasin' him but his shadow. It was havin' a hard time keepin' up."

The hostler met Andy as he dismounted at the stable door. His face flushed with excitement, he said, "I'm glad you got back. There's big trouble down the street."

Andy had seen no commotion at the fort. "Trouble?"

"That Burnsides, the one who shot the trooper yesterday. He got in a quarrel with a black soldier. Don't know who drawed first, but Burnsides took a bullet square in the brisket."

"Kill him?"

"He never took another breath."

"Sergeant Hamlin!" Andy declared. He remounted and moved down the street at a run.

He found a small crowd clustered around a body on the sidewalk. The deputy was there, his head bandaged from the previous night's ruckus. He looked up at Andy and nodded painfully. "Glad to see you, Ranger. We've got a messy situation here."

"So I heard." Andy dropped the reins and stepped up for a closer look. Burnsides was

116

slumped there, soaked in blood.

The deputy said, "People say a soldier came up on him and started callin' him names. Burnsides drew a gun, but he was drunk and missed. The soldier was sober and hit what he aimed at. He grabbed a horse from a hitchin' post and took to the tulies."

Andy said, "It was Sergeant Hamlin, the one we had in jail."

"How do you know?"

"Because I met him on the east road. He was cuttin' a hole in the wind."

"Why didn't you stop him?"

"I didn't know about this. Chasin' deserters is the army's job."

"It's my job now." The deputy looked anxiously at the men in the crowd. "I'll need a posse."

Andy said, "Are you sure you're fit to ride?"

"No, but I'm better off than the sheriff is. I'll wire the peace officers around us to be on the lookout. Then I'll take some men and hit the trail."

"In that case, I'll be gettin' on about my business, if it's not too late." Andy doubted that the deputy's posse would catch Hamlin. More than likely, officers in another county miles away would intercept him.

Meanwhile, innocent blacks were likely to suffer the painful consequences of mistaken identity.

He returned to the wagon yard to pick up his belongings and the packmule. The hostler seemed to be wrestling with a dilemma. He said, "I don't generally poke my nose into other people's business, and I didn't mean to tell you this. But you said it would be a favor to the lady if you took her husband back to stand trial. Maybe this'll help you a little. She asked me how far it is to Colorado City."

"Thanks." Andy paid him a dollar extra and struck off on the road north. His shoulder ached, but he pushed his mount into a lope. He had a lot of miles to make up.

CHAPTER 5

Geneva Bannister looked back occasionally, watching for any sign of pursuit. She had been nagged by a persistent feeling that someone was behind her, but she had seen nothing. The Ranger who had kept her under surveillance in Junction had not fooled her for long. She was sure she had shaken him off just as she had shaken off the Slocums. She did not intend to let anyone use her to get to her husband.

The long trip had given her plenty of time to think about Donley. She had loved him, or she would not have married him. Over time, however, she had found reason to question her choice. Usually when he left he did not tell her where he was going or how long he would be gone. From the first he had been vague about his business, making her wonder if he had good reason to avoid explanations. When he returned he usually brought back a string of horses for sale. He always gave her money enough for food and other necessities. She could not complain that he was a poor provider, though he would have been a better one had he stayed away from poker tables.

She wondered about other things. After the initial honeymoon glow of their marriage, his passion had cooled. She did not believe he was finding pleasure in other women during his travels. In most respects he had a Puritan sense of right and wrong. Several times she had heard him express disapproval of men who cheated, whether at cards or with women. He had even less respect for women who strayed from the narrow way.

She found herself thinking now and then about the rancher, Jess Nathan. He seemed stable, tied to his land and his memories. She wished Donley were more like him.

The stableman had said it would probably take her three days to reach Colorado City — four, if she wanted to be easy on the buggy horse. She decided not to push. It was still a long way to where Donley's letter had indicated he had gone. She did not want the horse to give out.

Unlike the night she had sought shelter at Nathan's place, the sky was cloudless, offering no hint of rain. As she had done most nights on the trail, she pulled off a short distance at dusk and stopped behind a cluster of trees that should hide her from anyone passing by. She fed the horse a bit of grain, then staked him to graze at the end of a long rope. She built a small fire and began to prepare a simple supper.

She had finished eating and was sipping coffee when she was startled by the sound of something moving through the grass. Setting the cup down, she fetched her rifle and waited with her back to the buggy. A horseman appeared around the trees and paused, looking first at the dwindling fire, then at her. Fear leaped into his eyes at the sight of the rifle pointed at him.

Quickly raising his hands, he stammered, "Ma'am, please don't shoot. I don't mean you no harm." He was black, and he wore an army uniform.

She asked, "What do you want?"

"I smelled the smoke of your fire and thought maybe I might find somethin' to eat. I'm powerful hungry."

Her strongest impulse was to drive him away, for she was afraid. Yet, she could sympathize with his hunger. Keeping the rifle trained on him, she said, "I didn't fix much, and I ate it myself. There is some bread I bought in town, and you can fry some bacon."

"I'd be mighty obliged, ma'am. My name's Joshua Hamlin. Don't be afeered of me. I'll eat, then be on my way." He dismounted, dropping the reins. The horse stood still.

She kept her distance while the soldier sliced bacon and dropped it into a skillet. She had been aware of trouble in Santa Angela but had not known the particulars beyond the fact that troopers from the fort had created a riot of sorts. The town had quieted down by the time she left soon after daylight. She suspected that this soldier had something to do with the trouble. He was probably running away.

The firelight revealed something she had not noticed. She said, "You have a stain on your uniform. Is that blood?"

He kept his head down, not looking her squarely in the eyes. "I'm afraid so, ma'am. I was in a fight."

"Is that your blood, or his?"

"His, ma'am."

She had a sudden hunch. "You've killed a man."

"He wasn't no man, hardly. But I expect there's folks huntin' me."

The soldier looked up. Geneva stepped backward, bumping against the buggy. She gripped the rifle harder and said, "Don't you come any closer."

The soldier said, "He killed one of my men. I knowed the law wasn't goin' to do nothin' about it. He needed killin', but I didn't set out to do it. I just figured to cuss him out real good. Then he drawed a gun, and I had to protect myself."

Needed killing. That was what Donley had said about Cletus Slocum. Geneva shivered, remembering.

The soldier said, "After I done it, I took out to the east, then cut back north. I reckon I shook them loose because I ain't seen nobody comin' up behind me."

That was similar to the tactic she had used to throw the Slocums and the Ranger off her trail. She said, "It's likely they've wired every sheriff around here. They'll be watching for that uniform."

"I ain't had a chance to swap for somethin' else."

She considered before offering, "I have a few of my husband's clothes in the buggy. See what you can find." She stepped away, giving him room. Almost immediately she wondered why she was aiding a fugitive. It was contrary to her normal inclinations. Perhaps it was because his situation seemed similar to Donley's.

The sergeant took a shirt and a pair of trousers. He was smaller than Conley, so they would hang loose on him. Even so, they would be less conspicuous than the uniform. He said, "Once again, ma'am, I'm obliged."

"Just take them and go." She let the rifle barrel sag a little, but she could raise it again in a second. "You'd better not stay on the trail. They'll be watching it."

"I've been hidin' durin' daylight and travelin' by night."

"Do you have anywhere to go?"

"Nowhere special, just someplace a long ways from here." The sergeant rolled the fresh clothes and tucked them under one arm. Mounting his horse, he said, "There's one more favor I wish you'd do for me, ma'am. If somebody was to ask, you might neglect to remember that you seen me." He rode away at a trot and was quickly lost in the dusk.

Geneva listened to the hoofbeats until they faded beyond hearing. Only then did she place the rifle back in the buggy. She was still trembling. In girlhood she had heard frightful stories about black men brutalizing white women. She had dismissed most of them as exaggerations, a holdover of old anxieties about slave rebellions. The soldier's sudden appearance had brought them rushing back, arousing old fears. Yet, the man had made no threatening move toward her. He had seemed as frightened of her as she was of him.

He had admitted to a killing. If the person killed was white, the soldier stood a poor chance of living long enough to go to trial. His remaining time was likely to be short, and the end terrible. Despite the fright he had given her, she felt sympathy for him.

She was up the next morning before full daylight, moving sluggishly, her eyes itching from lack of sleep. She had relived the previous evening a hundred times, occasionally slipping off into a nightmarish half sleep, dreaming of a shouting mob placing a rope around the soldier's neck and hanging him from a tree. Only, sometimes the victim was not the soldier — he was transformed into Donley Bannister.

Late in the morning half a dozen horsemen approached her from the north. As they pulled up beside the buggy, she saw a deputy's badge on one man's shirt. He touched fingers to the brim of his hat and said, "Pardon, ma'am, but we're lookin' for a man."

Geneva hoped nothing in her expression gave her away. "As you can see, sir, I am traveling alone."

"We got a wire to be on the lookout for a darkey soldier from Fort Concho. Seen anybody like that?"

"I can't say that I have." She consoled herself that it was not exactly a lie, just an evasive answer.

"There's a good chance he's ridin' north from Santa Angela. If so, he's probably still south of us." His voice darkened with concern. "You oughtn't to be travelin' alone, ma'am, with a murderer on the loose."

"A murderer! Who was killed?"

"A nobody who called himself Burnsides. We ran him out of our town a while back. But he was white, and a darkey shot him down while he was drunk. We can't let a thing like that just go by."

"I suppose not."

"If you're nervous, ma'am, I'll get one of these men here to ride along with you. Just in case."

"Thank you, but I have a rifle with me, and a pistol. I don't see that I have anything to worry about."

"Be on the lookout, then. No tellin' what a desperate man like that might do. Especially a darkey."

The posse continued south on what Geneva knew was a wild-goose chase. The lawman had indicated that the victim had been a man of no account. The soldier had told her as much too. She felt better about aiding him in his flight. Perhaps kind strangers had helped Donley in the same way. She would like to think so.

Donley had told her of a business acquaintance in Colorado City who owed him money. She needed it, for the trip had lightened the weight of her purse. Moreover, the buggy horse was wearing down from the steady pace all the way up from Junction. A couple of days' rest would be good for the horse as well as for her.

The western march of railroad building crews had prompted the birth of the town. Almost overnight, it had become a busy supply center as well as a cattle shipping point for a broad area of western Texas. Its buildings still looked new, the paint fresh. The lumber that had gone unpainted had not yet darkened from time and weather. She crossed the railroad tracks and picked out a likely-looking general store. Stopping in front, she started to climb down. A well-dressed man stepped up and extended his arms, offering to help her. She took him to be a banker or a lawyer. No one else wore clothes like these. Not many could afford to.

"That's kind of you, sir," she said. "Traveling alone, I have not had much help the last few days."

"You've been traveling alone?" The man looked shocked. "Madam, has nobody warned you that a black murderer is on the loose? He is being hunted in a dozen counties. Rumor is that he has killed two or three white men and forced himself on a couple of helpless country women."

She found it remarkable how quickly fear could create rumors far worse than the reality.

The man said, "They made a bad mistake sending those blacks out here to watch over us. It's they who need watching, not us. Anyway, you had better stay here in town till the killer is caught and disposed of."

Disposed of. The words gave her a chill. It sounded as if he were a mad dog to be dispatched without ceremony and dragged off somewhere for the buzzards to feed upon.

She changed the subject. "Do you know a man named Luther Fleet?"

The man frowned. "Fleet? Yes, but I can't imagine what a lady like yourself would want with him."

"My husband told me he owes us money."

"He owes money to many people. I would

not wager a nickel on your chance of collecting. But be that as it may, he lives in a nondescript shack south of the railroad tracks. You'll be able to recognize it by a belligerent bulldog he keeps chained at the front to ward off people who might want to do him injury. Those, I must say, are numerous."

The description took her aback. If Fleet were that disreputable, she did not understand why Donley would have done business with him. She asked, "What does he do for a living?"

"That, madam, is a question many have asked. Except for gambling, at which he exhibits some limited skill, he has no visible means of support." He tipped his hat. "You have my best wishes."

A little shaken, she contemplated moving on through town without bothering to see Fleet. But she needed supplies to continue her trip. The sergeant had almost finished the bacon, and she was short on flour, sugar, and coffee. She was unsure how far it might be to another town if she maintained her northerly direction. In the store she paid the merchant for the goods she bought, then counted the money that remained from what Donley had left for her. It was not much.

Like it or not, she needed to find Fleet.

The balding merchant, who reminded her a little of Addison Giles, loaded her purchases into the buggy. He said, "I assume your husband is waiting for you."

She said, "Yes, but farther on."

The merchant frowned as the other man had. "This is not a good time for a lady to travel alone."

"You're thinking about the fugitive soldier? The chances are that he is nowhere around."

"Then again, he could be watching us this very minute. Were I you, I would stay in town until he's caught. You can find good accommodations at Mrs. Kelly's boarding house, across the street and down yonder a way."

"I'll consider it. Thank you for your concern." She knew she could not afford to stay in the boarding house unless Fleet paid up.

The merchant gave her a lift into the buggy. She drove to the corner, turned and crossed back over the tracks. She followed a dirt street past a couple of low-order saloons and through what she easily recognized as a small red-light district. Two hundred yards beyond was an unpainted shack. Behind it stood a barn built mostly with used lumber, and a set of wooden corrals that held several horses. A bulldog waddled out from the shade of a narrow porch and strained against a chain, snarling as if it meant to do murder. Geneva had to pull hard on the reins to prevent the buggy horse from turning away.

She stopped in front of the house but did not climb down. She saw no way to reach the front door without passing too close to the dog. Soon she heard a man's voice from inside, "Dog, shut up out there!"

The dog did not let up. A pudgy, unshaven man came to the door and stood in his socks, his shirt unbuttoned most of the way down, the tail of it hanging out. Obviously the commotion had awakened him from a nap. "Damn you, dog, I'll take a whip to you if you don't quit that noise." He turned his attention to Geneva. "Who the hell are you, and what the hell do you want here?"

She was tempted to retort, *Nothing that you have.* But she could not turn away so abruptly. She needed the money. She said, "I'm Geneva Bannister."

"Never heard of no Geneva."

"Donley Bannister is my husband."

"Oh, Donley. Well, he ain't here. Ain't been here in a while."

"I know. I'm on my way to meet him."

"I don't see where that has anything to do with me."

"He said you owe him money. I need it."

Fleet scowled. "Who don't? Well, get down and come in. We'll talk about it."

Geneva nodded toward the dog. "Not till you tie him up short."

The dog continued a low growling. Fleet said, "Hush up, or I'll take a quirt to you." The dog quieted but watched Geneva with distrust. Fleet wrapped the chain around a post several times, shortening the dog's range of movement. To Geneva he said, "Now you can get down."

He did not offer to help her.

Though the dog could no longer reach her, she gave it a wide berth. She found the inside of the house as spartan as the outside. Newspapers had been pasted to the walls to serve as a cheap form of wallpaper, the house's only insulation. A half-empty whiskey bottle stood on a plain kitchen table.

"Drink?" Fleet offered.

The thought of drinking with him repulsed her. "No, thank you."

"Hope you don't mind if I take one. My stomach goes sour when I get woke up too fast from my nap." He uncorked the bottle and took two long swallows.

She said, "The money, Mr. Fleet."

"The money." He blinked as if he had already forgotten. "Well, now, that raises somethin' of a problem. I ain't got that much."

"How much do you have?"

"Just enough to start me in a game to-night. There's a couple of outfits in town to ship cattle. Their cowboys'll be ripe for the pickin'. I'll pay you in the mornin'."

"I do not intend to spend the night in this town."

"I don't see where you got any choice. I said I'll pay you in the mornin'."

"But I'm broke, almost. I can't afford a boarding house."

"You can stay here."

Her face warmed. "With you? Not on your life."

"Savin' it for your husband, are you? Well, you don't need to worry about sharin' the bed. I'll be playin' poker most of the night. When I come back, I'll sleep in the shed."

Geneva wanted to forget the money and rush out of this house, out of this town. But she could not get far with the little money she had left.

Fleet took the decision from her hands. He said, "Whatever you want for tonight, you better bring it in now. I'll put your buggy under the shed and throw your horse

133

into a pen with mine."

She brought in two blankets, her purse with the pistol in it, and her rifle.

Fleet noticed. "You figure on huntin' bear? I don't think you'll find any in this house."

Crisply she said, "You never know what kind of animal might come prowling around."

He was grumbling as he drove her buggy to a low shed. She took the pistol from her purse and checked to be sure it was fully loaded. That evening she cooked supper, never letting herself stray far from the purse.

Fleet drank much of the remaining whiskey, his flabby face reddening and his eyes watering. He loosened up and began to talk. "Old Donley, he's a good judge of horse-flesh. Him and me, we've made a right smart of money tradin' together. He knows where to get them for nothin' and where to sell them high. And he savvies how to steer clear of the sheriffs, too."

Geneva had suspected that Donley's horse business had a side that would not stand much daylight, but she had kept telling herself that her imagination was running wild. She tried not to hear everything Fleet was saying.

He slurred his words. "It's a long ways from Indian Territory down to that Junction country. Them Indians got more horses than they need, since they ain't goin' out on the warpath anymore. Fifty here, seventy there, they don't hardly miss them. And even if they do, the army won't let them off of the reservation to try and bring them back."

"You're telling me that you and Donley steal horses?"

"*Steal* is a strong word. After all, how else do you reckon them Indians got ahold of them in the first place?" Fleet gave Geneva a long, lustful study. "I can see why he picked you. He's always had an eye for good-lookin' horses. Women and horses ain't that much different. There's few things prettier than a slick, young mare."

Curtly she said, "I am not a mare, Mr. Fleet."

"But slick and young. I wonder how long it took him to unhook your buttons the first time."

Geneva felt warmth rising in her face. "You've said enough, Mr. Fleet. I thought you were going to a poker game tonight."

She wondered how he could expect to play successfully after putting away so much whiskey. But by the time he prepared to leave the house, his hands steadied, and he walked a straight line. Flexing his fingers, he said, "Whiskey sharpens me up. You watch, I'll trim those cowboys tonight. I'll take hide, hair, and all."

After he was gone, she checked the front door to see if she could secure it. There was no lock, nor was there a way to bar it. The best she could do was to brace a chair beneath the porcelain doorknob. She did the same for the back door.

She was tired, but she could not bring herself to lie in his bed. She spread her own blankets on the floor. She lay awake and fully dressed, listening to the sound of a train passing through town, to a piano playing somewhere down the dirt street, to boisterous laughing and whooping. Once she heard a couple of men talking loudly, approaching the house. The bulldog's chain snapped loudly as the animal ran to the end of it, giving the passersby a warning.

A man said, "That dog's lookin' for raw meat. This ain't the right house anyhow." The voices trailed away.

Geneva considered giving up and leaving before Fleet came home. She would have to go out the back door to avoid the bulldog. She could hitch her horse to the buggy and be a few miles north of here before sunup. But the purse contained little more than the pistol. She took it out for reassurance, knowing she might have to show it to convince Fleet to pay what he owed. She managed finally to fall into a restless half sleep, still hearing noises from outside, a night train passing.

She came suddenly and fully awake when she heard Fleet's voice. "Move aside, dog. I'm comin' in." Heavy boots tromped onto the porch. He pushed against the door. The chair held for a moment, then slid away and fell over with a clatter. A match flared. Swaying, Fleet lighted a lamp and held up a handful of bills.

"Told you, by God. I cleaned them boys to a fare-thee-well."

Geneva rose quickly to her feet, clutching the purse. "You were going to sleep in the shed."

"Changed my mind. You been lookin' down your nose at me like you was special and I was dirt. Now we'll find out which is the better man, me or Donley Bannister."

He lunged toward her as she dropped the purse and brought up the pistol. He grabbed her with strong arms, pinning her against him and forcing her back. She managed to place the muzzle against his leg as he pushed her onto the bed and fell on top of her. She jerked the trigger.

He screamed in pain and rolled away, his

eyes wide with surprise. "You bitch! You shot me."

On her feet, she pointed the pistol at his groin. "I'll do it again if you don't leave."

He fell to the floor, crying, gripping his upper leg with both hands. "My God, I'm bleedin' to death."

"You will if you don't go and find some help."

Whimpering, he dragged himself to the door on hands and knees, leaving a trail of blood. He picked up the chair and used it to support the wounded leg as he dragged himself out onto the porch, then to the ground. Perhaps because of the blood smell, the dog attacked. It dug its teeth into Fleet's leg and clung until it reached the end of the chain. Fleet was yelping as he dragged himself up the street.

Daylight was three or four hours away, but for Geneva the night was over. She grabbed up what belonged to her, including the wad of bills Fleet had brought. She did not take time to count them, for this was no time to quibble over small matters. She hitched her horse to the buggy and crossed the tracks at a brisk trot. The business houses were dark, the streets quiet except for a few noisy cowboys weaving their way toward the shipping pens where their chuck wagons were camped. The moon was dull but yielded enough light that the trail north was easy enough to see.

She doubted that her husband and Luther Fleet would ever trade horses together again. And for a while, at least, Fleet would have little interest in ladies' buttons.

CHAPTER 6

Andy had become acquainted with Colorado City during the long days he had spent there, being treated for the wound two stray outlaws had inflicted upon him. Geneva Bannister had a long head start, but he traveled faster on horseback than she could in the buggy on the road northwestward from Santa Angela. A posse riding south in search of the fugitive soldier had told him about meeting a lady traveling alone. He came within sight of her early on the third day and trailed well behind.

He shortened the distance as she approached Colorado City. He thought it conceivable, though unlikely, that she might meet her husband here. He watched her stop at a general store and talk briefly with a well-dressed man who definitely was not Bannister. Then she returned to the south side of the railroad tracks and pulled up in front of a plain shack that suggested something less than prosperity. Presently she unloaded some of her belongings. A man bulkier than Donley took her buggy and horse to a shed. Perhaps he was a relative, or at least a family friend.

Watching him from a distance, Andy realized he had seen him before. His name was Fleet, and his disposition was sour. At the sheriff's suggestion, Andy had asked him about Bannister. Perhaps it made sense that Geneva Bannister was paying him a visit inasmuch as he knew her husband.

Confident that she would not travel on for a while, Andy crossed the tracks and rode to the courthouse. The sheriff greeted him with a handshake that could crush walnuts. "Thought you had a gutful of this town already. How's the shoulder?"

"Pert near healed. Still aches a little now and again."

"Comes from sleepin' on the ground too much. You ought to have a decent bed at night."

"Hard to manage when you're trailin' somebody. Besides, Indians say sleepin' on the ground is the healthiest way. They claim that healin' powers rise up from mother earth."

"So, who are you after this time?"

"It's still Donley Bannister. I don't suppose he's been back?"

"We haven't seen or heard of him. Right now everybody's huntin' for a soldier out of Fort Concho. Killed a man, they say."

"So I heard, but my job's to look for Bannister." Andy told about trailing Bannister's wife up from Junction. He described the shack he had seen her enter.

The sheriff's eyebrows lifted. "Sounds like Luther Fleet's place. When Bannister was here, before I found out he was wanted, Fleet and him visited the whiskey joints and gamblin' tables. Fleet played pattycake with the ladies while Bannister just played poker."

"Bannister didn't pay attention to the women?"

"A man can have strict morals about one thing but not about another."

Andy thought Geneva Bannister would probably be pleased to hear about this side of her husband's character, if she didn't already know.

The sheriff said, "Tonight you can sleep on a soft bed over at my house."

"Thanks, but I've got to keep an eye on Mrs. Bannister. I almost lost her at Santa Angela on account of the soldier trouble. I don't want to chance losin' her again."

The sheriff shrugged. "You might not get

much sleep. Some cow outfits are in town. The only people who'll get much rest tonight are over in the cemetery."

"Sounds like Santa Angela after payday at the fort."

"You can't blame the boys for cuttin' loose. They don't often get to the big city."

The town had a long way to go before it could live up to the *city* part of its name, Andy thought. It was slim pickings compared to San Antonio, Fort Worth, or even Austin. But it must look like cowboy heaven compared to a ranch bunkhouse or lonely line camp.

He saw no reason to hurry, so he took time to drop in at the boarding house where Dr. Coleman had placed him for observation. Mrs. Kelly, the landlady, met him at the door, flour on her hands. She rubbed most of it into an embroidered apron tied around her ample middle, then gave him a brisk hug. Delighted at his recovery, the landlady asked about Bethel and Len Tanner. She told him in no uncertain terms that he was going nowhere until she fed him the best supper he had enjoyed since bidding farewell to his young wife. He did not object.

She said, "A drummer moved out yesterday, so your old room happens to be empty.

You'll sleep in a soft bed tonight."

He had to tell her, as he had told the sheriff, that duty prevented his accepting the offer. He said, "Maybe when this job is done I'll come back here and sleep for a week." He knew that was unlikely.

"Be sure and bring Bethel. I declare, I don't see how you can keep going off and leaving that girl behind. There ought to be something better for you than being a Ranger."

"There is, when I can afford it."

After supper he rode back across the tracks to be sure Geneva's buggy was still in the shed where Fleet had placed it. A little farther on he found a vacant shack from where he could watch the Fleet house without being obvious. As darkness settled in, he saw Fleet leave the house and stride toward a saloon south of the railroad. Horses were tied in front, indicating that several cowboys were already there.

Sidestepping a growling bulldog, Andy peered through a side window into Fleet's house. He saw Geneva block the front and back doors by wedging chairs beneath the door knobs. Then she spread blankets on the floor. That surprised him, for he could see what appeared to be a perfectly good bed. At least this indicated that she would not be going anywhere tonight. He decided to watch Fleet instead. The man might know Bannister's whereabouts. With enough whiskey in his belly, perhaps he could be induced to share that knowledge.

Hopeful that Fleet would not remember him, Andy followed the man to the saloon. He entered, plunging into an invisible wall of noise. Laughing, singing, clinking bottles and glasses together, many of the cowboys appeared to have made an early start on the evening. Andy ordered a beer at the bar and watched Fleet seat himself at a poker table, a small roll of bills in his hand. The bartender carried a full bottle and a glass, setting them on the table beside him. Three cowboys approached Fleet. One said, "You won everything I had the last time I was in town. I want a chance to win it back."

Andy thought of a spider welcoming a fly into its web. Smiling cordially, Fleet said, "Welcome, cowboy, take a seat. All of you take a seat. This is your chance, because I'm feelin' unlucky tonight."

Andy took his beer to a table in a dark corner away from the several lamps and sat down to watch. From time to time he touched the glass to his lips but swallowed little. The level of whiskey in Fleet's bottle went down and down. In spite of that, the cowboys' money inexorably moved toward the gambler's side of the table. Andy knew within reason that Fleet was cheating, but at the distance he could not see how he was manipulating the cards. The other players were too deep into their whiskey to realize it.

Two men came through the door and paused to look around. Andy recognized the chuck wagon cook and the kid who had brought him to town after his wounding. Andy pulled his hat brim down and lowered his head, but he was too late. They walked toward him.

The kid said loudly, "Howdy, Ranger. Looks like you healed up all right."

Andy made a sign for quiet. In a low voice he said, "I don't want everybody here to know I'm a Ranger. Just call me Andy."

The kid said eagerly, "You fixin' to arrest somebody? I want to watch you do it." Frowning, Cookie nudged the cowboy with his elbow.

Andy said, "Just watchin' a feller, is all." Motioning for the two to sit, he beckoned the bartender. "Bring them whatever they want."

The bartender demanded, "What about you? You've done nursed one beer for two hours."

Andy did not want to attract attention. "Bring me a fresh one." When the bartender turned away, Andy poured the remaining warm beer down a knothole in the pine floor.

The wagon cook licked his lips. "That's an awful waste."

"I need to stay sober."

Cookie turned to the kid. "That goes for you, too. We've got to herd these cowboys back to camp after a while. Otherwise they'll scatter like a bunch of Old Mexico steers."

The kid made no attempt to conceal his curiosity as he stared at Andy. "You ain't given up bein' a Ranger, even after gettin' shot? Next time, you're liable to end up with six foot of dirt in your face."

The cook said, "You've got no place to talk, tryin' to be a cowboy. If some bad bronc don't stomp your brains out, some wild cow will run her horn through your belly and out the tail of your shirt."

The men who sat in on Fleet's game dropped out one by one, their money gone. One groused, "You told us you felt unlucky. I'd hate to play you when you didn't."

The cook said, "Kid, it's time to haze them toward camp." Gradually the two managed to shepherd the cowboys out the door.

Fleet stuffed a large handful of bills into his pocket and told the bartender, "Look out there and be sure they're all gone. I wouldn't want them gettin' a notion to take it back."

The bartender stepped outside, then back in. He said, "All clear. Looks like you had a good night."

"It ain't over yet. I got somethin' even better waitin' at the house."

"Anybody I know?"

"Naw, she holds her nose too high for the likes of me and you. But I'll bring her down off of her high horse."

An ugly picture flashed in Andy's mind, sparking anger. Whatever she was or was not, Geneva did not deserve this. He realized that to intervene would tip his hand. She would know at once why he was here. Still, he could not simply stand back while Fleet carried out his intentions. He would do whatever he had to.

The bartender glared at him as he walked out the door. Andy had occupied space for perhaps three hours without adding enough to the till to pay rent on the table. He trailed fifty yards behind the staggering Fleet. Fleet cursed the dog and stomped up onto the porch. He pushed against the door. It resisted until he put his shoulder to it and forced it to give way.

Andy heard Geneva's voice raised in alarm and the sounds of a scuffle. Drawing his pistol, he sprinted up to the porch, ignoring the dog that nipped at his heels. As he was about to rush through the door, he heard a shot and Fleet's high-pitched scream. Fleet staggered to the door, squalling in pain. Andy realized that he need not show himself to Geneva after all. He jumped down from the porch and flattened himself against the side of the house as Geneva slammed the door behind Fleet.

The gambler stumbled across the narrow porch and down to the ground, trying to support himself with a chair. The bulldog attacked him. Fleet's cries ascended to a higher pitch.

Andy could only guess how badly the man was hurt. Fleet turned loose of the chair and began dragging himself on hands and knees, whimpering. Andy had come to help Geneva but now needed to help Fleet instead. He took the man's left arm over his shoulder. He said, "I see a light in that house yonder. Maybe they can give you some help, or send for it."

He helped Fleet onto the small porch and hammered his fist against the door. "Somebody! Got a hurt man out here."

Through the door's oval glass he saw the bobbing of a lamp being carried from somewhere in the back of the house. An angry-eyed woman in a low-cut nightgown opened the door and shoved the lamp into Andy's face. "We're closed for the night," she declared. "Go somewhere and sleep it off."

She was into her thirties, Andy guessed, with a hard mouth and too much color in her cheeks. He said, "This man's been shot."

She blinked. "Luther Fleet. Can't say I'm surprised. But what did you bring him here for? Look at him, bleedin' all over my clean porch."

"And apt to die here if we don't get it stopped."

The woman said, "Wait till I get an old blanket. I don't want blood all over the livin' room floor."

Andy said, "Grit your teeth, Fleet. Looks like the milk of human kindness has turned to clabber."

The woman brought a blanket, doubled it and spread it on the floor. "Lay him there."

Andy saw that the wound was in Fleet's leg, a long way from his heart. It could be dangerous, however. He could bleed to death, or he might even die from shock. Andy told himself he should muster some sympathy, but he regretted only that Geneva had not shot him a lot higher up.

He said, "Bring me some clean rags if you've got them. Towels would be better."

The bleeding slowed under the pressure of his hands and the towels. Andy said, "Fleet, I oughtn't to help you at all. I want you to tell me about Donley Bannister."

Fleet's face twisted in pain. He rasped, "Donley who? Don't know no Donley."

Andy squeezed the wounded leg. Fleet yelped like a kicked dog. Andy said, "Think a little harder. Maybe it'll come to you."

Fleet trembled, cold sweat glistening in his face.

Andy said, "For what you tried to do to that woman, I ought to let you lay here and die."

"Oh, God, no. You've got to help me."

"Only if you help *me.* Where can I find Donley Bannister?"

"I don't know, honest to God. All I know is that she's on her way to see him. Somewheres north, where he gets his horses. That's all she told me."

A man emerged from a back room, tucking his shirttail in. He was buckling his belt as he sneaked out the back door. An overweight young woman with tousled hair appeared from the same room, trying to close a flimsy housecoat. Wide-eyed, she bent over the bleeding man, then rushed out the front door to throw up. When she returned, the other woman said, "Flora, get some clothes on and go bring Dr. Coleman. I don't want this man to die here. It'd give the place a bad name."

Andy wondered what kind of name it already had.

The woman asked him, "How come I get the notion that you're some sort of a law?"

"You're right. I'm a Ranger."

"You must not be much of a shot, hittin' him in the leg."

Andy saw no reason to tell her the truth. He said, "I don't get to practice as much as I ought to."

The doctor came, grumbling about being rousted in the wee hours of the morning. He looked at Andy in surprise. "Ranger, I wouldn't expect to find you in a place like this. How's the shoulder?"

"A lot better than this man's leg."

The doctor knelt, setting his black bag on the floor. "Luther Fleet! I wondered when somebody was going to catch you drawing the wrong card."

Fleet whined, "She tried to kill me. Please, don't let me die."

Coleman said, "I'll do all I can. I know

152

several people who would like to have chance at you. I would not want to deprive them of that pleasure." He spent some time cleaning and dressing the wounds.

The woman said, "Doc, I want you to get him out of here."

Finishing up, Coleman said, "If I'm not mistaken, Fleet lives in that shack just down the road."

The woman nodded. "Him and that mean bulldog. A bullet in the brisket would be good for both of them."

The doctor said, "Andy, let's carry him out to my rig and take him home."

Andy had managed all the way from Junction to prevent Geneva's seeing him. He suggested, "What about the boardin' house, where somebody can look after him?"

Coleman shook his head. "This is one customer Mrs. Kelly would not make welcome. I do not wish to arouse her anger."

Andy beckoned the doctor out onto the porch and quietly explained his dilemma. He said, "I can help lift him into your rig, and help get him down. But I can't let Mrs. Bannister see me."

Coleman nodded. "Being a Ranger puts you into some unsavory situations, doesn't it."

"When you're huntin' a criminal, you

don't look for him in the church house."

With both Andy and the doctor supporting him, Fleet whimpered all the way from the doctor's buggy to his porch. "Damned woman," he complained, "I owe her for this."

Andy said, "That's one debt you'd better forget about. Next time she's liable to shoot you in the heart."

The doctor said, "That would require a good shot, for it would be a small target indeed."

The bulldog threatened but backed away when Fleet cursed it. On the porch, Andy freed Fleet's arm and said, "He's yours, Doc."

The doctor said, "I can handle him the rest of the way." He pushed the door open and helped Fleet inside. He deposited the wounded man on the bed, then lighted a lamp. Andy backed away into the darkness.

Coleman returned to the porch. He said, "You were worried for no cause. There is no woman here."

Andy swore under his breath and hurried into the house to see for himself. "She didn't waste much time gettin' away," he said.

Fleet whined, "I had three hundred dollars on the table. Robbed me, she did."

Andy said, "Like you robbed those cowboys tonight?"

Fleet cursed. "If I ever run into her again, she'll be sorry she ever saw me."

Andy said, "I'm sure she already is."

A partial moon showed him the way to the shed. He was not surprised that Geneva's horse and buggy were gone. He retrieved his horse and packmule from where he had left them staked. As he rode by Fleet's house, the doctor hailed him from the porch. Rolling down his sleeves, he said, "You are a peace officer. It is your place to give the sheriff a full report."

"I need to follow Mrs. Bannister."

"You won't be able to pick up buggy tracks in the dark."

Reluctantly Andy said, "I guess you're right." If he started now, in the dark, he might indeed take the wrong road, for several wagon trails led out of town in a more or less northerly direction. If he waited, other buggies or wagons might leave similar tracks. He would be unable to tell them apart. Still, protocol had to be considered. He would report to the sheriff, hoping he could find the right trail afterward. He seated himself on the courthouse steps. There fatigue caught up to him, and he fell asleep. He awakened to find the sun was up. He went to the restaurant and ate breakfast, watching through the window for the lawman to appear.

The sheriff arrived at his office after eight o'clock. Andy told him what had happened. He said, "She shot him in self-defense. I was fixin' to go in there and stop him, but she beat me to it."

The sheriff said, "I've been hopin' somebody would put Fleet out of my misery for a while. Too bad she left the job half done."

Andy laboriously scribbled a message on a sheet of paper. "I'd be much obliged if you'd wire this to Fort McKavett. They'll want to know where I'm at and where I'm headed."

"I'll take care of it."

"I hope Sergeant Ryker sends word to Bethel. I'd write her a letter, but God knows when she'd get it. Or if." He had rather dig a ditch than write a letter. Even to compose a brief message to headquarters was as slow as pouring molasses in January.

The sheriff asked, "How much farther do you think you'll have to go?"

Andy shrugged. "I've got my orders. I'll go wherever it takes."

CHAPTER 7

In her rush to get away from Fleet's house and escape the town, Geneva had no time to reflect on what she had done or give way to anxiety. When the town was behind her, however, the pent-up fear and anger burst loose in a torrent of emotion. Stopping the horse, she shook uncontrollably, a rush of tears burning her eyes. She leaned out over the side of the buggy and vomited. She covered her face with her hands and cried as she had not cried in years. She vented her hatred of the man who had tried to attack her, then yielded to a suppressed resentment against Donley. Because of him, she was forced to endure this long, sometimes frightening trip alone. Because of him, she had fallen vulnerable to the likes of Luther Fleet. Now, for all she knew, she would be regarded as a fugitive from the law, just as her husband was. She could not be sure Fleet would survive the loss of blood.

She became aware of a lighted lantern coming toward her, bobbing in rhythm with footsteps. Instinctively she reached for the rifle. The lantern stopped moving. Its yellowish light showed her a middle-aged man with a derby hat and a paunch. He asked, "Are you all right, ma'am?"

She had trouble finding her voice. "I'm fine."

"I heard you cry out. I thought you might be hurt."

She could not see past him in the darkness. She asked, "Where did you come from?"

"Chuck wagon camp, right over yonder. I'm the cook, about to start fixin' breakfast."

"Up early, aren't you?"

"The cook always gets up early. Fact is, though, I just got back to camp an hour ago. I had to herd a bunch of cowboys in from town. There wasn't much point in goin' to bed, so I didn't."

"I'm sorry I disturbed you. I'll be moving on."

"You're out awful early yourself, ma'am. Seems to me you might be in some kind of trouble. Anything I can do to help you?"

She found his voice to be kindly, but she

did not know if she could trust him. After tonight's experience, it might not be easy for a while to trust any man. She said, "It's my own problem. I'll work it out."

"Anyway, you look like you've been through a bad time. A cup of good, strong coffee might make you feel better. And I'll be fixin' breakfast before long."

The thought was tempting. Coffee might give her strength. "You're very kind."

"Swing that buggy off of the trail and follow me. It's just a little ways."

She saw the glow of a campfire, which laid a soft light on a wagon with chuck box attached.

The cook said, "Better stop here. You wouldn't want to run over any sleepin' cowboys, though there was a time tonight that I would've been tickled to do it myself." He helped her down from the buggy. He removed a wash pan from a three-legged stool and motioned for her to sit. "Hope you don't mind drinkin' out of a tin cup. I washed them all clean last night. Some of these cowboys don't care about such things, but I do." He grabbed the coffeepot by the fire and poured her a cup.

"Anything's fine," she said. The first taste burned her lips. She blew on the cup to cool it. Her hands still trembled.

The cook said, "I ain't pryin'. You don't have to tell me your troubles if you don't want to, but sometimes it's good to talk about what bothers you. It lets somebody else help you carry the load."

She said, "I shot a man tonight."

The cook looked startled. "Kill him?"

"I don't think so, but I should have. I just hit him in the leg."

The cook nodded. "I expect he had it comin'. Who is he?"

"His name is Luther Fleet."

She saw recognition in the arch of the cook's eyebrow. "I know him. Gambler. Thief. In bad need of a neck stretchin'. You sure you didn't kill him?"

"He dragged himself away from there, squealing like a pig caught under a fence. He tried . . ." She stopped, ashamed to bring out the words.

The cook seemed to sense the rest of it. "You should've stayed and told the sheriff. He'd find a way to finish where you left off and make it look like Fleet started the fight."

"There's a good reason I didn't want to see the sheriff. I'm on my way to join my husband, and there are people who would like to know where he is. They tried a while to trail me."

"Are you sure they're not still behind you?"

"I've watched, but I've seen no sign."

"Has your husband got a name?"

She nodded. "Donley Bannister."

The cook grunted. "I remember him. He came by our camp some time ago. Went on, then came back and left a wounded Ranger with us."

Geneva gasped. "He shot a Ranger?"

"No, he said somebody else done it. He just happened to be there. Like as not, he saved the Ranger's life. Not everybody would've done it in his situation. We gathered that he was on the dodge."

Geneva pondered the irony. Donley had saved a Ranger, yet other Rangers were looking for him. Life could be hard to figure.

The cook said, "You'll feel better after a good breakfast. I'll get it started."

Geneva was concerned about letting more people see her. "I'd best be on my way."

"Don't you worry about any of these boys talkin'. Most of them will be so hung over they won't remember you was here. The rest, well, they know I'd bend a pot hook over their heads if they told anybody whichaway you went."

Geneva looked toward the eastern sky. She saw no sign yet of sunrise. "Just a quick bite, then I'll be gone."

The cook busied himself with getting breakfast, greasing two Dutch ovens and molding balls of dough, fitting them into place. He heated gobs of lard in a deep iron skillet and dropped in strips of steak rolled in flour. He said, "It don't vary much from day to day, but neither does cow work." He frowned in thought. "Some of these boys have got a powerful grudge against Luther Fleet for cheatin' them at cards. Addin' what he done to you, I think the wagon boss'd allow them time today to pay the gentleman a visit."

Geneva was not prepared for that. "Surely you wouldn't lynch him."

"Nothin' that drastic. We'd just tickle him with the business end of a quirt and convince him that there's taller cotton someplace else."

She could see rough justice in the suggestion. "I wouldn't want you winding up in jail."

"The sheriff'd do this himself if the law didn't hold him back."

The cowboys were slow about emerging from their bedrolls, many groaning and belaboring the shortcomings of Colorado City whiskey. Geneva finished her breakfast before most got their feet under them. She told the cook, "I'm obliged for the breakfast, and the comforting words."

He gave her a lift into the buggy. "A pleasure, ma'am. And don't you worry about any of us talkin' out of school. We never saw nor heard of you."

First daylight was beginning to break in the east as she left the camp and took the trail northward. Some of her faith in men had been restored.

Andy was still in the sheriff's office when the madam rushed in, short of breath and face flushed with excitement. "Sheriff," she said, "you better get yourself down to Luther Fleet's house. The way he's hollerin', they must be killin' him."

"Who?" the sheriff demanded.

"A bunch of cowboys. Must be seven or eight."

"Did you actually see them doin' anything to him?"

"No, but I heard him squallin' like a baby."

Winking at Andy, the sheriff lighted a cigar. "Reckon we ought to go down there and do somethin' about it?"

"Soon as I finish my coffee." Andy refilled his cup from a pot on the lawman's round-bellied wood heater. "He cleaned out a bunch of the boys' pockets last night. They've probably sobered up and realized he cheated them."

"We'll need to go down there after a while and talk to them. More coffee?"

"I just got a full cup."

The madam stared at them in exasperation. "I risk life and limb runnin' up here to tell you, and you're not goin' to do anything?"

The sheriff said, "We'll get around to it."

She said, "I've done my part. They can hang his hide on the barn door for all I care. And yours too."

After she left, the sheriff said, "I reckon we'd better get down there before the boys carry things too far. I'd hate to have to feed them all at the county's expense."

Andy was concerned about the time he was losing here while Geneva was on the move, but he feared the sheriff might need help. They rode together in the sheriff's buggy, across the tracks, then west along a well-beaten trail past the house where Andy had taken Fleet after Geneva shot him. Half a dozen horses stood around Fleet's shack. Several cowboys came out and caught up their mounts. Andy saw a derby hat and recognized the wagon cook among them.

Cookie headed off any potentially incriminating questions. "Sheriff," he said, "you better go see about Luther Fleet. Looks like he's done somethin' to himself."

"Like what?"

"Best we can tell, he was whippin' himself with a quirt, like them penitentes over in New Mexico."

The sheriff asked without much show of interest, "Is he dead?"

"No, he's still breathin'. Keeps sayin' somethin' about God. Is it all right with you if we ride on? We need to get back on the job before the boss fires us."

"You-all go ahead," the sheriff said. "Me and the Ranger can take care of it from here."

"Muchas gracias." The cook frowned. "Bad enough him cheatin' the boys, but it was a lot worse what he tried to do to that woman."

The sheriff asked, "What woman?"

The cook caught himself. "One we heard talk about."

The cowboys rode away. Andy said, "The only way they could've heard about it was from Mrs. Bannister herself. She must've gone by their camp."

"It's north of town, just a little ways out."

Andy nodded with satisfaction. "Then I ought not to have much trouble pickin' up her trail."

The cowboys had shortened the leash so that the bulldog could do nothing more than threaten. Entering the shack, Andy and the sheriff found Fleet sitting on the edge of his bed. His shirt was off, his long underwear pulled down to his waist. He looked up bleary-eyed, having trouble focusing on them. He whined, "For God's sake, don't whip me no more."

The sheriff said, "It's me, and a Ranger. We came to see if you're still alive."

"Not by much."

Fleet's back and shoulders were raw, laced with quirt cuts long and deep, seeping blood.

The sheriff said, "You thinkin' about filin' charges?" He made it sound more like a warning than a question.

"If I did, I doubt I'd live to testify."

"Probably not." The sheriff's tone was matter-of-fact. "It seems to me that you've worn out any welcome you ever had here. Was I you, I'd hunt for a place where the water runs free and the sun always shines. Somewhere a long way from this town."

Fleet grunted. "Soon as I heal up enough to travel. Between gettin' shot and then bein' worked over with a quirt, I'm gettin' damned tired of this place."

166

The sheriff poked a finger at him. "If you ever come here again, you'd better just be passin' through on the train, and you'd better not get off."

Fleet hunched his shoulders and grimaced in pain. "I can't think of nothin' that would bring me back. But you've got to give me time to sell out."

"I'll give you till Saturday. If you can't ride a horse by then, you can buy a ticket on the train."

"You're a hard man, even for a sheriff."

"If I was a hard man, I wouldn't have waited for a woman to shoot you. I'd've done it myself."

Walking away from the shack, Andy said, "I hope you won't do anything to the cowboys."

"Why should I? They said he quirted himself. It'd be his word against theirs. Justice don't always move in a straight line, but it generally finds its way."

Andy said, "Sheriff, I like the way you think."

"I don't see any other way of thinkin'. What's right is right, and sometimes what's wrong is right, too."

Riding north, Andy found the cowboys breaking camp. The cook and the kid were loading pots and Dutch ovens into the wagon, behind the chuck box. The cook said, "We'd offer you coffee, Ranger, but we just poured out what was left."

"Much obliged all the same, but I need to move on. I don't suppose you'd tell me if you've seen a woman pass this way in a buggy."

The cook looked Andy squarely in the eyes. "I don't suppose we would."

Andy nodded. He took that answer to be as good as if the cook had said yes. He said, "Don't work too hard," and rode on. He had no trouble finding and following the narrow tracks of the buggy.

The trail led him close to the dugout where he had been shot, but he had no interest in seeing that place again. He passed it by. So far as he could remember, it was a long way north to a town of any consequence. From here on for several days he would see little but a thin scattering of ranches, established in the wake of the buffalo slaughter. There had been some hide camps in the past, but those would be gone now. Instead of gathering buffalo hides, men with no better work to do were gathering buffalo bones to be shipped to Europe for the making of bone china.

Remembering the great shaggy herds he

had seen as a boy, living among the Comanches who had captured him, he gave way to a fleeting melancholy for so much that had been lost.

At times the wagon road threatened to disappear, and with it, trace of the buggy. It was easy to imagine how the land had looked before, for it had changed but little. Cattle grazed now where the buffalo had been, but the landscape remained as he remembered it from boyhood, crisscrossed by narrow old trails beaten out by cloven hooves over uncounted generations. The Indian had survived here on what nature provided, little affected by distant events. The white man, living with and for his cattle, depended upon distant markets and took his chances upon prices set by others, hundreds and even thousands of miles away.

Andy had the feeling that he could even yet throw off most trappings of the white man's civilization and survive. That would not happen, however. For Bethel's sake, he had taken on responsibilities that would forever limit his personal choices. He might at times mourn the trading of complete freedom for a shared life, but he had resigned himself to it. He had chosen his path and could no longer change it.

He caught a hint of wood smoke. It was

169

so quickly gone that he thought at first he had imagined it. When it came again, it was stronger. Somewhere off the trail, a campfire burned. His immediate thought was that he had overtaken Geneva Bannister. He reined up, his gaze carefully searching for the source of the smoke. At length he found it, ahead and off to the right. So far, her buggy tracks had not left the wagon trail. This must be someone else, for a couple of traveling hours remained in the day. She had not been in the habit of stopping early.

Warily, remembering the incident in the dugout, he checked his rifle, then his pistol. He kept to the lower ground of the rolling terrain, hoping to see before being seen. He was surprised by the sudden appearance of a man on horseback. The rider was no less startled. He froze for a moment. Andy recognized him as Comanche and raised his hand. The Indian lifted a rifle, then lowered it partway.

Andy had had little occasion to use Plains sign language in recent years, but what he needed came back to him. He indicated that he meant no harm and asked permission to come into camp. The surprised Indian hesitated, then signaled a reluctant welcome without lowering the rifle further. Approaching him, Andy reached back into

170

memory for half forgotten words. They came haltingly.

"I am a traveler, like yourself," he said. The Indian wore no war paint. Andy guessed that he was a member of a small hunting party, off the reservation in violation of federal rules. Small groups now and then returned to old hunting grounds despite government prohibitions. Such forays were hazardous. Any whites they encountered were likely to assume they had hostile intentions and shoot them on sight.

The Indian's eyes narrowed in distrust. "How is it that you speak like one of us? You are Tejano."

"I was raised among the People. The Tejanos took me away from them."

"Did Father Washington send you to force us back?"

"I am with the government of Texas, not of Washington. I did not know you were here."

Sharply the Indian said, "This was our land. The Tejanos took it from us."

"I know." Andy also knew that the Comanches had taken it from the Apaches. He did not know who the Apaches took it from. "You are in danger here if anyone sees you."

"But there is hunger where the government wants us to live. We came here to find buffalo. All we find is bones."

"The buffalo are gone."

"Surely not all of them. There were so many."

"I have not seen one in years. I am sorry, Uncle, but they are truly gone. Only their bones are left." Andy saw sorrow in the man's face and felt sorrow of his own.

The hunter said, "I am tired of searching. You are welcome to come with me to camp."

Andy had never forgotten the contentment he had found in his brief boyhood years with the People. He felt a yearning to be in that company again, at least for a few hours. Wherever Geneva was, she would soon be stopping for the night. He could find her tomorrow. "It would give me pleasure."

The modest camp was well hidden in a hollow where its fires were unlikely to be seen unless someone came directly upon them. It consisted of a few buffalo-hide tepees smaller than those used in long-term camps.

Andy was the subject of intense scrutiny and some open expressions of hostility until he spoke in the Comanche language. As he explained the circumstances that had caused him to spend several of his boyhood years among the People, he sensed a positive change in the listeners' feelings toward him. He said, "If I had known you were here, I would have brought meat into camp." He had seen several antelope scattered to graze, watching him with curiosity, then flashing white rumps as they turned and fled. They would run a short distance, then stop to see if he was following. Finally they would cut in front of him and disappear over a hill.

An elder said, "We have antelope, but we had hoped for buffalo."

Andy could only express condolences. He smoked with them and listened to their unhappy talk about life on the reservation. They spoke longingly of better times when buffalo had been plentiful, before soldiers and government agents ruled their lives.

At length Andy asked, "Did anyone see a white woman traveling alone?"

The elder said, "We saw her. We did not allow her to see us."

"That is good," Andy said. "She might have shot at you." With Luther Fleet she had demonstrated her ability to use a gun.

"We feared she would bring the soldiers. Is she your woman?"

"No. I follow her because I need to find her husband. He has killed a man."

"The People kill our enemies, but we do not kill our brothers. The white man kills whoever stands in his way."

"Most don't. Those who do must accept punishment. It is my work to find them and bring them in."

"You are like a soldier, but you do not wear the blue."

"I am not a soldier. I am a Ranger." The old horseback warriors knew the Rangers from bitter encounters and shedding of blood by both sides.

The elder's face hardened. "Many times I have fought them. How can you be of the People, yet be one of those?"

"All things change. Now the People and the whites are friends."

"Only if we do what they tell us, and stay where they put us. It is a hard thing to live under the *teibo*'s rule and call him friend." He spoke of the whiskey peddlers, bringing with them degradation and despair. He spoke of horse thieves who raided the remudas and drove away the best of the People's mounts.

Andy shared antelope stew with the Comanches. These were not of any band he had known, though they recognized a few names he asked about. He was careful not to mention anyone he knew to have died. There was a taboo against speaking names of the dead.

He took a chance and asked about Steals the Ponies, who had been like a brother to him. The elder's eyes were clouded with sadness. "He lives, but he is sick of spirit. He has lost the one who was his wife. His son does not follow the old ways. He talks of going to the government school and becoming like the white man. It is hard for a boy to become a man now. He has no enemies to fight, no buffalo to hunt. They have taken all that from us. They are trying to make us all women."

Andy could only nod, for he had no argument to counter what the elder said. Someday, he thought, he should take time off and go to the reservation, to seek out Steals the Ponies and whatever others remained of those he had known. But it would not be a happy reunion. It would be more like a funeral.

As night fell and the fires died down, the Indians repaired to their tepees. They did not post a guard. Andy had long recognized this as a regrettable weakness that on occasion had brought disaster to them at the hands of their enemies. He rolled out his blanket and slept in the open. Once in the night he thought he heard a stirring of hooves. It did not happen again. He decided it had been caused by a couple of the Indian horses, staked beside their masters' tepees.

As first light spread across the rolling plains, he saw horsemen surrounding the camp. One glance told him they were soldiers, waiting for the Comanches to arise. That happened quickly as alarm swept like a whirlwind through the camp. Andy pulled on his boots and hat and walked out toward the nearest men. Several rifles were pointed at him.

"No need to shoot," he said, raising his hands. "I'm white."

A lieutenant pulled in front of the others, stopping just short of where Andy stood. "What are you doing with these Indians?"

"I happened across them late yesterday. I stayed the night with them."

"Man, don't you realize how dangerous that was? You are lucky you still have your hair."

"There's nothin' dangerous about these people. They're just hungry and huntin' for meat. They don't get enough on the reservation."

"How do you know?"

"They told me."

The lieutenant made no attempt to hide his suspicion. "*Told* you? How could you understand their language?"

"I lived with them when I was a boy."

"And you just happened across them? You weren't waiting here to sell them whiskey?"

"I wouldn't do that for all the money in Texas. Whiskey has been their ruination."

"We'd best take you back with us to the fort. You can plead your case to a higher authority than me."

Andy said, "I'm a Texas Ranger on official business." He took the hidden badge from his shirt pocket. "My name is Andy Pickard."

"I thought Rangers were supposed to shoot Indians on sight, not camp with them."

"That was a long time ago. Things are different now."

"Not all that much. What is your business here?"

"I've been trailin' a woman whose husband is a fugitive. I hope she'll lead me to him."

"What do these Indians have to do with it?"

"We just happened to cross paths."

"Then you will have no objections if we take them back to the reservation where they belong?"

"Objections? Hell yes, I've got objections, but I have no authority to do anything about it. I just hope you'll treat them decent. Try to look at the situation through their eyes."

The officer looked as if his stomach ached. "I have to look at it every day. Frankly, I don't like it any better than you do, but I am just a shavetail. The powers that be do not listen to second lieutenants." He gave a signal to the soldiers to start gathering the Indians. He asked, "Who is this man you're looking for?"

"His name is Donley Bannister. He killed a man down in Junction."

The lieutenant frowned. "Bannister? I know that name. As a matter of fact, we've been looking for him too. He's part of a horse-stealing ring that operates on the reservations and up into Kansas."

Somehow that was not a big surprise to Andy. "Down south he's known as a horse trader, but not as a thief."

"Where do you think he gets the horses to trade?" The lieutenant watched as the Indians finished gathering their scant belongings and mounting their horses. "By the way, we've been advised to watch out for a black soldier who murdered a man at Santa Angela. The authorities believe he came up this way. By any chance have you come across such a man?"

"I was at Santa Angela when it happened. I haven't seen him since."

"We'd like to find him before some lynch mob does."

"The outcome will be the same, won't it?"

"Hanging? Yes, but the army will do it with some civility."

Civility. Andy shook his head. No matter who did it, there would be no civility about it.

Flanked by the soldiers, the Indians began to move. Andy saddled his horse and rode up beside the elder. "I am sorry, Uncle."

Sadness dulled the old Comanche's eyes. "Nothing is like we knew it before. This land is no longer home. The reservation is not home. For the People there is no home anywhere."

Andy wished he could say something to bring comfort, but any such words would sound hollow and false. It was not in him to lie to this old man.

The elder said, "This is no life for one who has hunted his own meat and fought his own battles. This is a slow death, and we die without pride."

Watching the Indians move east with the soldiers, Andy allowed scenes and sounds from his boyhood to drift through his mind. For a few moments he lived in the past before the distant bawling of a cow jarred him back to the reality of now. His throat swelled in grief for what had been but would never be again.

He turned away and rode west, hoping to come across the tracks of Geneva's buggy.

CHAPTER 8

Andy's black horse was wearing down. So was Andy, but he was not yet ready to give up the search, though it had begun to appear a lost effort. He hoped to find a ranch where he might borrow, trade, or buy a fresh mount. The little packmule showed no signs of giving out, but a rest would be helpful for it too.

He had been seeing cattle, most bearing the look of longhorns brought up out of South Texas. Many ranches on the lower and high plains were being stocked with cow herds from the brush country below San Antonio. Some, showing English blood, were coming down from Colorado now that the buffalo slaughter had opened the range for cattle operations and the Indian troubles were over. He thought this was a likely-looking region for a ranch, but he already had his sights set on land far to the south, in the hill country.

He saw a wooden windmill tower and reined in that direction. He found that it served what appeared to be a ranch headquarters. A box-and-strip house stood surrounded by scrub oak trees common to the cross timbers area. Beyond it stretched a long building which he took to be a bunkhouse. Barn, sheds, and corrals were set off at a respectable distance. A ranch wife would want her house to be well away from the outdoor facilities' flies and dust.

Three men were in a corral, breaking a young horse. Andy rode up to the fence and watched a cowboy hold the bronc by the ears while another swung into the saddle and pulled his hat down tight. The bronc pitched out across the corral. The rider lost one stirrup, which flopped about wildly as the horse jumped. The cowboy took a firm hold on the saddlehorn and managed to keep his seat. Sweating, the bronc circled the corral several times, gradually slowing as it went around. Finally it stopped, heaving for breath. The cowboy dismounted and quickly stepped away to avoid being pawed.

Only then did the three notice Andy. An older man with a salt-and-pepper beard walked toward the fence, acknowledging him with a neutral nod neither friendly nor unfriendly. "Howdy. I don't believe I know you."

"Name's Andy Pickard. Are you the boss?"

"No, she's up at the house, fixin' dinner. Will I do? My name's Ben Danforth."

Andy dismounted and shook hands through the fence. "I'm a Texas Ranger. My horse is about ridden down. I was hopin' I might be able to swap for a fresh one."

The rancher nodded. "It can be done, but I wish you'd come yesterday. You'd've had more to pick from. Thieves ran off a bunch of our horses last night. Some of my boys are out now, scoutin' around and hopin' to find them."

"Do you have a lot of trouble with horse thieves?"

"They're worse than heel flies. They steal cattle, too, but they seem to like horses the best. They can get away with them faster." His eyes took on a hopeful look. "By chance are you on their trail?"

"I've been followin' a woman, hopin' she'd lead me to her husband. I don't know for sure that he's a thief, but he's wanted on a murder charge."

"Has he got a name?"

"Donley Bannister."

"Then you're lookin' for a horse thief. Every rancher around here knows his name, but not many have seen his face. Most of us would walk ten miles barefooted to see him hang."

Andy took a minute to digest that. He had heard from the army lieutenant that Bannister stole horses, so he was not exactly surprised. It disappointed him, nevertheless. He wondered if Geneva Bannister knew about this part of her husband's life. Though he would like to think she didn't, she would have to be naïve not to harbor some suspicions.

The three finished working with the bronc and turned it into a pen, where it went immediately to a wooden water trough serviced by the windmill. Danforth said, "That'll do till after dinner, boys." He turned to Andy. "Come on up to the house with me. The wife'll be ringin' the noon bell pretty soon."

He walked out of the corral and made a long study of Andy's horse. "Pretty good-lookin' animal," he said. "I don't know if we've got anything that'd be a fair swap for you. Tell you what: I'll make you a trade with the agreement that you can always trade back once your horse has rested up and taken on some feed."

Andy was pleased. "That's more than fair." They shook hands.

Mrs. Danforth was a plump little woman

with her graying hair rolled up in a bun and a smudge of white flour across her nose. She bustled around her simple kitchen with the energy of a bumblebee. She said, "Glad to have you, Ranger. We don't see much law around here except what our menfolks handle for themselves. I don't guess people back east would approve of how they enforce the law, but if they don't do it, it doesn't get done."

Danforth said, "There are times when we have to make a quick judgment and strike while the iron is hot. The law and the courts are too slow and too far away. If we don't take care of things ourselves, the lawless element runs over us."

Andy frowned. "You're talkin' about vigilantes."

"Call them what you want to, but sometimes they're the only law enforcement we've got."

Andy had seen examples of quick justice without benefit of a judge. It went against his grain, yet he could see the Danforths' viewpoint. A situation always looked different to a victim than to an outside observer who had experienced no pain.

Danforth said, "I don't suppose you've run into a rancher named J. Farrell Vanderpool?"

185

"I don't believe I have."

"Once we get some of these northern counties organized, he'll probably be elected a judge. He's already pronounced sentence on several renegades, and no pettifoggin' lawyers got a chance to muddy the waters."

Andy thought of an old legal adage: there is no appeal from the graveyard.

The cowboys came to the house, spurs jingling and boots clumping heavily on the porch. They paused outside to wash their hands and faces and comb their hair. This was not a bunkhouse cook shack. It was a woman's kitchen, and she expected civilized behavior.

Mrs. Danforth said, "I've cooked for everybody. When are the rest of the boys coming in?"

Her husband spooned a generous amount of white gravy over his fried steak and buttered a hot biscuit. "We won't know that till they show up."

They finished the noon meal. Saying they had another bronc to ride, the two cowboys returned to the corral. Danforth seated himself in a rocking chair on the front porch and motioned for Andy to sit too. He lighted a pipe and puffed quietly a while before asking, "You been up in this part of the country much, Ranger?"

Andy had not burdened him with the story of his years among the Comanches. He said, "A long time ago."

"I can see why the Indians didn't want to give it up. If the criminal element didn't pester us like horseflies, this'd be a grand place for a rancher. Good grass, good water even if sometimes you have to dig a hole for it. Hot in the summer, maybe, and a little cold in the winter, but show me any place that's perfect."

Andy felt at ease, sitting here with Danforth. For a little while he put Donley Bannister out of his mind. He said, "I've always wanted to have a ranch someday. I will, when I've saved enough money."

"You'll need a good wife."

"Already got her. She's waitin' for me down at Fort McKavett."

"Don't let her wait too long. One day you're young and frisky and can do anything. Next day you look in the mirror and your hair is turnin' gray. It takes you twice as long to do half of what you used to."

From the corner of his eye, Andy caught a movement. Three horsemen were coming in from the north, pushing their mounts. They circled around the corrals and stirred dust riding up to the house. Danforth pushed to his feet and walked down the steps to meet them. He asked, "Find anything?"

One of the cowboys declared excitedly, "Sure did. We found the thieves' camp hidden in a draw about seven or eight miles from here. They've rigged up a brush corral. Got a dozen or fifteen horses in it, and most of them ours."

Andy noticed how the cowboy referred to the horses as *ours,* though in reality they probably belonged to Danforth. Cowboys tended to take a proprietary interest in animals owned by whomever they worked for, caring for them as if they were their own.

Danforth knocked the ashes out of his pipe and turned to Andy. "Got time to chase some horse thieves?"

Andy said, "I'll *take* the time."

Mrs. Danforth came out onto the porch, drying her hands on a dish towel. She cautioned, "Ben, you be careful. Don't you get any of our boys hurt. No horse is worth that."

The cowboys took time to catch fresh horses from among nearly a dozen that had been placed in a corral as a protection against theft. Danforth pointed out a sorrel for Andy. "He's not the prettiest one in the pen, but he'll take you a long ways and bring you back."

Andy saddled the sorrel, then joined Danforth and his men. The cowboy who had brought the report took the lead. They left the corrals in a trot, then moved into an easy lope as their horses warmed up. Andy felt exhilarated after the monotony and frustration of trying to follow Geneva Bannister's buggy. The jolting brought pain to his healing shoulder, but he made up his mind not to let it slow him.

The men alternated between a trot and a lope. Late in the afternoon the cowboy in the lead raised his hand. The other riders stopped and circled around him. He said, "The draw is just past that hill yonder. How do you want to handle this, Mr. Danforth?"

Danforth looked at Andy and said, "My old cavalry captain always believed in chargin' right in amongst them. Throw them off balance before they have time to think about it, he said."

Andy shrugged. "I've got no quarrel with that."

Danforth had left the corrals in a high state of enthusiasm. Now his face was grim. "We'll form a line and sweep down on them in a run. Holler like rebels. If we can stampede their horses and set the thieves afoot, they'll be easy pickin's. Keep yourselves low. I don't want to explain to Mrs.

Danforth why I let one of you get killed."

They rode up on a rise. Below, a brushy draw a hundred yards wide crooked its way among the rolling hills. Andy saw campfire smoke rising from the middle of it. Beyond, he spotted a dozen or more horses standing in a crudely thrown-together corral of cut brush.

Danforth led the charge, firing a pistol and shouting like a Comanche. The cowboys struggled to keep up, yelling, firing, holding a ragged line as they plunged into the camp.

A man on a dun horse spurred out of the draw and galloped away, leaning over his saddlehorn, lashing the mount's hindquarters with a quirt. Two men seemed momentarily frozen in surprise beside the campfire. Afoot, they ran futilely toward their stampeding horses, then fired wildly at the oncoming riders. Andy concentrated on the man who was escaping. Remembering that Donley Bannister had ridden a dun, he vigorously applied spurs to the sorrel.

He soon saw that it was not going to be enough. Danforth had spoken about the sorrel's endurance but had not said anything about its speed. The dun was faster, quickly widening its lead. Andy drew the rifle from its scabbard, stopped the sorrel and stepped down. He knelt and drew a bead but missed.

The range was too great.

The rider had gotten away.

Remounting, Andy returned to the camp. The stolen horses had broken through the brush barrier. Three of Danforth's cowboys were circling them, gathering them up. Danforth and the other two stood in the middle of the camp.

One man lay on the ground. He was not one of the cowboys, so Andy surmised that he was a thief. Another man stood trembling, his hands raised. In a wavering voice he was pleading, "You got us all wrong. We don't know nothin' about no stolen horses."

Sternly Danforth said, "You lie. Most of the horses penned here belong to me."

"Me and Speck, we just rode in. We don't know nothin' about them."

Speck. Hearing that name made Andy take a better look at the man on the ground, then at the one standing. They were the two he had encountered along with Bannister in a dugout. The one called Ches had put a bullet through Andy's shoulder.

The man on the ground was unconscious. In rhythm with his heartbeat, blood pumped through a hole in his chest. It was obvious that he was dying.

Andy confronted the other man. "I know you," he said. "Your partner called you

Ches. If it hadn't been for Donley Bannister, you'd have killed me."

The thief seemed startled. "You're that Ranger."

"I am. Who's the man who left here on horseback just now?"

"You ought to've recognized him. If it hadn't been for him, you wouldn't be standin' here now."

Andy's suspicion was justified. "That was Bannister?"

"Yes, damn him. He ran off and left us. I hope you get him."

"I will, sooner or later."

One of the cowboys knelt beside the fallen man. "He's dead, Mr. Danforth."

Danforth said, "The wages of sin." His eyes smoldered with threat as he gave his attention to the surviving thief. "There's bound to be a bigger and better camp someplace. You want to tell me where it is?"

Ches said, "If it was just Bannister, I would, but I ain't goin' to inform on anybody else."

Danforth grunted. "So there's more. We're dealin' with a ring of thieves."

The three cowboys had circled the stolen horses and brought them up. Danforth looked them over with satisfaction. "Take them on back to the ranch, boys. We'll be along directly." To Andy he said, "There's a bay in that bunch that'll do you a better job than the sorrel you're ridin'. Why don't you go on with the horses? Me and a couple of my boys have got a job to do here."

Andy sensed what that was. He saw by the fear in Ches's face that he sensed it too. He said, "It'd be better if you turned him over to the local law."

"We would, if there *was* any local law. The courts are too far away, and like as not he'd be on the loose again in no time. Maybe in a few years it'll be different."

Andy could assert his authority and take the prisoner, but that would interfere with his search for Donley Bannister. At the moment, Bannister was the bigger fish.

He spurred to catch up with the cowboys driving the horses. They had traveled half a mile when two shots echoed behind him.

It was cold justice, but justice nevertheless.

CHAPTER 9

It was obvious to Geneva that Quincy Harpe tended to his horses' welfare better than to his own. After wasting much time crisscrossing the hills in what seemed a hopeless search, she had found Harpe's place many miles away from any recognizable road. It had an extensive set of sturdy horse corrals, but the picket cabin looked like a wreck almost ready to happen. Its walls were off plumb and leaned dangerously away from the prevailing winds. She guessed that it had originally been built as a buffalo hunters' camp without regard to permanence.

A letter from Harpe had set her off on the long search for Donley Bannister. It had assured her that her husband was in good health and hard at work. It had also said he wanted her to wait in Junction. Under no circumstances was she to follow him.

She had done so anyway. It was in her

nature to obey orders only when they suited her.

A heavy lump of a man stood on the front step, a rifle in his hand, watching the approach of Geneva's buggy. His wide mouth curved downward in a hostile scowl. As she drew on the reins, he demanded, "Who the hell are you, and why have you come here?"

"I'm Geneva Bannister. I've come to join my husband."

Harpe took a step forward. His belligerence made her want to shrink from him, but stubborness allowed her no retreat. He demanded, "Didn't you get the letter?"

"I got it, but my place is beside my husband."

"Ain't no tellin' who might've followed you here."

"Nobody followed me. I've been careful."

A large-boned woman, handsome in a rough-hewn way, stepped out of the house and stood beside Harpe. Her long black hair lifted and fell carelessly in the wind. She said, "Did I hear you claim to be Donley's wife?"

"I am. Is he here?"

"No, and I don't know when he's liable to show up. Best thing for you would be to turn around and go back where you came from."

"I've come too far to go back."

"Donley said you were supposed to stay put. Didn't you read the letter I wrote for him?"

"I thought your husband wrote it."

"He can't hardly write his own name. And who ever said he's my husband?"

"I just assumed . . ."

"Things here are different than you're used to. This ain't exactly a church encampment. Well, since you've come anyway . . ." She turned on Harpe. "How come you're standin' there lookin' like a fence post? Help her down. She's probably hungry."

He protested, "She can't stay here."

"She stays if I say so, and I say so. Now, go put her buggy away. You can bring her things in later."

Harpe did as he was told, and Geneva followed the woman inside.

Geneva said, "I want to go wherever my husband is."

"God knows where he's at right now. Could be over in Indian Territory or north as far as the Nebraska line. He don't let moss grow on him." She beckoned with a sweeping hand. "Come on in, and I'll fix you somethin' to eat. You're lookin' kind of lank. We'll need to fatten you up a little before Donley gets back."

Geneva admitted, "Meals have been a little skimpy on the road."

The woman said, "My name's Emmy. Just Emmy. Used to have a last name, but after two husbands I gave up usin' it." She busied herself at a cast-iron stove. "Can't say I blame you too much for followin' after Donley, even though he told you not to. He's considerable of a man. Wisht he was mine instead of the one I've got. You must be some woman for him to slip a ring on your finger. You must've put a hex on him."

Geneva had no satisfying reply. "I didn't do anything special. We met, and things just naturally happened."

Emmy sensed Geneva's discomfort. She said, "I don't mean to be a pryin' nuisance. It's just that I've been curious about what you've got that's taken such a powerful hold on Donley. It's hard to keep a stud horse in one pasture when there's mares across the fence. Yet, I've never known him to pay attention to another woman." She shouted, "Quincy, go fetch me some more firewood. Damned if you ain't let the wood box go nearly empty."

Geneva asked, "Why does he let you order him around like that?"

"He likes my cookin'. Quincy's got no hold on me, nor me on him. We stay together because it's convenient. I do the cookin' and keep the house. He takes care of business and brings in the money. A little bit, anyway."

"What kind of business?"

"I figured you knew. Horses. They gather them here, and Donley takes them down south where nobody knows the brands. Small investment, big profit."

Geneva wondered that she felt no resentment. "You're implying that Donley's involved in stealing horses." She had accepted his easy explanation for lengthy absences, that he was traveling far to buy horses for trading. She had loyally avoided dwelling on the possibility that he was stealing them, though an inner voice had been telling her for some time that everything did not add up.

Emmy frowned. "I ain't implyin' nothin', honey — I'm tellin' it to you straight. Donley may be a Bible-quotin' Puritan on some things, but he's got no compunctions about takin' other men's horses."

Geneva asked, "Did he tell you he's wanted for killing a man?"

"Yeah. Them Slocums have operated up in this country some. All of them need killin'. If Donley hadn't done it, the law would have to sooner or later. He saved them the trouble."

"Most people back there say he was justified, that a jury would clear him. I came all this way to talk him into going home and getting it over with."

"You can't ever be sure about a jury. Trustin' in a jury is how I lost my first husband. They hung him higher than the Confederate flag."

"That's terrible."

"And after we slipped them ten dollars apiece to turn him loose. Crooks, the whole bunch of them."

Harpe tromped into the house with an armload of wood. "When're you goin' to get my dinner fixed?"

Emmy said, "I'm busy takin' care of Geneva. You'll have to finish fillin' the wood box before I cook anything for you."

Harpe walked out, grumbling to himself.

Emmy said, "Men. You've got to keep jerkin' them up short. Otherwise they get the notion that they're in charge."

Geneva ate what Emmy placed in front of her. She was not sure what it was, but she was hungry enough not to ask questions.

Emmy said, "You'd best give up any notion of huntin' for Donley. Stay here with us and wait. He'll show up sooner or later, bringin' a bunch of horses."

"Quincy may object to my being in the way."

"He objects to just about everything. Don't pay no attention to him. I don't."

"I can pay for my keep. A man named Luther Fleet was in debt to Donley. I collected it from him."

"Luther Fleet? That four-flusher is in debt to just about everybody. How did you get him to pay?"

"I shot him."

"Dead, I hope."

"I just put a bullet in his leg."

Emmy's eyes brightened with admiration. "I don't know what Donley ever did to deserve you, honey. You're welcome to stay here as long as you want to, and Quincy be damned."

"Maybe a little while, till Donley comes or we hear where he is. I'll pay my way."

"Hang onto your money. You earned it fair and square."

The cabin was cramped and uncomfortable, but it offered rest and relief to Geneva after the grinding physical demands of the long buggy trip. In a day or so she settled into Emmy's routine, helping to keep the house and cook the meals. Nights, the horses being accumulated for trading were penned to keep them from straying or being stolen by a different set of thieves. Days, Harpe let them out of the corral to graze so they would hold their flesh and strength. He rode out occasionally to prevent them from drifting too far. The rest of the time he mostly loafed around the cabin or the barn, eating and drinking, grousing about one thing or another. Very little seemed to please him.

He made no effort to hide his resentment of Geneva. Her being here relegated him to sleeping in the barn. Whatever romance he was able to wheedle from Emmy was inconvenient and on her own terms. At best, the pair's relationship was an uneasy one of grudging mutual need, not strong affection.

One day Harpe opened the corral gate, then rode up to the cabin. "Horses comin'," he shouted. "Better start fixin' dinner."

Geneva felt a sudden excitement and ran outside. "Could Donley be with them?" she asked.

Harpe shrugged indifferently. "He ain't the only one does business around here."

Geneva hurried toward the corrals. Emmy caught up with her and said, "We better move back to the cabin. We wouldn't want to spook the horses away from the gate. If it's Donley, you'll see him soon enough." She frowned. "And you'd better hope he's glad to see you. When things go against his grain, he can scare a grizzly bear to death."

That was a side of him Geneva had rarely seen, though she knew he could be provoked to extreme reaction if the offense against him was strong enough. He had shown her no remorse over shooting Cletus Slocum, though he grieved about having to shoot the crippled roan. His only other expressed regret was that he had not been able to shoot the rest of the brothers and make a clean sweep of it.

She saw one rider take a position just past the gate to haze a dozen horses through. Two more men brought up the rear, pushing the remuda. The nearest man was dark, wearing a beaded vest. He wore a broadbrimmed hat with an eagle feather in its leather band. She thought he was probably Indian.

Watching the other two through the curtain of dust, she realized that neither was Donley. One was black. The other was white, a man in his thirties, sitting ramrod straight in the saddle.

Emmy said, "I don't know the darkey. The white one's Curly Tadlock. You better watch out for him. He's as handsome as a new pair of boots and slick as owl grease with the ladies. Don't give him so much as a wink, or he'll drag you to the haystack behind the barn."

Geneva could not help smiling. "You've been there?"

"Once. I was weak, and I reckon he was desperate. Anyway, he's good-lookin'."

"What did Quincy say?"

"Quincy doesn't say anything to Curly. He knows Curly'd clean his plow. And he knows I'd crown him with a skillet if he got high-handed with me. Donley was awful mad about it, though. He's like a Holy Roller preacher when it comes to he-and-she stuff."

"I'm not interested in Tadlock, or any other man but my husband."

"Then you'd better make that plain to him right off. I'll bet a dollar Curly makes a move at you before he ever sits down to dinner. He tries every woman that ain't old and ugly."

Once the driven horses were inside the corral, the Indian led his mount through and closed the gate.

Emmy said, "We call him Chief because none of us can pronounce his real name. He's pretty handy at gatherin' up Indian horses."

"But he's an Indian himself."

"A Tonkawa. They're friendly to the whites

and enemies to the other tribes. His bunch almost got wiped out a while back when the Comanches and some others made a raid on them. Slaughtered men, women, and young'uns like cattle."

Geneva shuddered. "I thought Indians just killed white people."

"There's been more Indians killed by other Indians than was ever killed by white folks. Or white folks killed by Indians, for that matter. Chief hates all tribes except his own. Takin' their horses is his way of gettin' even. He don't look at it as stealin'."

"I suppose he would call it an act of war."

"Yeah, but he don't mind takin' money for it. Indians have found out what a dollar is worth. They don't work for beads anymore."

Harpe frowned as he walked up to the Indian. "Ain't many horses for all the time you been out."

The Indian frowned back, a hard look in his eyes. "You no like, you go yourself."

Harpe held up both hands defensively. He was obviously afraid of the Indian. "No offense meant. Just noticin', is all."

Tadlock dismounted and tied his horse outside the corral. He said, "This ain't much to show for the risk. We had to outrun some awful mad Indians to get even this many."

Harpe said, "Looks like we may have to move the operation."

Tadlock said, "Country's gettin' settled up to where you can't ride ten miles anymore without somebody comin' to see what you're up to."

Harpe jerked his head toward the black man, still in the saddle and watching the horses across the fence. "Where'd you get him? You know it's risky to bring strangers here."

"He showed up where we were camped. He was lookin' for somethin' to eat, and we needed help with the horses."

Harpe looked eastward, his eyes worried. "You sure none of them Indians followed you?"

"They ran into soldiers takin' some breakouts back to the reservation. That's as far as they got."

Harpe said, "Maybe Donley will come in with a bigger string."

Tadlock said, "Not if he runs into the kind of trouble we had. Those Indians bayed after us like a pack of bloodhounds." He seemed to notice Geneva for the first time. A broad smile broke across his face, the teeth a bright white against the dusty, stubbled face. He said, "Well, now, the scenery has picked up considerable all of a sudden. Who is this beautiful lady?"

Harpe said sourly, "She's Donley's wife, and I hadn't noticed her bein' beautiful. Mostly she's been a nuisance."

"I'm surprised that Donley sent for her to come up here."

Harpe growled, "He didn't. She came on her own. A damnfool thing to do if you ask me."

"I don't believe I asked you." Tadlock removed his hat as he approached Geneva. Long, curly hair spilled down over his forehead. He said, "Ma'am, I'm known in these parts as Curly Tadlock. I'd be pleased to know your name."

She wondered if that was the name he was known by in other places. Remembering Emmy's admonition, she said coolly, "You may call me Mrs. Bannister."

Still smiling, he said, "Why is it that the best-lookin' ones are always *Mrs.*? It's like runnin' up against a locked door. But most doors have a key, if the right man knows how to find it."

Harpe looked from one to the other in confusion. "What's this about keys? There ain't no keys around here, nor locks neither."

Tadlock said, "Some locks can't be seen, but a man of experience can find a way to open them."

Even as she mentally rejected him, Geneva was physically stirred by Tadlock's boldness. She sensed that she needed to stay as far from him as possible, but it would be difficult in close quarters. She hoped Donley would get here soon.

Emmy said, "Come on, Geneva. We need to fix dinner for the workin' men." As they walked toward the house she said, "Like I warned you, he's already made a move. Watch that you don't let that smile and slick talk get you. Your husband ain't one for sharin' what belongs to him. Somebody could get hurt."

"I won't give Tadlock any encouragement."

"He's already got that. Seein' you was enough to touch him off."

While the biscuits browned, Geneva started to set the table. Emmy stopped her. "The Indian and the darkey ain't eatin' with white folks. They'll take their dinner outside."

Geneva knew the custom but questioned it. "They've all been working together, haven't they?"

Emmy shrugged. "That's different from

207

eatin' together. Work's one thing. Social life is somethin' else." She took the biscuits from the oven, almost dropping them as the hot pan burned her fingers. "How'd you come to meet Donley in the first place?"

"He stopped by our place in Erath County while he was on a horse-buying trip."

"Are you sure he was *buyin'* them?"

The black man finally turned so Geneva was able to see his face. Recognition gave her a light shock. This was the soldier who had ventured into camp early in her trip. Joshua Hamlin still wore the shirt and trousers she had given him to replace the uniform that would have identified him. "Mr. Hamlin."

Open-mouthed in surprise, he touched fingers to a floppy old hat he had picked up somewhere. "Ma'am," he said. "Looks like we been travelin' the same road."

Tadlock asked Geneva suspiciously, "You know him?"

"We crossed trails some days ago. I gave him something to eat."

"It's a bad habit, feedin' strays. They take to followin' you. Are you sure he didn't?"

"Nobody followed me."

Hamlin and the Indian filled their plates and carried them outside. Harpe had eaten a large breakfast, but he heaped his plate with all the food it would support. He and Tadlock hunched at the table together. Midway through the meal Harpe said, "I still don't like it, Curly, you bringin' that darkey here. First time a lawman questions him, he'll spill all he knows."

Tadlock said, "Don't worry about it. As soon as we're through with him . . ." He left the rest unspoken.

Geneva was stunned. She knew she had not been meant to hear that. Donley would not be a party to such treachery, using a man's labor, then disposing of him like a worn-out boot. But he might not get here in time to stop it.

She wondered if she should talk to Emmy about this. The woman gave no sign that she had heard, or perhaps she had but chose not to acknowledge it. Likeable though she might be, she was hardly an innocent party here.

And I won't be either if I stay long, Geneva realized. She decided to take a chance and speak to Tadlock. "You wouldn't really kill him, would you?"

He said dismissively, "The world ain't goin' to miss one burr-head. There's too many of them as it is. Besides, we can't have him talkin' about us."

"But he won't. The fact is that he's running from the law."

"How do you know?"

"He told me he killed a man."

"White?"

"As far as I know."

"All the worse. Him bein' black, they're probably lookin' high and low for him. They'd hang him, but not till he told everything he knows. Since he's goin' to die anyway, I don't see nothin' wrong with us rushin' it a little." Tadlock turned away from her, a signal that the subject was closed.

After eating, Harpe and Tadlock took a nap on the floor. The Indian and Hamlin rested a while on the porch, then went back to the corrals. There they sorted through the horses, saddling them one at a time and trying them. The Indian did much of the riding. A few pitched, but he stuck like a cocklebur. The horses gave up before he did.

Geneva watched Hamlin. He rode several horses while the Chief rested. One managed to pitch him off. He climbed back into the saddle, dismounting only when the horse had worn itself down.

Tadlock had finished his nap and was watching over the fence. He said, "That's enough, boy. We'll work them another round in the mornin'. Then we'll pay you off and let you go on your way."

Geneva shuddered.

The sergeant wiped sweat onto his shirtsleeve and walked toward the cistern beside the house. Geneva waited until she felt confident no one was paying attention, then moved close to him.

He said, "Ma'am, I sure was surprised when I seen you this mornin'. I want to thank you again for your help. I was pert near done in."

She said, "I've come to help you a little more. You've got to slip away from here the first chance you get. Travel as fast and as far from this place as you can."

The sergeant appeared startled. "They fixin' to turn me in to the law?"

"Worse than that, they intend to kill you. You've fallen into a den of thieves. They're afraid you'll tell what you know about them."

"I don't know much to tell. Mr. Tadlock promised to pay me twenty dollars to help him with his horses. Took me a while to figure out they was stolen."

"Don't sell your life for twenty dollars. Get away."

Hamlin murmured, "Yes'm. Reckon I better." He looked up, concerned. "I hope you won't get in trouble over this."

"They won't know I told you."

"God's blessin' on you, ma'am." He started to turn away, then hesitated. "Since you had a warnin' for me, I got one for you. I heard Mr. Tadlock makin' bad talk about you to that Indian. He don't mean you no good."

She nodded solemnly. "I know."

When Emmy called that supper was ready, three men responded. Emmy asked, "Where's that darkey? Didn't you tell him supper's ready?"

Harpe grumbled, "No, and I ain't goin' out after him. He ought to know when it's time to eat."

The Indian took his plate onto the porch. Harpe and Tadlock seated themselves at the table without waiting for Geneva and Emmy. Harpe demanded, "Bring that coffee over here."

Emmy said, "It's on the stove. Go get it yourself. I ain't no waitress."

Harpe mumbled under his breath and filled his cup at the stove. "Women these days have got it too easy. Not like my old mother. When Papa spoke, she jumped."

Tadlock said in a gentle voice, "Emmy, would you mind bringin' us the coffee, please?"

Emmy smiled. "I'd be tickled to."

After she poured coffee for him, Tadlock said, "There's women even talkin' about wantin' to vote. They don't know a damned thing about politics."

Harpe nodded agreement. "What with uppity women and high taxes and darkies free to do whatever they want to, the world is slidin' straight down to hell. It's harder and harder for an honest workin' man."

Geneva and Emmy changed glances. Emmy flung a challenge at Harpe. "What would you know about honest workin' men?"

The men finished eating. Emmy stepped out onto the porch and said, "Chief, I wisht you'd go tell that darkey to come get his supper before it's all cold. I ain't cookin' twice."

The Indian returned after a time. "Don't see him."

Harpe snickered. "Probably laid up someplace asleep. It's hard to get a decent day's work out of them people."

Tadlock's eyes showed concern. "Maybe he's run off."

Harpe blinked. "How come? You think somethin' spooked him?"

"It don't take much to spook a darkey. Chief, go take another look."

The Indian was soon back. "Horse gone.

213

He gone."

Harpe began looking worried. "We'd better track him down."

Tadlock frowned. "It's comin' on dark. Looks like rain too. By mornin' he'll be long gone." Facing Harpe, he clenched a fist. "You sure you didn't say somethin' to scare him away?"

"I never spoke six words to him since he came here."

Both men turned toward Geneva. Trying to hide a quick rising of anxiety, she said, "When would I have had a chance to say anything?"

Emmy motioned with a cast-iron lid lifter from the stove. "Nobody had to say anything. You two had murder in your eyes, plain as if you'd wrote him a letter. Don't you be layin' the blame on Geneva."

Harpe grumbled, "Blame ain't all I'd like to lay on her."

Tadlock said sharply, "Watch your mouth. She's a lady." His voice softened as he spoke to Geneva. "You'll have to pardon Quincy for his poor upbringin'. He grew up in a cow lot."

She knew his smile was false, meant to reassure her. She saw something ugly in his eyes.

The soldier was right about him, she thought. *It's time Donley got here.*

CHAPTER 10

Andy had spent a miserable night in the rain. He had unpacked the mule the evening before and spread his tarp between two bushes, trying to simulate a tent, but he was wet in spite of that. Now it was morning, and he shook with a chill. He had gathered dry wood before the rain started, managing to keep it fairly dry through the night while he sat cramped beneath the tarp, covering himself the best he could with a slicker. He built a fire and made coffee while he tried to warm up.

Geneva Bannister's trail had simply disappeared. Too many wagon and hoof tracks had been made after her passage, covering up those left by her buggy. He had cut a zigzag pattern back and forth, covering many miles over several days, hoping in vain to find where she had gone. He had visited several ranches and cow camps, inquiring if anyone had seen her. Now he feared the rain had obliterated whatever sign she might have left.

Somewhere to the north was an army post where he might be able to send a wire back to headquarters. He dreaded having to admit that he had spent so much time and had traveled so far on a failed search. He was aware that many Ranger missions came up dry, but those were other men's, not his.

He vaguely remembered this area from his long-ago time with the Indians, but settlement had brought wagon roads, a haphazard scattering of ranches, even a few small villages. Some he knew about, many he didn't. Landmarks were limited. To the east lay Indian Territory and its tribal reservations. To the west stretched the far-reaching Llano Estacado. He was east of the escarpment in a hilly, often sandy, thinly wooded area known as the Cross Timbers.

Geneva and Donley Bannister could be anywhere in this vast, thinly settled region. Much of it was only sketchily documented so far. Some recent maps still left it largely blank except for one word printed across it: *Comanche.* Less than a decade had passed since the horseback tribes had been driven from it.

He finished the little that passed for breakfast. The clouds were breaking off.

Morning sunshine pierced them here, there, and yonder. He decided to let his bedding and tarp dry out rather than pack them wet. He spread them on bushes to give them air and sunshine. The site resembled a careless nester's camp, he thought, but who was to see it besides himself?

After a time, somebody did. Half a dozen horsemen topped over a hill to the west, paused there, then moved in his direction. His first thought was of Indians. He was not alarmed. They should give him no trouble unless they came shooting without allowing him a chance to talk. The few who ventured into this region anymore were usually harmless hunting parties, sadly doomed to failure like the one he had encountered several days ago. Occasionally they had a military escort. More often they were off the reservation illegally.

He discerned that these were white men. He knew of no one who might have reason for hostility toward him except perhaps Bannister. He raised his right hand to demonstrate friendly intentions as the riders came close. He saw no friendliness, however, in a man with a fierce black beard who pushed out a little ahead of the rest. He carried a rifle across his lap. The rider gave Andy a challenging study with bullet-gray eyes beneath heavy brows black as pitch. He demanded, "Who are you, sir? Give an accounting of yourself."

All the men were well armed. Andy could see that they were not merely ranch hands out on a cow hunt. He said, "My name is Andy Pickard, and I'm waitin' for my beddin' to dry."

"But why are you here? What is your business?"

His manner aroused a flare of defiance in Andy. "Maybe I'd better ask about yours. How come all the questions?"

The man shifted the rifle slightly toward Andy. "I am J. Farrell Vanderpool. My ranch is north of here. These men and I have been on the trail of horse thieves. In the absence of information to the contrary, we must suspect that you may be one of them."

Andy knew the name. Ben Danforth had told him about Vanderpool and his lethal campaign against thieves. He could see that these men were deadly serious. Stalling them could be hazardous. Though he had been coached to say no more than necessary about whatever mission he was on except to fellow lawmen, Andy said, "I'm a Ranger. I'm on the hunt for a fugitive." He opened his jacket to show his badge.

Most of the larger plains ranches were

financed by English and Scottish investors and by Eastern banks. The man who faced him had the look of a Chicago or St. Louis banker sent out here to manage investments for speculators hoping to cash in on what was being called the beef bonanza. Vanderpool studied Andy a minute longer. "Who is the fugitive you are after? Perhaps one of us knows something of him."

"Donley Bannister. I had him in sight once, but his horse outran mine."

"We are familiar with the name."

Andy explained that he had been trailing Bannister's wife in hope she would lead him to her husband. "I lost track of her some days ago. I don't suppose any of you have come across a woman travelin' by herself in a buggy?"

Vanderpool looked to the other riders. None had anything to contribute. He said, "I am sorry. However . . ." He turned in the saddle. "Bring that boy up here."

Andy had not noticed a black rider who remained behind the others. Recognition jolted him. This was the army sergeant accused of killing a man in Santa Angela. Andy struggled to remember the name. Hamlin, that was it. Joshua Hamlin.

Vanderpool said, "We came across this boy yesterday. He said he was running away from some horse thieves who intended to kill him. He has been trying to take us to their camp, but has had trouble finding his bearings."

Andy saw that Hamlin no longer wore the uniform. His clothing hung loosely, at least a size too large. His horse was a sorrel, not the brown he had been riding when Andy had seen him making his escape.

Andy asked, "Do you remember me, soldier?"

The reluctant sergeant nodded. "Yes, sir. You're the Ranger that throwed me in jail."

Vanderpool seemed intrigued. "How is it that you know this boy?"

"He's a soldier at Fort Concho, or was. Shot a man and lit out runnin'."

Vanderpool was surprised. "I took him perhaps to be a thief, but I did not take him for a killer."

Andy said, "The man he killed had murdered a soldier. I reckon he deserved what he got." He turned back to the sergeant. "How did you come to get mixed up with horse thieves?"

Downcast, Hamlin said, "I didn't know they was, at first. They offered me twenty dollars to help them drive some horses they said they had bought. Then this lady come to me and said they figured to kill me when they didn't need me no more. They was afraid I'd talk to the law."

"What lady?"

"They called her Miz Bannister. That's all the name I heard."

Andy felt a surge of hope. "Was her husband with her?"

"No. They said he was comin' with some more horses, but I didn't see him. I lit out when nobody was watchin'."

A grim smile creased Vanderpool' face. "These thieves have been a plague to my neighbors and me for much too long. We'd welcome your company if you would like to come along and help us, Ranger."

Andy said, "I'd be tickled to."

Hamlin said, "I rode all night long. It was cloudy, so I couldn't see the stars. Come mornin', I was plumb lost. Still am."

Vanderpool told Andy, "We don't give a damn about some shooting that took place two hundred miles from here. I'd like to hold on to this boy till he finds the thieves' camp for us."

"He's yours till then. After that, he's my prisoner."

Vanderpool extended his hand. "Deal."

Andy reached back into a saddlebag and brought out a set of handcuffs. He thought better of it and put them back. "We'll trust you, Joshua, not to try and run away. To do it would just get you shot."

The sergeant's shoulders sagged. "I shot that man in self-defense. But when everything's done, they'll hang me, won't they?"

"I can't speak for a judge and jury."

"They'll all be white. Sure they'll hang me."

Vanderpool said, "You can cross that bridge when you get there. Right now, boy, let's find those horse thieves."

Geneva walked to the window and looked toward the corrals.

Emmy said, "No use workin' yourself into a lather. Donley will show up in his own good time."

"I wish he were here now."

"Curly Tadlock's been after you again, ain't he?"

Geneva nodded. "Every chance he gets, he puts his hands on me. I pull away, but he keeps pushing."

"He always did fancy himself as God's gift to womankind. He can't understand why they don't all see him like he sees himself. Your husband'll set him straight. Curly won't admit it, but he's afraid of him."

"Then why does he keep making a try for me?"

"Because Donley's not here. Curly is one to get while the gettin's good."

Geneva thought of Luther Fleet. "I'll shoot him if I have to. Not to kill him, but to put him in his place."

"It'd be a service to womankind."

"I don't understand Donley, partnering with a man like that."

Emmy gave her a pitying look. "It's the money. Curly's good at what he does. He knows where to find horses and how to get away with them. Donley knows where and how to dispose of them for a good price. They don't like one another much, but as long as the partnership pays a profit, they'll act like they was born twins."

Tadlock and the Indian — mostly the Indian — rode the horses each day, giving special attention to those not yet well-broken. Tadlock had commented, "We don't want some farmer throwed off on his head before we get all the horses sold. It's bad for business."

Harpe had done no riding. He usually sat on the fence, making critical comments about the others' horsemanship. The three were discussing the black soldier as they came into the cabin for supper. Pouring a cup of coffee for himself, but not for Harpe or the Indian, Tadlock said, "We could've got a few more days' work out of him, ridin' those horses."

Harpe said, "I still wonder how come he left."

"No tellin'. Them people are superstitious, you know, like Indians." He caught himself. "All except the Tonks."

The Indian shrugged.

Tadlock said, "The trouble is that he's apt to fall into the hands of the law. When he does, he's liable to bring them down on us like a thunderstorm."

"Business is dryin' up around here anyhow," Harpe said. "It's time we quit this place for good."

"Soon as Donley shows up. We'll throw his horses in with these and leave here."

Emmy was disturbed. "You'd abandon this camp?"

Tadlock said, "It's been abandoned before. Look at it. Some windy day this rickety cabin'll fall in and hurt somebody."

She said, "I'll admit it ain't much, but it's all the home I've got."

Tadlock shook his head. "In our business it don't pay to get attached to one place. A change of climate from time to time can be healthy." He turned to Geneva with a sly grin. "Same thing goes for people. Sometimes it's good to change things around and have some variety. It keeps us from gettin' stale."

Geneva gave him a look of silent contempt.

They saw the dust first, and Harpe's voice trembled with nervousness. "What if it's a posse? That black boy could be fetchin' a hangin' party here."

Tadlock tried to calm him. "It's probably Donley, bringin' in a bunch of horses."

Harpe argued, "But what if it ain't?"

"Then we'll fight them off. Most posses break up pretty fast when they smell gunpowder." He calmly took his rifle from the corner where he had placed it.

Geneva's heart lifted at the thought that Donley might be coming. She would no longer have to put up with Tadlock's sleazy innuendoes, his unwelcome hands taking every opportunity to touch her as if she were a lady of the line. She opened the cabin door.

Tadlock demanded, "Where do you think you're goin'?"

"To meet my husband."

"Better be sure it's him before you run out there. If it ain't, you might take a bullet before they see that you're a woman."

She realized Tadlock was right to be cautious. She retreated to where Emmy waited near the kitchen stove.

Watching through the window, Tadlock sighed in relief. "Everything's all right. It's Donley." He walked outside, carrying the rifle.

Geneva was close behind him. She could not see Donley's face, but she recognized him by the erect way he sat on his horse, as if he owned the world. A half-grown boy helped Donley push a small gathering of horses through the gate, then stepped down inside to close it. Donley dismounted outside the corral and tied his horse to the fence. Geneva began walking toward him, then moved into an eager trot.

Donley turned, stiffening in surprise. He was too startled to respond as she threw her arms around him. He did not return her joyous kiss. Instead, he said, "Geneva, what the hell are you doin' here?"

His angry reaction took her by surprise. "I wanted to be with you. I was afraid you couldn't come back to get me."

"But I sent word that you wasn't to come. Don't you know it's dangerous up here?"

She glanced back toward Tadlock, coming along with Harpe and the Indian. "I didn't know *how* dangerous till I came."

Tadlock looked into the corral and

grumbled, "Is that all the horses you could find? Hardly worth the time and trouble."

Donley bristled. "You don't know how much trouble. I was lucky to get away with these. It don't look like you got many more."

"We had to shake off half the Indian nation. What's your excuse?"

"Ranchers. They think a lot of their horses. They got Speck and Ches. Damn near got me too."

Tadlock pointed his thumb toward the boy in the corral. "Who's that? Where'd you get him?"

"Orphan boy. He's all right. He's been a help to me."

"But he's apt to have a long memory. That's dangerous."

Geneva shuddered, remembering that Tadlock and Harpe had planned to kill Hamlin when they were through with him. She feared they might decide upon the same treatment for this sandy-headed kid. He looked to be only fifteen or sixteen, too young to realize what a dangerous situation he had stumbled into.

She said, "Donley, we've got a lot to talk about."

Donley's voice was still sharp. "We damned sure do. I thought you had more sense than to follow after me. Them Slocums could've trailed you, or the law." He spotted the buggy parked beside a shed. "You came in that? It leaves tracks a blind mule could follow."

"Nobody followed me. I saw to that." His reaction stung her like a lash. She said, "I thought you'd be glad to see me."

"Somewhere else, but this is the wrong place."

"Everybody says no jury would convict you for killing Cletus Slocum. I want you to go back with me and give yourself up. A quick trial, then you won't need to run anymore."

Donley's eyes were fierce. "You must be crazy if you think that's all there is to it. Ain't you figured out yet what we've been doin' here?"

"I have, I'm sorry to say. But perhaps they don't know about it down there."

"Even if the court turned me loose, I'd have the Slocum brothers waitin' to shoot me in the back first chance they got. I doubt I could get them all."

"We wouldn't have to stay there. We could go somewhere far away and make a new start."

"Doin' what? All I know is horses."

"You could settle in one place and raise them honest."

"A black horse can't change his color." Donley turned his back on her and spoke to Tadlock. "Curly, the climate around here has turned hotter than hell's hinges. We've got to quit this place."

"I already decided on that. Just been waitin' for you to come in." Tadlock's expression turned dark. "You think somebody's on your trail?"

"Nobody I've seen, but I feel it in my bones. Every time I look back over my shoulder, my hair starts to raise up. Soon as we get some dinner, we'll take all these horses and head west."

Tadlock cast another glance into the corral. "With such a piddlin' few, there won't be much money to split."

"In this kind of business there always comes a time when your luck goes cold. You pick up what chips you've got left and run like the devil was after you. Chances are that he is." Donley beckoned to the boy. "Come on, kid, let's get somethin' to eat. Don't unsaddle your horse."

Emmy was not keen about leaving. "It ain't much," she said, "but it's got four walls and a roof."

Donley said, "So's a jailhouse. Besides, what would you do here without menfolks to take care of you?"

She glanced at Harpe. "Better than I've done *with* some I could name."

Harpe growled, "Then stay here. There ain't nobody cares."

Geneva and Emmy prepared a hasty meal for the men and the boy. Geneva thought it odd that Tadlock and Harpe took theirs out to the narrow porch and ate with the Indian. They talked in low tones that did not carry back inside. Their conspiratorial manner made Geneva uneasy.

Emmy gathered the food that remained in the cabin. She put it into a cloth sack.

Donley said, "Good idea. We won't be passin' any stores for a while."

Tadlock and Harpe came back inside, the Indian moving up beside them. All three held pistols, aimed at Donley. Tadlock said, "We ain't all goin'. Us three are, and that woman of yours, but you're stayin' here."

Donley's face flushed. Instinctively he started to reach for the pistol on his hip but stayed his hand. Three muzzles were pointed at his stomach. He declared, "I always knew it, Curly. You're a damned thief."

"I learned from a good one." Tadlock nodded at Geneva. "Get over here, woman. I'm takin' you along."

Donley grabbed her arm and pulled her up against him. "Like hell you are."

Tadlock said, "Sorry it's worked out like this, but I don't want to keep lookin' back, wonderin' when you're comin' after me."

He fired. Donley staggered. He bent forward from the waist, then fell on his face. Screaming, Geneva dropped to her knees beside him. Before the shot's echo died, the panicked boy bolted out the door and ran for the corral.

Tadlock said, "Go after him, Chief. Don't let him get away."

The Indian hurried outside.

Tadlock grabbed Geneva's wrist and roughly pulled her to her feet. He said, "Donley's dead. You don't have to hold yourself back for him anymore. You're goin' with me."

Geneva tried to reach Donley's pistol. Tadlock jerked her away from it. "Come on, I ain't got time to fool around." He threw an arm around her waist and drew her toward the door. He said, "I tried bein' nice to you and got nothin'. Like it or not, you're mine now."

He shouted back over his shoulder for Harpe to pick up the grub sack. Emmy followed Harpe out the door, crying in anger and holding Donley's pistol with both hands. She called, "You turn Geneva aloose!" She fired a wild shot in Tadlock's general direction.

Tadlock shouted, "Quincy, do somethin' about that crazy woman before she hurts somebody."

Harpe swung the food sack and knocked Emmy down. He picked up the pistol she dropped and shoved it into his waistband. He said, "Just for that, you're stayin' here."

The kid was on his horse and out of the corral in a run, leaving the gate open. The Indian ran to close it before the penned horses could escape. He took one futile shot in the boy's direction.

Tadlock cursed. "Damned Tonk never could shoot straight."

The boy was quickly gone, lost from sight amid a scattering of oak timber. The Indian asked, "You want me get'm?"

Tadlock said curtly, "You couldn't catch him now. Let's saddle our horses."

In the corral, Harpe led up a horse for Geneva. "I put Emmy's sidesaddle on him," he told her. "She ain't goin' with us. I wisht you wasn't neither."

"So do I," Geneva said. Harpe gave her a boost into the saddle. She weighed her chances of doing what the boy had done. Perhaps when they were out of the corral.

Tadlock shouted, "Open the gate, Chief." He circled the horses and started them toward the opening. Geneva moved in among them. When she was clear of the gate she put her horse into a run northward, the direction the boy had taken. The wind whipped her face and tugged at her hair. She felt a momentary exhilaration as it seemed she had broken free. But she heard a horse rapidly coming up behind her. Tadlock cut in front and grabbed her reins. He jerked them out of her hand and wrapped the ends around the horn of his saddle. He brought both horses to such an abrupt stop that Geneva was hurled to the ground. She felt a sharp pain in her shoulder as she rolled.

He dismounted and pulled her to her feet. Crying in frustration, she doubled her fists and beat them against his face and chest. He slapped her so hard that her head snapped back. She thought for a moment he had broken her jaw.

Angrily he said, "You'd just as well make up your mind right now. You'll do what I say and go where I tell you. I'm not puttin' up with any more nonsense." He boosted her onto her horse, then cut two long leather strings from his saddle and bound her hands. He tied them to the horn over which her right leg was bent. Leading her horse, he cut across country and caught up to the fast-moving westbound remuda.

Harpe scowled. "If it'd been me, I'd've given her the back of my hand and left her afoot."

Tadlock said, "Like you did Emmy?"

"You've got to keep women in their place, or they'll take over the world."

Sourly Tadlock said, "I saw how well you kept Emmy in her place. She had the Indian sign on you from the start."

"It don't bother me one bit to leave her behind. There's always a better one down the road."

Moving in a long trot, Tadlock holding her reins, Geneva had time finally to think about Donley, lying facedown on the floor. She wished she could cry for him, but she did not want Tadlock to see her tears. She wanted him to see only strength and defiance. She thought too of Emmy, left by herself with not even a horse to carry her away from that awful place.

She had to concentrate on staying in the saddle. She felt awkward and out of balance with her hands tied to the horn.

The Indian rode near the lead horses. Suddenly he turned in the saddle. He pointed and shouted excitedly. "Riders come!"

Geneva looked back. Behind them a quarter mile or less came a cluster of horsemen moving in a lope. She felt a sudden exhilaration. This must be the posse Donley had dreaded. Perhaps they would set her free.

Tadlock swore. "Hangin' party, sure as hell." He seemed torn for a moment, looking toward the driven horses in front of him, then back to the pursuit rapidly coming up behind him. Indecision did not delay him long. "Let the horses go," he shouted. "Every man for himself."

He spurred savagely, forcing Geneva's horse to keep up. The terrain was hilly and rough. The horses had to dodge their way among the oaks and scrub brush. Geneva feared she would lose her seat and be dragged, or trampled beneath the hooves.

She heard shots. The Indian stiffened, then slipped out of the saddle. He lay crumpled, not moving. His horse galloped on to join the others, the stirrups flopping.

In a panic, Harpe cried, "They got Chief!"

Tadlock urged his horse and Geneva's to more speed. She tried to work her hands free so she could jump off, but the bonds were too tight.

He warned, "I know what you're thinkin'. You'd just break both legs and maybe your head."

Harpe yelped in surprise as his horse suddenly went down. Legs flailing, it pitched its rider out into the grass. Harpe rolled, then was on his feet, yelling for Tadlock to help him.

Tadlock kept riding.

Running afoot, arms outstretched, Harpe begged, "Pick me up. For God's sake pick me up."

Tadlock ignored him. He spurred toward an oak thicket that stretched for several hundred yards.

Geneva managed a quick glance back. She saw Harpe raise his hands as the posse surrounded him. She could not hear him, but she imagined he was pleading for his life.

Tadlock said, "Maybe they'll waste a few minutes with Quincy and give us a longer lead."

Geneva protested, "He's your partner. Don't you care what happens to him?"

"I care about what happens to *me.* Quincy never toted his weight in the first place."

He plunged into the thicket. Geneva had to duck her head and bend low to keep heavy limbs from dragging her out of the saddle. Lighter ones cracked and splintered under the impact. They pulled her hair, tore at her dress, and deep-scratched her skin. Pain made her want to cry out, but she would not allow herself to show weakness to Tadlock.

They had ridden several miles, much of it through thickets that slowed them to a walk but hid them from sight. Finally Tadlock stopped. "Got to let the horses rest," he said. "Looks like we've shook loose." He untied her hands. "Get down if you want to. Just don't get no ideas."

Geneva hurt all over. She bled in a dozen places where rough limbs had cut into her skin. Her dress was torn, leaving one shoulder bare and badly scratched. She slipped from the saddle and felt her legs give way as her feet touched the ground. She went to her hands and knees. She felt dizzy and for a bit was unable to gain her feet. Tadlock did not help her up.

He said, "We left a trail. If they've got a good tracker, they'll be comin' on."

"I don't know if I can go any farther."

"You've got a lot of travelin' left in you yet."

"Do you have any idea where you're going?"

"Someplace where it'll just be me and you. You've been with the wrong man up to now, but I'm twice the man Donley Bannister ever was. I'll make you forget you ever knew him."

"One thing I'll never forget is the way you

238

shot him down in cold blood."

"He'd've done the same to me, soon as we didn't need one another anymore. I just did it to him first."

"Like you tried to do to that black man, and to the kid?"

"Odd about that darkey — like he knew what we had in mind for him. I always wondered if somebody warned him." He frowned at her. "You maybe?"

Pride made her straighten her shoulders. "Yes, I did it, and I'm glad."

He nodded toward their back trail. "I wouldn't be surprised none if he led that posse here. If so, it's your doin'."

"I just wish they had gotten here sooner, before you shot Donley."

"He'd likely be dead by now anyway. They'd've hung him. Me and Quincy and the Indian too. This way, he died quick. He didn't have time to think about it."

Geneva made up her mind that if the chance came, she would not give Tadlock time to think about it, either.

He pointed his thumb toward the horse. "Climb on. It's time we got movin' again. They ain't made a rope yet that fits my neck."

CHAPTER 11

Hamlin had begun to recognize landmarks. He assured Andy and Vanderpool's posse-men that they were near the thieves' camp. "I remember that lightning-struck tree yonder. I was thinkin' I was glad I wasn't there when it happened."

A rider approached from the south, his horse running hard. Andy drew on his reins and said, "He's awful anxious to get away from somethin'. He's ridin' like he's seen Indians."

Vanderpool leaned forward in the saddle. "There are worse things around here than Indians." He squinted. "He's nothing but a kid."

The boy reined up in time to keep his horse from running headlong into those of the posse. His face glistened with sweat. His eyes were alive with excitement. He blurted, "They tried to kill me back there."

Andy asked, "Who did?"

"Feller named Tadlock. He killed Mr. Bannister, and he was fixin' to kill me."

The name struck Andy hard. "Bannister? Donley Bannister?"

"Yes, sir. Shot him in the belly for no reason a'tall."

"How did you come to be with Bannister?"

"He said he'd pay me a dollar a day for helpin' him drive some horses to a camp. We hadn't much more than got there when the killin' took place."

Andy felt an unexpected regret. "You're sure Bannister is dead?"

"I seen him go down. I was next, so I left there."

Vanderpool glanced toward the sergeant and said, "That sounds very much like the soldier's story."

Andy nodded. "Hire them, then kill them before you have to pay up. That's one way to hold on to your money." He turned back to the frightened boy. "Who else was there?"

"An Indian and a man called Quincy. And two womenfolks."

"Could you lead us to the place?"

The boy vigorously shook his head. "I don't want to go back there."

Vanderpool said, "Now, son, we're your friends. We won't let anybody hurt you. I'll pay you ten dollars to take us to that camp."

The boy thought it over. "Ten dollars?"

"Cash money. I have it right here in my pocket."

"Have I got to go all the way in?"

"Just show us the place."

Andy asked, "Boy, didn't you know you were dealin' with horse thieves?"

"Yes, sir, I kind of figured that's what they was. But a dollar a day . . ."

Vanderpool lost most of his fierce expression. "I hope this is a lesson to you. Running with the wrong people can get you killed. How old are you, son?"

"I ain't for sure, but I think I'll be sixteen along about Christmas. I used to know, back when Mama was alive. But she died, then Pa went off huntin' for a job and never came back. I've got nobody to ask."

"Are you looking for work?"

"That's how come I joined up with Mr. Bannister."

"When we're through here, you can go with me to my ranch. I'll start you at twenty dollars a month. I may raise that once I see what you can do."

"I can do most anything."

"Right now you can lead us to that camp."

The boy took the lead, Hamlin riding beside him and confirming the directions.

Andy pulled his horse in close by Vander-pool's. He said, "You're not as fierce as I took you to be, hirin' that boy."

Vanderpool shook his head. "If nobody helps him, likely as not he will turn to thievery and become another thorn in our sides. But if he takes to honest work, he can be an asset instead of a liability."

Assets and liabilities sounded like banker talk to Andy, but he understood what Vanderpool meant.

Vanderpool said, "I can sympathize with his situation. I was an orphan boy myself, but I was fortunate. A good-hearted man befriended me. He set my eyes to the future and my feet on the road to prosperity. Perhaps I can do something for this boy before he drifts beyond salvation."

Andy could relate to that. He said, "A lot of generous people helped raise me. Some Indian, some white."

"Then you and I both know how difficult it is for an orphan boy to make it over to the green side of the hill."

The boy and the soldier stopped and waited for the rest to catch up. The boy pointed. "That's the place, that cabin down there. They had maybe twenty horses in the corral when I left. They're gone now."

Vanderpool swore. "And the thieves with

them, I'd wager."

Andy said, "Just the same, we'd better ride careful goin' down there."

The posse moved their horses forward in a walk, rifles and pistols drawn and ready. The boy stayed behind for a few minutes, then became nervous about staying by himself. He spurred to catch up.

Hamlin said, "Boy, you stay behind me. If there's any shootin', you skin out like a scared rabbit."

The boy looked to Vanderpool for confirmation. Vanderpool said, "Do what he says, son. He's been in the same fix you were, and got out of it just like you did."

Andy carried his rifle across his lap. He had always felt more comfortable with a rifle than a pistol, though he was proficient with both. A rifle had more authority.

The picket cabin's roof sagged, and the front wall seemed bowed a bit. The door was open. A raw-boned woman stepped out onto the shaky porch, one hand shading her eyes. Vanderpool signaled for the posse to stop. He and Andy rode forward.

Andy spoke first. "Anybody in there with you, ma'am?"

The woman looked him over critically before she spoke. "One man. He's not in any shape to give you trouble. If you're a posse lookin' for horses, they've done left."

Andy said, "I've been lookin' for a man named Donley Bannister. The boy back yonder says he's been killed."

"Come in and see for yourself." She turned back inside.

Andy and Vanderpool glanced questioningly at each other, then dismounted and walked cautiously to the cabin. Andy carried his rifle, Vanderpool a pistol. The woman waited just inside the door. She said, "You won't need them guns. For once in his life, Donley's harmless."

Bannister sat on the edge of a sagging bed, his long underwear peeled down past his waist, his trousers around his ankles. He held a folded cloth against his groin. His pinched face bespoke pain. He squinted, trying to get a good look at Andy. "Well, I'll swun. You're that Ranger I took pity on. Thought you might've died."

Andy said, "I heard you'd been killed."

"It ain't because the son of a bitch didn't try. He shot my pocket watch all to hell. If it hadn't been for Emmy, I'd've bled to death."

Emmy said, "The bullet just went in a little ways. I dug it out, along with the innards of his watch. He's about quit bleedin'."

Andy said, "I've been huntin' all over for you, Bannister."

"It's a sorry state you've found me in. If I'd had any notion he'd shoot me, I'd've shot him first."

Vanderpool broke in. "You've got your man, Ranger. Now we want to move on and get our horses back. Are you going with us?"

Andy considered. "Bannister, it doesn't look to me like you're goin' anyplace for a while."

Bannister grimaced. "How could I? They carried off every last horse on the place." He took a deep and painful breath. "Kidnapped my wife too. I want you to bring her back."

That disturbed Andy. Trailing Geneva Bannister so far, he had taken a proprietary interest in her welfare. "We'll do what we can." To the woman he said, "Patch him up good. When we get back, he'll be needin' to ride."

Emmy said, "I want you to know that Geneva's a good woman. Much too good for the likes of Curly Tadlock to be layin' hands on her. Kill him first, then arrest him."

"You're askin' me to be judge, jury, and executioner."

"I've heard that's what Rangers do."

246

"It's been known to happen, but it's not supposed to." Andy followed Vanderpool out the door. He started to tell the boy to stay behind, but it occurred to him that Bannister might take the youngster's horse and escape before the posse returned. Afoot, he could not get far.

Vanderpool told the boy, "Stay with us. If there's any shootin', you drop back out of range."

"Yes, sir. I don't want to lose that job."

The trail was easy to follow. It was impossible to hide the tracks of twenty or so horses. Vanderpool spurred into a lope, the posse stringing out behind him. Andy tried to pull even with him, but he could not catch up to the vengeful rancher.

Andy saw the dust before he saw the horses. He heard Vanderpool's exultant shout: "There they go, boys. Let's get them."

The pursuers tore through brush thickets and around the rolling hills. Andy could see the horses plainly now. The thieves had abandoned them and were running for their lives.

Vanderpool pulled his horse to a sliding stop, jumped to the ground with his rifle, took deliberate aim and fired. Two hundred yards ahead, a man toppled from the saddle. The rancher remounted, shouting with enthusiasm. Following his example, one of the possemen was on the ground, kneeling with his rifle braced on his knee. He fired, and a thief's horse went down. Its rider jumped up and went running, arms outstretched. Andy could not hear his voice, but he judged that the man was begging the remaining two riders to pick him up. They did not acknowledge him. In a few moments the posse surrounded him. His hands up, he cried for mercy. Andy half expected one of the possemen to shoot him.

Vanderpool said, "Riley, you and Boyd stay here with him. We're going after the other two."

Andy had slowed but not stopped. He put his horse into a full run again. He had seen that one of the two riders was a woman. She had to be Geneva Bannister. He had also seen that her hands were tied to the saddle. The other rider was leading her horse.

He tried to level his rifle, but the muzzle danced crazily as the horse cut to one side and then the other, avoiding the scrub brush. Firing from a running horse would waste ammunition. Worse, he might hit the woman by accident.

The pair disappeared into a dense thicket. Andy was tempted to plunge in after them, but Tadlock could hide in the timber and set up an ambush. He slowed to a trot. Vanderpool and Hamlin pulled up beside him. Vanderpool said, "I hate to leave him unhung, but he could be drawing a bead on one of us right now."

Andy said, "I don't like leavin' that woman in his hands."

"She's a horse thief's wife. I doubt he can do anything to her that hasn't been done before."

"Everybody told me she's a lady."

"If so, she shows poor judgment in the company she keeps. We've got our horses back. We've killed one thief and caught another. The boys and I are going home." He nodded toward the sergeant. "What about him?"

Andy said, "He's my prisoner. So is Donley Bannister."

"They're no longer of concern to me . . . us. You can have both of them so long as you take them far away from here."

"That I'll do."

"We'll stop at the cabin and get something to eat before we go on. You're welcome to join us."

Andy looked toward the thicket. "What do you think, Joshua? Are you game to go in there?"

The sergeant nodded. "I owe that lady."

Nerves tingling, Andy entered the thicket where he had seen the two horses go. Though he searched diligently, he could find no tracks, no clear sign of their passage. The fugitives had broken off small tree limbs in their passage, but he realized that many more had been broken by wind and last winter's ice. He could not distinguish one cause from another.

He admitted, "We'll never trail them through this mess. Not unless you're a better tracker than I am."

Joshua said, "What we need is an Indian, but he's layin' out yonder dead."

Andy knew further search would be futile. He said, "We'd just as well turn back. Maybe Bannister will have some idea where they might be goin'."

Approaching the cabin, he saw that the recovered horses had been placed in a corral. The posse's mounts were tied to the fence. Andy dismounted and tied his horse outside the cabin. Inside, he found Emmy cooking at the iron stove. The captured man — name of Quincy Harpe, he was told — sat on the floor, against one wall. His expression was bleak, his eyes downcast.

Vanderpool appeared buoyant. "From now on the thieves will know they can find no safety in our part of the country. We have broken them for good."

Andy doubted that. He suspected that the ranchers would continue facing the same problems. Only the culprits' faces would be different.

Bannister still sat on the edge of the bed. He had pulled his underwear back up. A bulge showed where Emmy had placed a large bandage. His anxious eyes focused on Andy. "You didn't find her?"

"We lost them in the brush."

"Couldn't you follow the tracks?"

"We didn't find any."

"I could've. I wish I'd been with you."

Andy's hopes improved. "You're a tracker?"

"Damn right. How do you think I managed to find so many horses?"

Andy asked, "Do you have any idea where Tadlock might be headed?"

"I know half a dozen places he might try for. If I could get a line on his direction, I'd have a better notion where to look for him."

"Do you think you're able to ride?"

"To get my woman away from that snake before it's too late? You bet I can ride."

Andy said, "Just don't forget that you're under arrest. If you try to escape, I'll have no choice but to shoot you."

251

"I'll stick to you like a cocklebur till we find Curly and my woman. After that, we'll see."

Andy looked at the sergeant. "And you, Joshua?"

"Like I told you, I owe the lady."

The meal used up most of the food from the bag Harpe had dropped when his horse was shot from under him. Emmy said with resignation, "I can't stay here by myself without any grub. The cabin is fixin' to fall down anyhow."

Bannister said, "You're a good scout, Emmy. You can take my woman's buggy, and her horse." He glanced up at Andy. "Unless you're arrestin' Emmy too."

"She's not in my fugitive book. She's free to go wherever she wants to."

Emmy nodded. "Thanks, Ranger." She looked gravely at Harpe, hunched in fear against the wall. "I guess you know that posse won't let him get to town alive."

Andy knew she was probably right. These men were in a mood for revenge against horse thieves. He was fortunate to keep Bannister from their grasp. He said, "He knew what the chances were when he chose this business."

She said, "He's a weaklin' and a coward, but he *is* a man. Somebody ought to cry over him. I reckon I'm the only one that will."

Finished eating, the possemen hitched Geneva's horse to the buggy for Emmy and gave her the little food that remained. They put Harpe on one of the recovered horses, bareback. A posseman hinted that he would not have to travel that way long.

Emmy stood beside Harpe, tears on her cheeks. She clung to his hand until the posse took him and moved out, driving the rest of the recovered horses except one left for Bannister to ride. Bannister helped her into the buggy. He kissed her hand and said, "You've got a good heart, Emmy. Give it to a man that deserves it."

"If I ever find one," she said. She flipped the reins and moved away.

Bannister climbed painfully into the saddle, biting his lower lip. His face was pinched from the effort. He said, "All right, Ranger. Show me where you lost that trail."

"You don't look fit to ride."

"I'm a long ways from dead yet."

The three rode out, Andy's packmule following. Andy showed Bannister where he had lost the fleeing Tadlock. Walking his horse back and forth in a zigzag pattern, Bannister managed after a time to find the tracks. He said, "At this point, Curly was just tryin' to get away. He hadn't settled on a direction. We'll have to follow the tracks a while before we can figure out which way he means to go."

Andy glanced at the sun, by this time low in the west. He said, "The day's gettin' short. Night'll be on us before long."

Bannister looked somber. "I expect my woman's thinkin' about that too." He grumbled in a voice too low for Andy to hear.

Andy asked, "Did you say somethin'?"

"No, just cussin' myself for all the times I could've shot him and didn't." Riding pensively, Bannister said, "My woman told me she thought a Junction jury would turn me loose."

Andy said, "That's the way everybody was talkin'. They were sayin' you acted in self-defense, and the community was better off with one less Slocum to worry about."

Bannister asked, "I suppose now you'll charge me for horse-stealin'?"

"Junction is a long way from here. Maybe if you come clear on the murder charge, they'll forget about the horses."

Wincing, Bannister pressed his hand against the bandaged wound. "Damned horses didn't come cheap. They cost me a bad bellyache and a perfectly good pocket watch."

"If it hadn't been for that watch, the slug might've gone through your gut."

"Looks like those horses have cost me my woman too."

It seemed peculiar to Andy that Bannister was not calling his wife by her name. He kept referring to her as *my woman,* as if she were a piece of property, like a horse. Andy said, "I can tell that you're hurtin'. I don't think you can ride much more till you've rested."

"I couldn't rest, thinkin' of him havin' her, doin' what he wants to with her. Damn it, I had Emmy write and tell her not to come up here in the first place."

The statement surprised Andy. He said, "When she got the letter, I took it for granted that you wanted her to join up with you. I counted on her leadin' me to you."

"I'm sorry you didn't find me sooner. Curly might have an extra hole in him now, instead of me." Bannister bent forward, pressing his hand against the bandage. He sucked a sharp breath between his teeth.

Andy said, "Any time you want to stop . . ."

"Not as long as there's light enough to see by."

Bannister lost the tracks twice. Andy wondered if he could find them again. He did, but only after losing time.

Bannister said, "At first Curly was just runnin'. Now he's takin' pains to make himself hard to follow."

Andy asked, "Do you have any idea where he's headed?"

"Not yet, but he can't go far enough to get away from me. I could've overlooked him takin' all the horses. I might even forgive him for shootin' me in the belly. But then he stole my woman. By the time he gets done with her . . . she'd be better off dead."

The tone of Bannister's voice troubled Andy. He heard no affection in it, only a strident possessiveness. Andy could not conceive of feeling that way toward Bethel.

Joshua said, "She was kind to me when I was hungry. And she gave me warnin' that Mr. Curly figured to kill me when the work was over with."

Andy noticed that Joshua deferentially used the term *mister* even in speaking of a man who had planned his murder. For himself, he would have used some of Bannister's more pungent terminology.

He said, "We'll get her back."

Bannister's expression was dark. "After

Curly's finished with her? She won't be the same."

Eventually it became clear that the tracks were leading westward. Bannister leaned forward in the saddle and pointed. He said, "Now I've got a notion where he's goin'. A worn-out reprobate named Wilkes is livin' in an old buffalo hunter camp. He was of help to me sometimes in the horse business."

Andy asked, "How far to his place?"

Bannister's face creased with frustration. "Too far. There ain't no way we can get there before night."

"Dark shouldn't stop us if you know where it is."

Bannister clenched a fist. "It's a dugout. We could pass right by and not see it."

Andy said, "Maybe it won't be like you think."

"It will. I know Curly. I'll kill him if it takes the rest of my life to run him down."

Bannister's mood became increasingly desperate as the sun dropped behind low-lying clouds that indicated rain somewhere to the west. At full dark he made an anguished cry, then conceded that traveling farther would be useless. He was slow and easy in climbing down from the horse. Turning his face away to hide the pain, physical and emotional, he said bitterly, "Curly's got her at Wilkes's place by now."

Andy asked, "What kind of a man is Wilkes? Maybe he'll take up for her."

"He couldn't stand up against Curly. Even if he tried, it'd be because the nasty old fart wanted her himself."

"We'll catch up to them tomorrow."

"Tomorrow will be too late. It would've been better if he'd killed her instead of draggin' her away with him."

The bleak tone of Bannister's voice increased Andy's uneasiness. He said, "I can't imagine wishin' Bethel was dead, no matter what somebody did."

"You can't imagine it because you ain't been there. I have." Bannister poked at the little fire they started for coffee. "I never told her, but she wasn't my first wife. The other one . . . she was a pretty little thing. Made me think of pink roses. She'd never been off of the farm before. A slick lawyer come along, whisperin' pretty words in her ear. Talked her into runnin' off with him. After a while she came back, carryin' his baby and beggin' forgiveness. I tried, God knows, but every time I touched her, I'd think about her layin' with him. I wanted to strangle her. When she died birthin' the baby, it was the best thing for both of us. Otherwise, there's no tellin' what I might have done."

Bannister's words were chilling. Andy said, "But that one left of her own choosin'. This one was taken by force."

"In the long run, it all comes out the same. I don't know if I could look her in the face again."

As Andy lay down on his blanket, Joshua leaned close and said quietly, "I got a cold feelin'. I'm afraid Mr. Bannister may do somethin' awful when we find her."

The same thought had begun to haunt Andy. "It'll be up to us to keep it from happenin'."

The soldier brooded, staring into the flickering coals as the campfire burned down. Andy sensed that he was thinking ahead to what awaited him upon his return south. A legal hanging was probably the best he could hope for. A lynching was more likely.

That thought, and concern for Geneva Bannister, left Andy sleepless. He sat up, poking wood into the fire a piece at a time to keep it going. Joshua left his blanket and sat beside him. He said, "It sure is a dark night. I ain't been able to sleep none either."

Andy said, "We'll pay for it tomorrow."

"I always slept good of a night when I was a soldier. Always felt like the army would see to it that I had somethin' to eat and a place to lay my head."

Andy asked, "How'd you come to join up?"

"I was still a growin' boy when emancipation come. I got awful tired of draggin' a cotton sack. I sure didn't want to be doin' it the rest of my life. A recruiter come along and gave me a bunch of talk. Said all I had to do was put my X on a piece of paper and I'd be a soldier. I'd have plenty of money and plenty to eat. He stretched that story some, but he was right about one thing: I could make somethin' of myself in the army. Long as I wore that uniform, I wasn't just another field hand. I was special. It ain't just everybody that gets to be a sergeant, neither." His expression turned melancholy. "Now I've lost all that on account of a nogood piece of white trash that needed killin'. I wish somebody else had done it instead of me."

Andy nodded with sympathy. "I do too."

"Now it looks like the devil has got ahold of Mr. Bannister, like he taken hold of me. He may do somethin' he'll always be sorry for."

"That's why we have to make sure he doesn't get out of our sight."

CHAPTER 12

Geneva was desperately tired, and she hurt all over from the fast, rough ride. She was not accustomed to traveling on horseback. Only the fact that her hands were tied to the saddle had kept her from falling — that and the dread of being dragged.

She said, "Can't you untie me? My wrists are bleeding."

Tadlock offered no sympathy. "You'd try to run away again. That's how come I tied you in the first place."

"Where would I go? I have no idea where we are. I'd have nothing to eat, and what money I had was left in the cabin."

"Good. Maybe now you'll do what I tell you to."

"At least let me get down and stretch my limbs. They feel paralyzed."

Reluctantly Tadlock conceded. "I reckon if anybody's still trailin' us, they're way behind." He pulled in close and untied her hands. "I'm holdin' onto your horse. Don't get any notions about runnin'."

She rubbed her wrists. They were sticky with blood and burned as if she had held them too close to a fire. It would be useless to try to get away from him now. But she would keep alert. Sooner or later she might get her chance.

Never had she seriously wished she could kill someone. She had that thought now about Tadlock. When she had first seen him, he had struck her as handsome in a rough sort of way. Now she could see only the ugliness beneath. Donley Bannister's blood was on his hands. She had no doubt about Tadlock's plans for her. The thought brought revulsion.

She said, "There are certain things a woman should be allowed to do in private."

He pointed toward a clump of brush. "Go on. I need to do the same thing. But if you're tempted to try and run, forget it. I could catch you before you took twenty steps."

"I know that. I'm not stupid."

"Then how come you got hooked up with somebody like Donley?"

"Because he's a man." She corrected herself. "Was."

"I'm a man too, a better one than him."

"Some man! You shot my husband without giving him a chance."

"I'm an old poker player. I understand odds. There's times to take an honest chance, and there's times to pull one out of your sleeve. With a man like Donley, it's always paid to hold out an ace."

She knew Donley's faults. At times he drank too much, gambled too much. Now she knew he had also been a horse thief.

But God help me, she thought, *I loved him in spite of all that.*

She straightened her dress the best she could. The brush had torn it in several places. It hung loosely off one bare shoulder. She wished she had a pin to fasten it in place.

"Feel better?" he asked when she returned to where he waited with the horses.

"Some." She stalled for time, in no hurry to get back in the saddle. She hoped someone was catching up. She asked, "Are we going anywhere in particular, or are we just wandering around?"

"It's comin' on night," he said. "We've got nothin' to eat, thanks to that damned Quincy keepin' the grub sack. Besides, it looks like it might rain. I know a feller who lives a little ways on."

"Friend of yours?" That thought brought

her no comfort.

"I wouldn't call him a friend. Done business with him now and again, but I never let him get close to my money." He held the leather strings that had bound her. He said, "I won't tie you if you'll promise to behave yourself. I don't fancy havin' to chase you through the brush again."

She said, "I won't run." To herself she added, *Not yet.*

She did not see the dugout until they were almost at its door. It had been built into a hillside. A crude rock chimney protruded from the dirt-covered roof. She smelled wood smoke. Near the dugout was a well, its circular stone wall rising three feet up from the ground. A little farther away a sagging shed was topped by a tangle of brush, next to a nondescript corral of scrub oak branches and trunks.

Tadlock said, "There used to be buffalo bones scattered all over these hillsides till the bone pickers gathered them up."

Born in Texas, Geneva had seen the great buffalo herds grazing free and had been told unbelievable stories about them. She said, "It's hard to imagine all those thousands wiped out in a few short years."

"Money," Tadlock said. "Some people will do anything for money."

Like steal horses? she thought. *Or kill a partner so you can grab his share?*

Tadlock said, "It don't pay to ride up to a camp without lettin' them know. Some people shoot first and then ask who you are." He shouted, "Hello the house!"

A shaggy black dog trotted toward them, barking. It stopped short, turning halfway around and tucking its tail as if prepared to run in event of a threat.

"A coward," Tadlock said. "A lot like the man that owns it."

The wooden door opened slightly, and the muzzle of a rifle poked through. A gravelly voice called, "Who's that out there?"

"It's Curly Tadlock. You know me."

The door swung inward. A gray-whiskered man in grimy clothes cradled a rifle in his arms, his hand on the trigger guard. "Damned right I know you. You done wore out your welcome around here."

"Just a little misunderstandin', Wilkes. You goin' to let this lady wait out here with night settin' in?"

The man lowered the rifle, squinting to see better. "A lady? That changes the complexion of things. Send her in while you put your horses in the pen out yonder."

Geneva did not like this man's looks any better than she liked Tadlock's. His ragged beard had felt neither scissors nor razor in weeks and was a stranger to a comb. He looked her up and down as if he were appraising a mare. "A fine figure of a woman," he said. "Don't you know better than to run with the likes of Curly Tadlock?" She flinched as he touched a rough palm to her bare shoulder. He took her hand and examined the abrasions left by the leather strings that had bound her wrists. "It don't look like you've come of your own free will and accord."

She said, "He killed my husband, then dragged me with him."

He said, "Appears to me like you're in somethin' of a fix. But say the word and I'll blow his lamp out. He's overdue for a reckonin'."

The longer she studied him, the more uneasy she became. She sensed that Wilkes could be as bad a bargain as Tadlock. She said, "Badly as I hate him, I wouldn't want his blood on my hands."

"It wouldn't be on your hands, it'd be on mine. They've been bloodied before."

She did not doubt that. His eyes were those of a wily old coyote.

The tiny room was a boar's nest, just large enough to accommodate a small, rough fireplace, a table with one chair built from wooden crates, and an unmade bed with wide rawhide straps instead of slats. A stained canvas was stretched across the ceiling to catch dirt that might otherwise filter in from the sod-covered roof. On a grate in the fireplace, hot grease sizzled in a cast-iron skillet.

Wilkes said, "I was about to fry up some venison to go with my biscuits and beans. I hope that suits your fancy, because I ain't got much else."

"Venison will do," she said, noting that he picked up the sliced meat with dirty hands. She did not feel hungry.

He said, "Sad to say, it's been a long time since a woman set foot in this place. All I ever see is renegades like Curly. Not what you'd call the salt of the earth."

"Do any lawmen ever come around?" A bit of hope was behind the question.

"Not since I've been here. I've known people to ride by within fifty yards and not see this dugout. I don't get much company unless it's on business."

She could guess what kind that was. "Curly says you've done business with him."

"And generally wished I hadn't. He don't give nobody an edge." Wilkes frowned. "You say he killed your husband. Would I know him?"

268

"Donley Bannister."

"Donley!" The man's face registered surprise. "He wouldn't be an easy man to kill. Curly must've shot him in the back."

"No, but he took Donley unaware. He didn't give him a chance."

"That's Curly's way." Wilkes glanced toward the rifle he had set beside the door. "What would you give to be free of him?"

"I don't have anything to give you."

"I ain't talkin' about money."

"I don't know what you mean."

"I think you do. You're a grown woman." He gripped her bare shoulder again, harder this time.

Geneva felt ill. To trade Tadlock for Wilkes would hardly be a gain except that Wilkes might be easier to get away from. He was many years older and probably slower in his movements. She said, "That's asking too much."

"It ain't a lot. I may not be the man anymore that Donley was, but the fire ain't plumb out. I could show you a thing or two."

Geneva shrank away from him, but the room was too small for her to go far.

Wilkes said, "You keep thinkin' about it. Right now why don't you finish fryin' up that venison and fix us a pot of coffee? I'm hungry."

The fire had burned low. A small shovel leaned against the fireplace. Geneva used it to stir the coals and coax them to greater heat.

Tadlock entered the dugout, carrying his saddlebags and a blanket roll that had been tied behind the cantle of his saddle. He saw Geneva at the fireplace and said, "Hurry up with that supper, woman."

Wilkes watched him narrowly. "What you got in them saddlebags?"

"That's my business."

"I'll bet it's all the money you've cheated out of poor folks like me."

"You always had both eyes wide open. I was just faster on my feet than you were." Tadlock fetched a tin plate from a small shelf on the wall and speared the first piece of venison with the point of a knife. "Pour me a cup of that coffee," he commanded.

Geneva remembered the way Emmy had talked to Quincy Harpe. With a flare of resentment she said, "You're not crippled. Get it yourself."

Tadlock slapped her, hard. She stumbled backward, almost falling onto the bed. He said, "Now get me that coffee."

Hands shaking, she poured it. Her face was aflame.

Tadlock said, "I like spirit in a woman, but I want her to always remember who the boss is." Finishing the coffee, he said, "Wilkes, I've never seen a time when you didn't have some whiskey around. Where's it at?"

Hesitantly Wilkes reached under the bed and brought forth a bottle. He thrust it at Tadlock and said curtly, "You owe me for this. Careful you don't choke on it."

"If it's like most of the stuff you get, I probably will." Tadlock took two long swallows without stopping for breath. Grimacing, he wiped his mouth on his sleeve. "Even worse than I thought."

Wilkes reached for the bottle, but Tadlock withheld it from him and took another drink.

Wilkes brooded, watching his whiskey slowly disappear, swallow by swallow. He said, "What would you take for your woman, Curly?"

"She ain't a mare for buyin' and sellin'. Even if she was, you wouldn't have enough money to buy her with." Tadlock cut a quick glance at Geneva. "What would you want with her, anyway? You're too old for a woman like her."

"I ain't *that* old."

"Just when you thought you had her, she'd

skin you and hang your hide on the door."

Wilkes's eyes narrowed. "I might decide to take her away from you."

"Big talk for a burned-out old renegade. I've got a notion to boot you halfway to the Pease River." He gave Geneva a long, hungry study. "Wilkes, this bed ain't big enough for three. You're sleepin' outside tonight."

Wilkes reacted with anger. "You eat my grub, you drink up my whiskey, and now you're takin' my bed?"

Tadlock jabbed a forefinger against Wilkes's chest. "You heard me, old man. Take your damned greasy blankets and go, unless you want me to grab you by your scruffy neck and throw you out."

Wilkes trembled with rage. "Damn you, Curly!" He grabbed the rifle from beside the door and swung around.

Tadlock was too fast for him. He grabbed the rifle and twisted it from Wilkes's hands. He opened the door and kicked Wilkes out through it. He shouted after him, "For that, you'll sleep outside tonight without any blankets." He set a bar in place against the door.

The dog set up a frenzied barking.

"Damned old fool," Tadlock said. "He's lived too long." He turned an angry gaze upon Geneva. "Did you put him up to that?"

Geneva felt as if the blood had drained from her face. "It was his own doing."

"It looks like I've got to watch you every minute. I hope you're worth it."

Wilkes was beating on the door, demanding to be let back inside. Tadlock tried to ignore him but finally cursed and gathered the blankets from the old man's bed. He opened the door and threw them outside, shouting, "Take them and go sleep under the shed."

Geneva demanded, "You're going to make him stay outside? This place belongs to him."

"It doesn't. He found this empty dugout and just squatted here. Be thankful I didn't shoot him. I may decide to do it anyway before we leave here."

She struggled to keep some semblance of composure, but she lost control. She slumped into the chair and let her tears spill in a rush.

Tadlock said, "I never saw a woman yet that didn't break down and cry at the least little thing." He studied the nearly empty bottle and said, "Look under that bed and see if he had another."

She found one and handed it to him. He

opened it, letting the cork fall to the dirt floor. He dragged the chair against the door and seated himself so that she could not escape. He motioned toward the narrow bed. "Sit down there," he said. "I want to look at you a while." He tipped the bottle upward and wiped his mouth again.

Geneva's hope gradually began to rise. If Tadlock kept working on that bottle, he might drink himself unconscious. Then she could get away.

But after a while he set the bottle on the floor and moved toward her, arms outstretched, his eyes burning. Desperately she attempted to duck past him, but he caught her arm and twisted her around. He pushed her backward onto the bed and fell on her with all his weight. His breath was heavy with whiskey as he forcibly pressed his mouth against hers. She struggled until he slapped her again, harder than the last time.

"It's payday," he said.

After a long time she became aware of daylight showing through the cracks in the wooden door. He lay beside her, his eyes open, trying to focus on her face. He brought a rough hand up to caress her cheek. He said, "I told you I'm a better man than Donley ever was." Slowly he moved his hand down to her shoulder, then to her thigh.

Turning her face away, she closed her eyes, hating him, wishing him dead.

He attempted to arise, but his legs betrayed him. He sat down heavily on the edge of the bed and rubbed his forehead. "Sorriest whiskey I ever drank. It's a wonder it didn't kill Wilkes a long time ago." He jerked a thumb toward the fireplace. "What I need is black coffee. Stir them coals and get a fire started. And fry up some of that meat. My stomach feels like there's two cats fightin' in it."

He drank the first cup of coffee in several long gulps without stopping, though it was steaming hot. He wolfed down a strip of venison and demanded more. Satisfied, he appeared to be almost sober. He reached for her. She backed away, looking for something she could use to protect herself.

He said, "You can't go nowhere till I'm ready to let you. Then we'll go together."

She saw the fireplace shovel with which she had stirred the coals. Her first intention was to strike him with it. Instead, she pushed the shovel deeply into the fire, then hurled live coals and hot ash into his face.

Tadlock screamed and brought his hands up to cover his eyes. Some of the coals had gone down into his long underwear and set it to smoking. Dancing wildly around the room, he bumped into the bed, then the table, and almost fell into the fireplace. Howling like a wounded dog, he found the door and staggered outside. He cried, "My eyes! My eyes!"

Shaken, Geneva pitched the shovel away and quickly put on the tattered dress that Tadlock had thrown on the floor. She dropped a slab of bacon and a bag of coffee beans into a cloth bag. Tadlock's pistol and gun belt lay across the back of the chair. She shoved those into the sack. As an afterthought she picked up his saddlebags. Wilkes had speculated that they contained profit from Tadlock's sales of horses. However much or little it might be, he owed her that for his brutal treatment and for killing her husband.

Tadlock was at the well, his underwear smoldering. He wailed loudly as he emptied a bucket of water over his head. She hurried past him, pausing to drop Wilkes's rifle down into the water, out of reach. She ran to the pen where three horses stood waiting for feed: hers, Tadlock's, and one she supposed belonged to the old man.

Wilkes slouched out from under the shed, rubbing his eyes. He appeared to have slept in his clothes. He demanded, "What's Curly hollerin' about? You didn't shoot him, did you?"

She did not answer him.

He said, "You ought to've. He'll be comin' after you."

Saddling her horse, she said, "Not for a while, he won't." She unfastened Tadlock's rifle scabbard from his saddle, carrying it and the rifle with her. She opened the gate and drove the other two horses out ahead of her. She intended to take them far enough that Tadlock would have to waste a lot of time trying to catch them afoot.

She had no clear idea where she was going. Her intention at the moment was simply to put as much distance as possible between herself and Tadlock. Later she would decide what to do.

She wished now that she had killed him.

CHAPTER 13

Bannister was up and saddling his horse when dawn was still a distant promise. Andy could not see twenty feet.

Bannister said, "Come on. We're losin' daylight."

Andy said, "You can't even see yet. Let's make some coffee first."

"I can see enough. Ain't got time to waste for coffee." Bannister mounted and rode off. Andy and the sergeant saddled quickly.

Joshua said, "He's ridin' like he knows where he's headed."

"I hope when we get there that we can see the place. He talked like it'd be easy to miss."

"Might be better for Mrs. Bannister if we do miss it. I don't know which man to be the most scared of — Mr. Bannister or the man that carried her off."

As light began to spread across the hills, Andy saw a scattering of bleached buffalo bones, all that remained to show for the great slaughter of a few years ago. He thought of the Indians he had encountered earlier in their futile search for the sacred animal. Most of these buffalo had been killed for their hides and nothing more. The meat had been left to feed wolves and other prairie scavengers. Facing starvation, the People had eventually been forced to give up the struggle for freedom and drag themselves to the reservation.

Andy could see why Bannister had not wanted to risk missing the dugout in the dark. It would have been easy to miss even in daylight had Bannister not led the way. Andy saw a rock chimney first, its top extending only a couple of feet above a small hill into which the rude dwelling had been built. Next he saw the brush corral.

"No horses in the pen," Bannister said grimly. "They're already up and gone."

A black dog came from beneath a shed and began barking. A ragged old man followed warily, stopping twice to give the visitors a careful study as if ready to turn and run. He stared at Bannister in disbelief. "Donley!" he exclaimed. "Curly claimed he shot you dead."

"Wilkes, you ought to know not to believe everything he says. How long has he been gone from here?"

"He ain't gone." The old man nodded uneasily toward the cabin. "He's in yonder, ravin' out of his head. I think he's dyin'."

"And my wife?"

"She rode off after daylight and took the horses with her. I'd be gone from here myself if she hadn't left us afoot. Curly went plumb crazy after what she done to him."

Bannister demanded, "What did she do?"

"Throwed fire in his face, a shovelful of coals and hot ashes. Burned him awful bad."

Bannister muttered, "Just a taste of what he's got comin' when the devil gets ahold of him." He turned toward the dugout's wooden door and shouted, "Curly, drag yourself out here."

Wilkes said, "I doubt he can do that. Last time I looked in on him, he was barely able to move. He found my old six-shooter and tried to aim it at me. I took it away from him." The pistol was in Wilkes's waistband. Andy quietly relieved him of it.

From inside, a hoarse voice called, "Who's that?"

Andy called, "Texas Ranger. Come out with your hands up."

"I can't," Tadlock answered. "You'll have to come in."

Andy shoved the door open. His jaw

dropped as he saw a man lying on a crude bed, his swollen face spotted with deep and ugly pits. One eye appeared burned beyond healing, the other pinched almost shut. From the waist up, much of Tadlock's long underwear was gone, blackened remnants clinging to an angry mass of blistered skin. The dingy little room smelled of burned flesh.

Tadlock asked plaintively, "Who are you? I can't hardly see you."

Bannister approached the bed, his voice crackling with fury. "I'm Donley Bannister. You never expected to see me again, did you?"

"Donley!" Tadlock rasped. "But I thought . . ."

"Thought you killed me?" He grabbed Tadlock by his shoulders and shook him violently. "What did you do to Geneva?"

Tadlock shrieked in pain. "Nothin' to what she done to *me*. Burned me to death, pretty near."

Bannister shook him again. "Tell me what you did to her. Answer me, damn you!"

Andy pulled Bannister back from the edge of the bed and said, "Go easy. He can't tell you anything if you kill him."

Bannister's face was scarlet. "I'll kill him, all right, but he's goin' to talk first. Where is she, Curly?"

Tadlock's voice broke. "She done this to me, then she rode off."

Andy decided he had to take charge, for he saw murder in Bannister's eyes. "Tadlock," he said, "I'm a Texas Ranger, and you're under arrest."

"Get me away from Donley. He'll kill me."

"Looks to me like he's got good reason."

"She didn't have no call to burn me alive. My God, look at my eyes."

Bannister said, "Lend me that six-shooter, Ranger. I'll finish what she started."

Andy stepped in front of Tadlock, shielding him. He told Bannister, "You've got a good chance of comin' clear for killin' Cletus Slocum, but this man is helpless. Killin' him would be plain murder."

Bannister stood fuming, his legs braced, his feet a little apart. He said, "Looks like he's near dead already. How was she, Curly? Was she worth it?"

Tadlock whimpered. "Somebody do somethin'. I can't stand this pain."

Wilkes said, "I tried to rub hog lard on him. He screamed like a baby."

Joshua was moved by Tadlock's plight. He said, "Maybe we can take him somewhere."

Wilkes said, "You wouldn't get two miles with him. He was afire when he come runnin' out of that dugout. He sucked in a lot of smoke and flame. I reckon they burned out his innards."

Tadlock coughed up blood. In spite of himself, Andy felt a grudging sympathy for Tadlock. This was a hard way for a man to meet his final reckoning.

He said, "You-all go back outside. There's no point in tormentin' this man any further."

Bannister was grim. He leaned over Tadlock and whispered something Andy could not hear. Andy assumed it was a curse. Then Bannister walked out with Joshua and Wilkes.

Andy stood at Tadlock's bedside, staring at the ruined face, the blistered body. If this had been a wounded animal, he would not have hesitated. But a man, even a wretch like Tadlock . . .

He removed all but one cartridge from Wilkes's pistol and laid the weapon near Tadlock's head. He said, "There's just one bullet. Don't waste it."

Outside, Andy found Bannister digging a grave. He said, "I wouldn't have expected this of you."

Bannister grunted. "I want the pleasure of droppin' him in the hole and throwin' dirt in his face."

A shot sounded from inside the dugout.

Startled, Bannister demanded, "What the hell did you do?"

Andy said, "I gave him a choice."

Reluctantly he reentered the dugout, followed by Joshua and Wilkes. He had seen men die, but he had never seen what could happen when a man held a pistol to his own head and fired. He thought for a moment that he would gag.

Wilkes cursed softly. "This place ain't goin' to be fit to live in now."

Andy went back outside and found Bannister still digging, a bitter look on his face. Bannister said, "I wanted him to die slow, screamin' with every breath. You cheated me out of that."

Andy said, "At least nobody can say that Mrs. Bannister killed him. The only bloody hands are his own."

They wrapped Tadlock in his blankets and lowered him into the grave. Andy said, "I don't know much about prayin'. Anybody want to say somethin'?"

Joshua waited for someone to speak. When no one did, he removed his hat, bowed his head, and said, "Lord, there ain't none of us can say we ain't sinned in your sight, so it ain't our place to speak bad about this man. Whatever wrongs he's done, they're over with now. I hope you can see your way clear to forgive him, and I wish everybody here would too." He glanced at Bannister. "The grave makes everybody equal — saint and sinner, black man and white. Praise the Lord. Amen."

Andy said, "I've heard some high-paid preachers, but I never heard a prayer said better."

Joshua shrugged. "I've talked to the Lord a right smart lately, since I killed Mr. Burnsides."

"Does he ever answer you?"

"Every time."

Andy had checked his fugitive book but found no one in it who fitted Wilkes's description. Two prisoners were enough anyway. He handed the empty pistol to Wilkes and asked, "What are you goin' to do?"

Wilkes said, "I don't think I'll want to stay here anymore. I figure when the lady turns my horse loose, it'll drift back here for feed. Then I'll go look for a better place."

Andy turned to Bannister. "Where do you suppose your wife has gone to?"

"I imagine her first thought was to put as many miles between her and Curly as she could. After that, she might decide to go back to her old home in Erath County.

That'd be southeast of here. Or she might decide to go back to Junction. That'd be pretty near due south. We'll have to try and follow her tracks till we get a clear idea whichaway she's headed."

"You're the tracker. Go ahead."

They traveled until nearly dark before making camp. Andy arose at daybreak. He was dismayed to find that Bannister had slipped away sometime in the night, taking Andy's pistol.

Joshua gazed with worried eyes at Bannister's tracks. "I'm afraid he figures to find her before we do. You reckon he's still got notions about doin' her harm?"

"It's hard to say what's in a man's mind when he's been through as much as Bannister has. We'd better saddle up and go."

In their haste, they skipped breakfast.

After a couple of miles Geneva quit driving the horses that belonged to Tadlock and Wilkes. They followed her a hundred yards, then stopped to graze. She looked back, half expecting to see Tadlock trailing her but knowing he couldn't catch her afoot. She wondered how badly he was burned. Not badly enough to pay for the shame and humiliation he had visited upon her, she thought. She shuddered, remembering the animal violence, as if through her he was taking out all of his angers and pent-up hatreds. She still felt the hurt, the nausea, the loathing.

Despite her eagerness to get far away, she considered waiting in ambush and killing him with his own pistol when he came for his horse. The weapon was still in the sack she had brought from the dugout. She discarded the idea, knowing that to see him would probably set her to shaking so badly she could not hold him in the sights.

She looked about, trying to find her bearings. The rolling plains stretched in all directions as far as she could see, a choppy land of sand and grass, mesquite and scrub oak. Somewhere to the west lay the rugged breaks that marked the eastern edge of the higher and even more extensive staked plains, until recently the domain of Comanche and Kiowa. Surely somewhere in the midst of this far-reaching prairie must be a town where she could buy supplies, and new clothing to replace the tattered and torn remnants that barely covered her.

She would need money, and she had none of her own. She had not yet looked in Tadlock's saddlebags. She unbuckled one side and lifted the broad flap. Wilkes had been right. There *was* money, perhaps several hundred dollars. She felt a momentary lift, tempered only a little by the knowledge that Tadlock had gained it by stealing and selling other people's property. At least now it was in needier hands than his.

When she found a town, perhaps she could buy a buggy. Her body was sore from the unaccustomed horseback travel as well as from Tadlock's harsh treatment. But money was useless unless she could find a place to spend it.

She had been seeing cattle. Where there were cattle there must be a ranch, with people. And she began to feel thirsty. It stood to reason that if she followed a cattle trail it should lead to water. She chose one that appeared to have been heavily used. She gambled that the southward direction would lead her toward water rather than away from it. She hoped that cattle moving along the trail after her would eliminate her tracks and thwart any effort by Tadlock to follow her.

She came eventually to a stream angling southeastward, as they tended to do in this part of the country. It might be a tributary to the Brazos, she thought, or one of the other major rivers that angled across Texas on their long course toward the Gulf of Mexico. At this moment it did not matter which river.

Several cows loafed on the bank, having drunk their fill and now placidly chewing their cud. A couple rose to their feet in alarm and trotted away. The rest watched her with suspicion but chose comfort over flight. She moved upstream from them and dismounted. Her horse dropped its head and began to drink. She lay on her stomach and cupped her hand in the water, sipping eagerly.

Her thirst satisfied, she considered how comforting a bath might feel. Her hands and arms were grimy from two days of travel and dust and sweat. She was eager also to rid herself of whatever physical stain Tadlock had left with her. She feared the emotional stain would remain a long time.

After unsaddling and staking the horse to graze, she removed the badly torn dress and her underclothing, then waded into the water. It was pleasantly cool but not cold. She scrubbed the garments as best she could without soap, then carried them out and spread them across a clump of brush. She reentered the stream and soaked in leisure while her clothing dried in the sun. The water relaxed her. She felt that along with the sweat and grime it carried away whatever remained of the long night with

Tadlock.

Dressed, she built a small fire. She realized that she had left the dugout too hastily. She had grabbed what little food appeared handy, but she had no knife to slice the bacon, nor a pot or can for boiling coffee. She decided to ride farther in hope of finding a house or a cow camp.

Her horse, picketed on the stream bank, jerked its head around and poked its ears forward. A horseman was coming in her direction. For a panicked moment she thought of Tadlock. Reason quickly told her it was unlikely that he was this close behind her.

A small man, not much over five feet tall, rode up with a "Howdy, ma'am."

She was conscious that her remnant of a dress gave her only partial cover. The torn skirt revealed one leg up past the knee. Hunching, trying to cover both the leg and her bare shoulder, she demanded, "What do you want?"

The rider was quick to recognize her embarrassment. He discreetly looked away and said, "Didn't mean to take you by surprise. Looks like your horse might've throwed you off and dragged you. Maybe this'll make you feel more at ease." He untied a yellow slicker from behind the cantle of his saddle and handed it down to her, turning his head while she put it on.

Still not trusting him, she stammered a little. "Th-thank you. I'm sorry you had to see me in this condition."

"I didn't see a thing. I don't need the slicker right now noway. It don't look much like rain."

She guessed him to be in his forties, thin, wiry, his hair partly gray and in need of cutting. His whiskers had not felt a razor in a while. He was a long way from handsome, but his eyes were kindly. He said, "By the looks of things, you've been through a right smart of trouble. Is there any way I can help you?"

"You could tell me how to reach a town. Any town."

"There's one in every direction, but none you could get to between now and night. It ain't far to our house, though. I'd be glad to take you there."

Suspicion still lingered. "*Our* house? Who else besides you? A wife?"

"No, ma'am, just me and my brother Jock. Neither one of us has ever found a woman willin' to put up with two old Scotchmen." He seemed to sense what troubled her. "You don't need to fret about us doin' you harm. We're just a couple of stove-up cowpunchers. Been years since we done any carousin' and carryin' on. McPherson's my name, Scotty McPherson."

Geneva began to ease. Instinct told her this little man was just what he said he was. She said, "I hope you'll pardon me if I seemed rude, Mr. McPherson. You're right, I've been through so much the last couple of days that I don't know up from down."

"You'll feel better when you've had a good supper. I'll saddle your horse for you while you gather up your possibles. I don't believe I heard your name."

"It's Geneva Bannister." As an afterthought she added, "*Mrs.* Bannister."

Geneva had to keep tugging at the slicker to keep it from falling away from the leg crooked over the sidesaddle's horn. McPherson must have had a lot of talk bottled up in him for a long time, for he kept a one-sided conversation going as they rode southward. In time they cut into a wagon road that showed it was used frequently.

He said, "We see a lot of traffic on it. Somebody passes by our place every two or three days. If it's gettin' toward evenin', we invite them to stay all night. Me and Jock love company."

"Do you have many neighbors?"

"Quite a few. A couple of them ain't more than twelve or fifteen miles away. It's a caution how this country's settlin' up."

"What made you and your brother decide to come here?"

"We came down from Kansas with a buffalo skinnin' outfit. When the hide trade dried up, we put our money into cows. Our old daddy always taught us to be of a savin' nature. With hard work and the Lord's help, we're pretty well fixed now."

Geneva expected to be greeted by a barking dog, but their arrival was announced by a screeching peacock instead.

McPherson said, "Don't pay any attention to old Loudmouth. He's our watchdog, but he doesn't bite."

The house was not large. It was built of lumber, box-and-strip style, with a porch facing east, away from the afternoon sun. A little distance in the back were a barn, also of lumber, a low shed, and a set of cattle pens. Chickens pecked around the yard. A milk cow stood waiting at a corral gate.

McPherson said, "We've got just about anything we'd ever need — milk, fresh eggs, a few hogs so we can put up plenty of salt pork. Even got a little garden. Ain't nothin' beats fresh tomatoes."

With two old bachelors living alone,

Geneva expected to see the kind of boar's nest that Wilkes's dugout had been. She was pleasantly surprised to find the homestead neat and well-kept, as if there was a place for everything, and everything was in its place.

A man came out of the house with a milk bucket in his hand. Seeing the riders approaching, he stopped and stared. He was not much taller than Scotty McPherson. The resemblance in their faces told Geneva that this was the brother.

Jock McPherson stared at Geneva. "Where'd you find the stray, Scotty? And why the slicker? It ain't rainin'."

"I'll tell you later. Help her down and I'll put the horses up."

Jock gently eased her to the ground. "I'm Jock. I'm a bit older than my little brother, and a sight better lookin'."

Geneva would not have said that. Like his brother, Jock had neglected the razor for some time, and a haircut would have been a considerable improvement. But crow's-feet crinkled at the edges of the same kindly blue eyes. His broad smile revealed a gold filling in one front tooth.

He said amiably, "You go on in the house and make yourself to home. I'll be in as soon as I finish milkin' the cow."

The inside of the house was as neat as the outside. The furniture was spare but utilitarian. There were only two rooms, one with a pair of cots, a bureau and a mirror. The other was kitchen and living room combined. A coffeepot sat steaming on a wood-burning range flanked by a deep wood box. Shelves lined one wall. A water bucket and a wash pan sat atop a flat cabinet. The kitchen table had only salt and pepper shakers and an empty cup from which Jock had evidently been drinking.

Geneva thought the well-kept house had one thing missing: there were no curtains on the windows. Otherwise it would be easy to believe a woman lived there.

Scotty returned before Jock did. He said, "Ma'am, we need to do somethin' about that yellow slicker, but I'd bet there's not a dress to be found in less than fifteen miles."

She said, "If I had a needle and thread, maybe I could sew this one up a little." That was a forlorn hope. The dress was beyond salvation.

He said, "Would you object to wearin' man's clothes? I'm thinkin' Jock's would be a fair fit."

It would hardly meet the demands of propriety, but neither did her present situation. "Anything would be better than this."

He went into the bedroom and opened a standing cabinet. Rummaging, he brought out a shirt and a pair of trousers. "You might try these, ma'am."

"Are you sure Jock won't mind?"

"Not a bit. They'll look better on you than they ever did on him."

He closed the door to give her privacy. She took off the slicker and the dress, then donned Jock's clothes. They fitted except that the shirt was tight. She had to strain to close the top buttons. She looked at herself in the mirror and wished she hadn't. Her hair was stringy and windblown. She borrowed a comb that lay atop the dresser and did what she could to bring about some order.

Jock had returned from the milking by the time she walked out into the other room. The two brothers looked at her, then at one another. Both grinned. Jock said, "I'll never wear them clothes again. I'll just hang them up to look at and try to remember how good they looked today."

Scotty asked, "Mrs. Bannister, are you a good cook?"

"Fair to middling, I suppose."

"Would you mind takin' charge of the stove this evenin'? We've batched here so long that we've forgotten what a woman-cooked supper tastes like."

"For all your kindness, I'd be glad to."

Scotty brought a ham from a smokehouse out in back while Jock filled the wood box and peeled potatoes. Then the two disappeared outdoors while Geneva kneaded dough for biscuits and cut several slices from the ham. Later she would make gravy from the grease.

She stepped out onto the porch and said, "Supper will be ready in a few minutes."

Both men had shaved off their whiskers. Scotty sat on a bench with a towel over his shoulders while Jock snipped away at his hair. From the looks of things, Scotty had already done the same favor for Jock, if it could be called a favor. Neither man was likely ever to earn a nickel as a barber.

Her heart warmed. These gentle brothers were as far from Curly Tadlock or Quincy Harpe or Wilkes as daylight was from darkness. They revived some of her shaken faith in men.

But she felt she should give warning. Tadlock would not hesitate to kill them if they tried to oppose him. She sat in silence while the McPhersons enthusiastically dove into her cooking. They took turns complimenting her.

Finally Scotty shoved his plate back and

said, "Mrs. Bannister, I wish you could stay here forever."

"But I can't," she said. "I've got to move on." She explained about Donley, leaving out the fact that he stole horses. She told about Tadlock and his shooting Donley, then dragging her away. She did not tell all that he had done to her, but she supposed they sensed the rest of it. "I left him afoot, but I have a dread that sooner or later he'll come looking for me. If he were to find me here . . . I would not wish that kind of trouble on you gentlemen."

Jock shook his head in sympathy. "So now you're a widow lady, and there's a rattlesnake slitherin' around, lookin' to find you. Me and Scotty would be glad to shoot him for you, same as we'd shoot a mad dog. We were both dead shots back in the buffalo days."

Scotty nodded. "We've still got our old Sharps fifty. It'd blow a hole in him you could drive a wagon through."

She argued, "But he might shoot you first. I couldn't let that happen on my account."

Jock said, "At least think about it, ma'am. You could have a home here as long as you want it."

She had stated her case. She knew further argument would be of no use. She would have to leave tomorrow no matter what they said.

Scotty said, "Enough of this gloomy talk. What we need now is some music. Do you like music, ma'am?"

"I do, but I haven't heard any in a long time."

Scotty brought a fiddle down from the bedroom wall. Jock had a harmonica. They played, stomping the wooden floor in rhythm to the music. At times, the wail of the fiddle sounded almost like the bagpipes the men's father would have known. Geneva felt her heart lift. In the warm glow of their friendship, she was able for a while to push Donley and Tadlock to the back of her mind. She even sang along on a few tunes she knew.

She felt she had moved out of a nightmare and into a benevolent dream.

She protested, but they gave her the bedroom and took blankets out onto the porch. "We're used to sleepin' outdoors," Jock said. "We do it for months at a time when we go with our neighbors on roundup."

The bedroom door had no lock. For that matter, the front door did not either. That did not trouble her. She instinctively trusted these men. They gave her a comfortable feeling of safety.

Hating to leave, Geneva stayed longer than she intended the next morning. Breakfast was a slow, drawn-out affair at the kitchen table. At length she asked the brothers, "Don't you intend to go out to work this morning?"

Scotty smiled. "Those cows don't need to see us every day. They take care of themselves pretty good."

Jock said, "It's hard to strike up a good conversation with a cow."

Geneva sensed that they were stalling to keep her as long as they could. She felt flattered, but she could not put down a rising concern that Tadlock might be coming. "I have enjoyed your hospitality, but I had best be moving on."

Outside, the peacock set up a loud screeching. Jock turned his head to listen. "May be somebody comin'."

Geneva's heart leaped. Jock motioned for her to keep her seat. He lifted a rifle from its place on the wall. It was as large as any she had ever seen. She guessed it was the buffalo gun Scotty had spoken of.

He said, "Don't worry. If it's Tadlock, he'll never get a chance to touch you." Jock stood in the doorway, the rifle balanced across his

300

left arm. After a few moments he eased. "Ain't nothin' but Old Man Feeney on his way to town. It must be Saturday."

He went outside. Shortly Geneva heard him inviting the traveler in for breakfast. Feeney turned out to be somewhat older than the McPhersons, thin-shouldered, with a high-pitched voice. He said, "Can't stay but a few minutes. I ain't been on a good drunk in a long time, so I'm overdue." He added, "I sure do dread it."

That this had turned out to be a false alarm gave Geneva partial relief, but a remnant of fear still haunted her. This time it was a harmless neighbor, but the next time it could be Curly Tadlock.

She shuddered. Half an hour later, she regretfully said her good-byes to the McPherson brothers and was on her way south.

The visit with the McPherson brothers gave Geneva a happy glow that lasted a few miles, until it began to be dispelled by the repulsive memory of Curly Tadlock and the horror of seeing Donley shot down before her eyes. She resisted these images, but they came nevertheless, and with them renewed grief over her husband.

Her memory of Colorado City was darkened by her experience with Luther Fleet. In spite of that, she knew she had to pause there for supplies. Her first stop was a ladies' clothing store. The proprietress looked her over critically, for she was still wearing Jock McPherson's shirt and trousers.

Geneva said, "I need to buy a couple of dresses."

"I'll say you do." The woman shook her head as if in sympathy. "Where in the world did you get those clothes?"

"It's a long story. Just get me into something that won't scare the horses."

"Anything would be an improvement. Let me show you what I have."

Geneva walked out wearing a new dress, paid for with a little of the money from Tadlock's saddlebags. The dress was creased where it had been folded and placed on a shelf. She carried a second dress and some undergarments in a bundle beneath her arm, along with Jock's things.

She went then to a livery stable. The stableman gave his first attention to her horse rather than to her. She said, "Would you know where I might buy a buggy and a buggy horse?"

"You've come to the very place," he said, perking up at the prospect of a sale. "I don't have a new buggy, but I've got one here that seldom got out of the barn except to carry an old lady to church. You can't hardly tell it was ever used."

He showed her the buggy. She had no difficulty in seeing that it had been used, though it appeared to be sturdy enough. She had to haggle with him over the price but settled on a figure. At last she could get out of the saddle and ride more comfortably the two hundred or so miles down to Junction.

He said, "I've got a good buggy horse here. I might make an even swap for that saddle horse you've been ridin'."

Geneva had already decided against selling or trading the horse. She reasoned that by all odds it was probably stolen. She had no right to sell it. She intended when she got out of town and out of sight to turn it loose. Perhaps it would return to wherever it had been stolen from. At any rate it would no longer be on her hands and her conscience.

The buggy horse was a brown, none too young but probably serviceable enough. After settling on a price, the liveryman told her, "I forgot to mention that this horse leans a little to the lazy side. You'll need to pop him with the whip now and again.

Horses will take advantage of you if you let them."

"So do some people," Geneva said.

She stopped next at a general store. The balding merchant studied her closely, then said, "I remember you from a while back. You were on your way to meet your husband. I suppose you found him?"

Tight-lipped, she said, "Yes, I did." She did not feel like confiding any more information. Thinking about it brought pain.

He said, "I remember because it was about the same time that some lady put a bullet into a gambler named Fleet." His eyebrows lifted in an unspoken question.

She did not intend to admit anything. "Did it kill him?"

"Sad to say, it didn't. But he'll have to be careful who he cheats from now on. He can't outrun them anymore."

"This lady . . . are the authorities looking for her?"

"If they are, it's to give her a medal. A bunch of people were at the railroad station to watch the sheriff put Fleet on a westbound train. They cheered his leavin'."

Geneva felt some relief in the knowledge that Fleet had not died, though at the time she had wished him dead. At least she did not have a murder charge hanging over her.

She asked, "Do you know a couple of brothers named McPherson?"

"Sure do. Nice fellers, but I can't rightly call them customers. A customer is supposed to spend some money. A merchant will starve to death waitin' on those two."

She handed him a bundle containing Jock's clothes. "Would you set this back somewhere and give it to Jock McPherson the next time he comes? Tell him Geneva said thanks."

Loading the groceries into her buggy, the storekeeper asked, "Whichaway are you headin' now?"

It was conceivable that Tadlock might come along and ask the storekeeper the same question. She told him, "East, toward Fort Worth."

"It'd be a lot easier trip if you took the train. Faster too."

"I'm in no hurry."

But she was. She had the horse moving in a trot as she crossed the railroad tracks. She tried not to look up the dirt street toward Fleet's shack but could not help herself.

She was still glad she had shot him, but glad also that he had not died.

CHAPTER 14

Andy knew the two brothers were lying to him about Geneva. Following what they hoped were tracks of Geneva's horse, he and Joshua had come upon the McPherson place at midday. They found the pair in their house, having their noon meal.

"I'm Jock McPherson," one said, answering Andy's knock on the door facing. "You-all are welcome to have dinner with me and my brother Scotty." He gave Joshua a quick study as if having to make a decision. "Both of you."

Andy reasoned that they had cooked just enough for themselves. He declined the invitation. "We need to be travelin' on. We just want to know if you've seen a woman pass by here on horseback — a woman alone."

Suspicion came into McPherson's eyes. His brother appeared beside him in the doorway and said, "What's this about a woman?"

Jock said, "He wants to know if we've seen one. We ain't, have we?"

The second brother said, "We're two old bachelors. Do you think if we'd seen a woman that we'd've let her get away?" He stepped back inside for a moment, reappearing with a big buffalo rifle in his hands. He demanded, "Would your name be Tadlock?"

That dispelled any doubt Andy might have had about Geneva passing this way. "Tadlock is dead. My name is Pickard. I'm a Ranger. I'm tryin' to find the lady before her husband does."

"Her husband? We thought he got killed."

"She thinks so too. We're tryin' to catch up to her and let her know she may be in some danger."

"Who from, if Tadlock is dead?"

"From her husband."

Jock said, "That doesn't make sense."

"Not to me or you, but we're afraid he's not thinkin' like normal people. He took a crazy notion that she might be better off dead after what Tadlock did to her. We need to catch up to her before he does."

The two brothers stepped back inside and conversed quietly. Returning to the porch, Jock said, "We'll take you at your word."

Scotty McPherson said, "If it'll be of help

to you, Ranger, she was headed from here to Colorado City. Past that, she didn't say, and we didn't ask her."

Jock offered, "We'd be glad to go along and help you find her."

"That won't be necessary, but thanks just the same." Andy started to turn away but paused to say, "She must've made a real impression on you-all."

"That she did. Find her, Ranger, and keep her safe."

Andy stopped just north of Colorado City. He said, "We'll need to pick up some grub. The mule's pack is almost empty."

Joshua said, "I don't dast go into town. They'd grab me for sure."

Andy recognized the risk but saw no safe alternative. As a black, Joshua was likely to arouse less suspicion by riding through boldly with Andy than if he were seen circling the town by himself. He said, "Nobody knows you here except by description. If anybody asks, I'll tell them you're a new cook for the Ranger company."

"I can't even boil potatoes."

"We won't have to give them a demonstration."

Reluctantly Joshua rode into town at Andy's side. The few people they passed on the street gave them no more than a moment's notice. Stopping at a store, Andy said, "You'd better go in with me. You'd draw too much notice waitin' out here by yourself."

Nervously Joshua took his place behind Andy and walked into the store, taking off his hat. He was careful to show the deference expected of his people so nobody would pay him undue attention. The storekeeper, paunchy and balding, laid out the items Andy asked for and added their prices on a piece of butcher paper.

Andy took pains to speak to Joshua like a boss to a servant: "Go open the pack and put these things in it while I settle up the bill."

"Yes, sir," Joshua replied quietly, bowing in the traditional manner carried over from slave times.

Andy glanced at the three other people in the store. All seemed to accept without question the boss-servant relationship he and Joshua presented.

The proprietor recognized Andy. He said, "Ranger, aren't you? As I remember it, you spent some time at Mrs. Kelly's boardin' house, recuperatin' from a bullet wound."

"Yes, I did."

"I suppose that boy is a prisoner?"

"No, I picked him up to cook for my company." Andy considered before he asked, "I don't suppose you've seen a strange lady travelin' through alone? A right nice-lookin' lady?"

"As a matter of fact, I loaded her buggy with groceries."

So Geneva had acquired another buggy. That should mean her trail would be easier to follow, Andy thought.

The storekeeper said, "I remembered her because she'd been here before."

"Did she say what her name was?"

The man thought about it. "I believe she said it was Bannister. If she ever told me her given name, I've forgotten."

"Did she say where she was goin'?"

"Said she figured to head east, toward Fort Worth, but she didn't. A customer told me he met her on the road south. He was taken by her good looks."

Andy understood why she would have lied about her plans. He told the storekeeper, "If anybody asks you, you never saw her, and you've got no idea whichaway she went."

"Does that mean somebody is after her?"

"There's a good chance somebody is."

"I'm deaf, dumb, and blind," the store-keeper said.

As Andy walked out, Joshua was re-tying the mule's pack. Uneasy, Joshua said, "Did he ask you anything more about me?"

"No, I think my first answer satisfied him."

They rode on through town, crossing the tracks. Andy glanced up the dirt street toward the house where Geneva had shot Luther Fleet in the leg. He smiled, mentally revisiting that long night and its aftermath. No jury would have convicted her, he thought.

They cleared the town, but Andy could see that Joshua was troubled. He tried to calm him. "We got away with it that time."

Joshua shook his head. "But Santa Angela lays ahead of us. The closer we get, the more I feel like Daniel goin' into the lion's den. The army'll be lookin' to catch me for desertion, and the law'll be wantin' me on account of Mr. Burnsides."

"We could circle west of town and pick up the trail farther south."

Joshua thought about it. "Everybody is the same color in the dark. Maybe we'll be lucky and get to town in the nighttime. But what if Mr. Bannister gets to his missus before we do?"

"We're travelin' as fast as we can without breakin' down the horses. I don't see how he could be movin' any faster."

"Except he got a head start on us."

They were within twenty miles of Santa Angela when they unexpectedly encountered an army patrol — a white lieutenant and six black troopers. Andy and Joshua had no chance to pull off the trail and avoid them. As the patrol advanced, Andy said, "I'll do the talkin'. You just try to look like you don't understand what it's all about."

Joshua appeared ill. "I know a couple of them men, and they know me. I'm as good as dead."

The lieutenant raised a hand, signaling the men behind him to stop. His expression was severe as he rode a few steps farther. He focused his attention mostly on Joshua. He said, "We are on the lookout for a deserter. Your servant fits his description."

Andy noted that the officer automatically assumed Joshua to be a servant. It would not occur to the lieutenant that a black person might be independent and not be in some way responsible to a white. Trying to present a poker face, Andy said, "I'd bet every man you've got with you would match the same description. They all look pretty much alike to me."

The lieutenant said, "The fugitive is also wanted by civilian law enforcement here on a charge of murder."

"Then it couldn't be this boy. I can't even get him to wring a chicken's neck. Besides, him and me just came down from the plains. Ain't likely he could've been up there and killed somebody down here all at the same time."

The lieutenant signaled for his troopers to pull up even with him. "Some of you know Sergeant Hamlin. Is this he?"

Andy held his breath. Joshua somehow managed to sit stone still, staring at the soldiers, awaiting their answer.

After a long silence one said, "It ain't him, sir. The sergeant is a younger man than this'n."

The lieutenant seemed convinced, if disappointed. He gave Andy a curt nod. "Very well, you may be on your way."

Andy and Joshua rode a hundred yards before either spoke or looked back. Both were sweating. Joshua said, "They knowed, all right. They just wouldn't peach on me."

"He said the sergeant is a younger man."

"I've aged considerable in the last few days."

Darkness fell as they followed the North Concho down to the outer reaches of the village. Andy said, "Looks like we timed it right. We'll ride through the edge of town where they haven't got any streetlamps.

Nobody'll pay us any attention."

Joshua tilted his hat down low and dropped his chin. Andy said, "Make like we're just a couple of cowboys ridin' through." Despite his show of confidence, his nerves were as taut as a fiddle string.

They crossed the Concho on a bridge and cut around to the east of the fort. A sentry challenged them. "Halt! Who goes there?"

Andy's mouth went dry, but he managed to say, "Me."

The sentry stepped closer, so Andy could see him better. The soldier said, "That's no answer. Who are you?"

"John Smith. Me and my hired hand are on our way down to help on the Bismark farm." Andy had heard about the farm. It furnished foodstuffs and horse and mule feed to the army. He added, "If you want anything to eat next winter, you'd better let us pass. Weeds are takin' the corn crop."

"I won't be here next winter. I'm fixin' to get my discharge. But go ahead on before the corporal sees you. He likes to bedevil civilians."

They camped south of the fort and were on their way again by the time the sun was up. To the southeast lay Fort McKavett, where the Ranger company was stationed and where Bethel waited alone for his return. The thought of passing by without seeing her brought sadness to Andy. But he remembered that he had stayed overlong the last time. Moreover, the fewer people who saw Joshua, the better. They would skirt around McKavett, then cut back into the road to Junction.

Just as they reached the point where Andy had decided to leave the trail, they came upon a slow-moving wagon, carrying a farmer and his wife. Andy hailed them. "Pardon me, folks. I'm a Ranger."

Defensively the man said, "I ain't done nothin'."

"I never thought you did. Are you goin' in to Fort McKavett?"

The farmer said, "Yep, we're about to run out of flour and beans, among other things." He gave Joshua a quick study. "Is this boy your prisoner?"

"No, he's my helper."

"Thought you might've caught the boy everybody's been lookin' for, the one that did the killin' over in Santa Angela awhile back. The way they talk, there's some that've already got a rope stretched and ready for him."

Andy hoped his face did not reveal his uneasiness. He dared not look at Joshua. He said, "I'm on a different case. Since you're headed for McKavett, would you mind takin' a couple of notes there for me? One's for my wife, the other for the Ranger camp. The storekeeper'll see that they get to where they belong."

The farmer looked at his wife. She nodded. He said, "I don't reckon we're in any hurry."

On blank pages torn from the back of his fugitive book, Andy scrawled a note to Sergeant Ryker, informing him that he hoped to intercept Donley Bannister at Junction. The other note told Bethel that the mission was taking longer than expected, but he hoped it would end soon and he could return to her. He thought about adding *I love you,* but he suspected the farmer, his wife, the storekeeper, and no telling how many others would read it before Bethel did. Anyway, she should know by now. Once they were married, a man ought not to have to keep telling his wife that he loved her.

The farmer placed the folded notes in his shirt pocket. He said, "We're all keepin' an eye out for that soldier boy. They say some of the sportin' crowd has put up a reward for him. It was one of them that he killed."

When the wagon rolled on, Andy turned to Joshua. "You're too popular around here. I ought to've sent you packin' when we were still up north, and pretended like I never saw you. Come night, you'd better slip away."

"That'd cause trouble for you, wouldn't it?"

"I could truthfully say nobody ever told me officially that you're a wanted man. All I've heard about you has been hearsay. They can't convict a man on hearsay."

"They're liable to try."

"By then you can be long gone. There's a lot of black folks in the East Texas cotton country. You could lose yourself amongst them till the law has given up on you. Then you could go just about anywhere."

"I'd like to go back to where I was before these troubles. I liked bein' a sergeant. The army's one place where a black man can make somethin' of hisself. That's all ruined for me now."

"I wish it was otherwise, but that's how the world is. Maybe someday it'll be different."

"Someday I'll be dead. I'm livin' *now*." Joshua paused. "I reckon I'll stay till we know the lady is safe."

Dusk caught Geneva between Fort Concho and Fort McKavett. Clouds were restless and darkening in the east, suggesting the possibility of a storm. She did not relish the prospect of camping in the rain. She had thought often about rancher Jess Nathan and the hospitality he had shown when she was traveling northward. She had been thinking of him again today, knowing this trail led by his ranch. Her heart lifted as she recognized his place off to the side of the road.

A faint wagon trail led past his barn on its way to the frame house. She pulled onto it. As she passed a goat shed, she saw Nathan by the barn, feeding grain to his chickens. He lifted a hand in greeting and tossed away what remained of the grain. Wiping his dusty palms on his trouser legs, he walked briskly out to meet her.

"Mrs. Bannister," he said, a broad smile creasing his weathered face. "Welcome to a poor man's castle."

She said, "It looks like a castle to me after the nights I've spent camping beside the road. Do you think you could find room for a visitor who wants to keep out of the rain?"

"The house is yours. Go on over. I'll put up your horse and buggy." He took a closer look. "Different horse, isn't it?"

"Different everything." She removed a small bag from the buggy. "Different me too, I'm afraid. But it's a long story."

"I've got all evenin' to listen to it."

His smile gave her more comfort than she had felt since she had left the McPherson brothers' place. It went against her nature to impose on the kindness of people she did not know, but with Nathan it seemed different. Like the McPhersons, he plainly welcomed her company. Her leaning upon him for help did not seem an imposition, at least not a burdensome one. She knew he was pleased to see her.

She carried her bag to the house. Inside, she saw that it was not as neat as the McPhersons', though it was not the boar's nest that Wilkes's dugout had been. It was evident that Nathan regarded the outdoors as his province. The house was primarily a convenience for eating and sleeping out of the weather. What it needed — what Nathan needed — was a woman, she thought.

Maybe this *woman.* She considered the idea but pushed it aside. Donley was too recently dead for her to entertain any such whimsical notions.

Nathan's noon dishes sat in a dry pan, unwashed. She could imagine his rushing through the meal so he could get back out to tend the livestock or his small field. Such niceties as washing dishes could wait for nightfall. She started a fire in the cookstove and set a pan of water on it to heat. She found a broom and began sweeping the floor.

Nathan came in, saw her at work, and said, "You don't need to be doin' that. I'll take care of it in my own time. You're a guest."

"I like to earn my keep." She swept the small accumulation of dirt out the door. "I take it you haven't had supper yet. I'll fix it."

Nathan grinned. "Lady, I wish I could hire you to stay here all the time. But I don't suppose your husband would take kindly to that."

Geneva's face fell. Nathan sobered quickly. He apologized: "I'm sorry if I said somethin' wrong. I meant it as a compliment."

With a catch in her throat, she said, "You couldn't have known. Donley is dead. Murdered."

Nathan mouthed the word *murdered* but did not say it aloud. "That's too bad." His voice was subdued. "Do you know who did it?"

"A man named Curly Tadlock. I'm afraid he's after me now."

"Why would he be after you?"

Geneva did not know how to answer him,

but her silence seemed to tell him enough. He nodded gravely and said, "He won't get you if I can do anything about it. Do you have an idea where he is now?"

She shook her head. "I haven't seen him, but I've had this feeling, this tingling at the back of my neck. I'm being followed."

Nathan's voice hardened. "If he follows you here, he'll wish he hadn't." His gaze went to a rifle hanging on pegs beside the door.

She said, "I'm on my way back to Junction. The sheriff will watch out for me, and I have friends there."

"You've got a friend here too."

Unconsciously she touched his hand, then quickly pulled back. "This is my trouble. I don't want to draw you into it."

"You already have, just tellin' me about it."

They fell silent while she cooked supper. They ate quietly, most of the time avoiding looking at each other. Nathan finally broke the silence. "I'm sorry about your husband. I can imagine the shock that must've been for you, havin' it happen all of a sudden. With my wife, she was sick a little while. At least I had some time to get used to the idea before she died."

"His death wasn't the only shock I had."

She looked at the floor. "I found out he was a horse thief."

Nathan took a minute to absorb that. "I'm sorry. You deserve better."

Geneva sat, hands clasped around a cold coffee cup, and told Nathan what had happened since she left here. She did not describe Tadlock's assault, but smoldering anger in his eyes told her that he sensed what she left out.

He said, "Too bad you stopped at throwin' coals in his face. You ought to've emptied a gun into him."

"I thought about that later. At the time, I just had to get away from there."

As before, he gave her his bed. Instead of sleeping in the barn, however, he carried blankets out onto the porch. He said, "Tadlock might sneak past me at the barn, but he won't get by me on the porch."

For the first time since leaving the McPhersons, she felt comfortable and safe. She did not drift easily into sleep, however. She lay thinking of Donley and trying to remember happy times, but instead she relived the pain and terror Curly Tadlock had forced upon her. Finally, for refuge from the dark memories, she thought of Nathan sleeping peacefully just outside the door. She imagined how her life might have been had she married him instead of Donley. It might not have offered much excitement, but it would not have been lonely. She would always have known where her husband was and when he would be home. She wished Nathan could have come into her life earlier. She might well have made a different choice.

She became aware of raindrops beating against the window. She realized that the slightest wind would blow rain onto the porch where Nathan lay. She arose and lighted a lamp in the kitchen, then threw a wrap around her shoulders and opened the front door. She asked, "Aren't you getting wet out there?"

From beneath a blanket he admitted, "A little."

"Come in here where it's dry."

"I'm in my underwear."

"We're grown people."

He gathered his blankets and brought them inside, covering himself with them. Geneva stoked the coals in the stove and added extra wood. She said, "You're shivering. Come over here where you can get warm."

He put on his trousers, kept dry beneath the blankets. He said, "I'm much obliged."

"Nothing to be obliged for. It's your house."

He said, "It's not the first time I ever slept in the rain. I've seen a lot worse than this one."

"It's enough to give you a chill. I'll fix some coffee."

She was keenly aware of his gaze following her while she ground the coffee and put the pot on the stove. She was pleasantly warmed by his attention.

He said, "Seein' you here in the kitchen takes me back. It reminds me how lonesome this place can be."

"Haven't you ever thought about getting married again?"

"Thought about it, but never done anything about it. I get shy around most womenfolks. Even you, a little."

"There's no need to be shy with me. I've never hurt a man in my life. Well, maybe one or two."

"I'm sure they deserved it. You're a good woman, Geneva."

She brought him a cup of coffee, then dragged a chair up close to his. She felt strongly drawn as she stared at him. He was not handsome in the way Donley was. Time and hardship had cut lines in his face, and she saw loneliness in his eyes. But he had a determined chin that told her he still had a lot of fight in him. Life might have beaten him down some, but it had not defeated him.

She noticed a badly skinned knuckle and took his hand. "You should have done something about this. How did it happen?"

"Tryin' to shut a gate on a cow that didn't want me to stop her. She won." He shrugged it off. "This kind of thing happens all the time when you deal with animals. I don't pay much attention to it."

She let her fingers run slowly over the knuckles, the palm. "They're rough," she said. "They've seen a lot of hard work."

"The Good Book says, by the sweat of thy brow . . ."

"They're honest hands. I like them."

He squeezed her fingers gently. She squeezed back, not wanting to let go.

She awakened at first light and heard Nathan putting wood in the stove and starting a fresh pot of coffee. As she entered the kitchen, he went outside to look around. He returned to say, "I don't see anything amiss. I'll be back as soon as I've done the milkin'."

"I'll have breakfast ready."

He picked up his rifle from beside the door and carried it with him.

At breakfast, they exchanged glances but little conversation. There was much Geneva wanted to say, though she could not bring out the words. She felt that Nathan was struggling with the same problem. She wished she could feel the strength of his arms around her, but she held back, as she knew he was holding back.

She said, "While I clean up the kitchen, would you mind hitching my horse to the buggy?"

Nathan frowned. "Are you sure you want to go?"

"It's best. The sooner I leave, the sooner I can get to the sheriff in Junction."

"This county has a sheriff too."

"But the one in Junction knows me." She remembered the young Ranger who had watched her before she began her journey. "And there is other law around there if he needs help."

Putting away the breakfast utensils, she heard him bringing up the buggy. She saw that a saddled horse was tied on behind. As Nathan came into the house, she asked, "Why the extra horse?"

He said, "I'm goin' with you."

"There's no reason for you to do that."

"There's plenty of reason. I wouldn't want Tadlock to catch you out on the road by yourself."

"I've traveled alone for days."

"You aren't alone now, and you won't be from here on."

She worried. "He would kill you without giving you a chance."

"Not if I see him first."

Geneva was torn between gratitude toward Nathan and fear that he would not be a match for Tadlock. She said, "You're a rancher. What do you know about gunfighting?"

"Enough. I lied about my age and went into the Confederate army durin' the last of the war. I learned to do what I had to, like it or not."

"Even to risking your life for me?"

Nathan hesitated. "You've just lost your husband. It's way too soon for me to be sayin' this, but you're a widow, and I'm a widower. After a suitable time . . ." He left it there.

She felt tears warm in her eyes. "I'm all mixed up inside. So much has happened to me. As you said, we can talk about it, after a suitable time . . ."

Nathan gathered up a blanket, some groceries, and a rifle. He climbed into the buggy and took the reins. Geneva tilted her head to look into his face. It was somber.

Someday, she thought, when a proper time had passed . . .

CHAPTER 15

Andy did not worry much about following the buggy tracks, for he was sure now where she was going. He noted at one point that Geneva pulled off the main trail and went up to a ranch house he remembered from the trip north. The rancher's name, as he recalled, had been Nathan. Geneva had spent the night in the house while Nathan had slept in the barn. From that, Andy had concluded that Geneva was a lady, and Nathan was a gentleman.

A nighttime rain had compromised the tracks leading to the house, but mud had preserved those leading southward away from it. They told him the buggy had been beneath the shed during the storm. He guessed that Geneva had probably spent the night here again. The condition of the drying mud indicated that the tracks had been made as recently as this morning.

He rode up to the front of the house and

shouted, "Anybody home?"

He was not surprised that no one answered. A responsible rancher should be somewhere out on his land at this time of day, not lazing around the house.

He told Joshua, "We've made up a lot of time. Maybe we can catch her before dark."

After a while he noticed something that intrigued him. He said, "See anything about the buggy horse's tracks?"

Joshua said, "Can't say as I do."

"It looks like a second horse is followin' the buggy."

"Mr. Bannister, you think? Maybe he's got between her and us."

Andy saw concern in Joshua's eyes. He knew it reflected his own. Searching for another explanation, he suggested, "It might be there's a horse tied behind the buggy."

"How could that be?"

"That rancher Nathan. I suspected he was taken some with Geneva Bannister the last time. Maybe he's decided to go along and protect her."

"But they think Mr. Tadlock is trailin' her. If Mr. Bannister catches them, they won't be expectin' him to give them any trouble. They'll let their guard down."

"He's apt to figure the worst if he finds her with Nathan."

"Then we'd better lope up."

They put the horses into an easy gallop. At the top of each hill Andy hoped to see the buggy ahead, but again and again he was disappointed. He and Joshua alternated between a lope and a trot, trying to cover distance, yet spare the horses. Finally, toward dusk, he saw a dark form a mile or so ahead. He asked, "What does that look like to you?"

Joshua squinted. "Either a buggy or a wagon. I hope it's the right one."

Closing, Andy saw that it was indeed a buggy. As he had guessed, a horse was tied behind it. He said, "We'd better slow down and announce ourselves before we get too near. I don't know how good a shot Nathan is, but Mrs. Bannister has proven she knows how to handle a gun."

They were more than two hundred yards out when he saw a man jump from the buggy, then help a woman down. He slowed his horse to a walk and motioned for Joshua to trail a little way behind him. A hundred yards out, he shouted, "We're comin' in peaceful."

Joshua said, "That man has got a rifle."

"I saw it. Raise your hands so they can see we mean no harm."

They were within twenty yards before

Nathan stepped out from behind the buggy. He lowered the rifle to arm's length. He said, "We couldn't tell who you were." He frowned, his eyes narrowed. "Seems to me I remember you. Ranger, aren't you?"

"Yes. Andy Pickard's my name."

"Last time I saw you, you were trailin' Mrs. Bannister."

"Still am, or was. I see I finally caught up with her."

"She's done nothin' wrong. You've got no call to badger her now."

Geneva came out from the protection of the buggy and gave Andy a long study. She said, "I remember you from Junction. You trailed me when I left. I thought I lost you a long time ago."

"You did, off and on. I always managed to pick up your tracks sooner or later."

"There's no need now. My husband is dead."

Andy had been trying to think of a gentle way to tell her but had not come up with any that suited him. He decided the best course was to come right out with it, point-blank. He said, "I've got news for you, Mrs. Bannister. Before I tell you, you'd better grab ahold of that buggy and hang on tight. Your husband is not dead."

She shook as if he had struck her. "But

Curly Tadlock shot him. I saw him fall."

"His pocket watch took the slug. He was stunned, but he came around after a while."

Geneva swayed. Nathan put an arm around her shoulder and steadied her. She murmured a few incomprehensible words, then said, "Curly dragged me away so quickly, I didn't know. I thought he was dead."

"He's not, but Tadlock is."

She gasped. "Curly is dead?"

"Stone cold. Shot himself in the head."

"Then I've done all this running for nothing."

"Not for nothin'. You may still be in danger. Last time we saw your husband, he was talkin' wild. He might have it in mind to kill you."

Her face seemed to lose color. "Kill me? Why?"

Andy explained as best he could, though he could not quite understand it himself. "He said after what happened, it might be better if you were dead."

The news seemed to strike Nathan almost as hard as it struck Geneva. He removed his arm from her shoulder and said, "I'm sorry. You don't deserve this."

She said, "Maybe you'd best go back.

There's no reason to get yourself involved in this."

"I'm not leavin' you."

Andy considered their words to one another and the expressions in their faces. He needed no explanation. He said, "We won't make Junction tonight. We'd best find a decent place to camp."

Geneva's pulse raced as they descended the last long limestone hill before entering the outskirts of Junction. She wished for the comforting presence of Nathan beside her, but since breaking camp he had been on his horse, riding beside the Ranger. He had avoided looking her in the eyes. He had entertained a dream, only to see it shattered by the fact that Donley was still alive. She had lost a dream as well.

Joshua trailed behind the buggy as a rear guard. Once when Geneva thought Andy and Nathan were beyond hearing, she summoned Joshua to pull up beside her. She said quietly, "There's enough brush here to hide a herd of elephants. You could disappear in the blink of an eye."

"Yes'm." Joshua's voice was solemn. "Reckon I could."

"Then why don't you? You know what'll happen if you're arrested. They'll send you back to Santa Angela to stand trial . . . if you even live that long."

"If a man's vow ain't worth nothin', then he ain't either. I made a vow to Mr. Andy that I'd stick till we seen this thing through. The minute it's done, I'm gone."

"You may not get the chance."

"That's up to the good Lord. He freed Joshua from the lion's den."

"I believe that was Daniel. Joshua fought the battle of Jericho."

"That's all right too. My name's Joshua."

They heard the sound of a horse, galloping. Andy warned, "Get down from the buggy, Mrs. Bannister, till we see who this is. Anything happens, run for the brush." He drew his rifle and stepped down. Joshua and Nathan followed his lead.

The rider slowed his horse and yelled, "I'm friendly."

Relieved, Andy broke into a smile. "Everybody take it easy. It's just Len Tanner. He's an old Ranger."

Tall, lean, hungry-looking, Len Tanner stopped his horse and bent forward to pat its shoulder. "I was afraid I wouldn't catch you-all. I had to lope up a right smart."

Andy strode forward to grip Len's hand. "Did Sergeant Ryker send you?"

"He got your note. Said I'd better come

and help because you've got a nasty habit of gettin' yourself shot. Headquarters is tired of payin' your doctor bills."

"You've been shot before too."

"Seldom ever. One advantage of bein' skinny is that I don't make much of a target. You-all got anything to eat?"

Andy turned to Geneva. "Would you get him a can of tomatoes or somethin', please? Otherwise he'll complain all the way in to town."

If not that, Len would talk about something else. His jaw was not often at rest except when he was asleep, and not always then.

Andy had to ask, "Have you seen Bethel?"

"Why? Do you think she's gone and left you? She ought to, the way you keep ridin' off and leavin' *her*. If she was mine, I'd set her up on a shelf over the fireplace and just look at her all the time. Or put her in my pocket and carry her with me."

"I wish I could."

Andy and Len trailed far enough behind the buggy that Geneva would not hear their conversation. Andy explained what had happened and what he feared might when they reached Junction.

Len wanted to know about Joshua. He said, "I figured him for that Fort Concho fugitive soon as I took sight of him. How'd you manage to catch him?"

"I didn't." Andy told him all of it.

Len seemed dubious. "You mean he's come all this way with you and not once tried to get away?"

"I haven't even put him under arrest. I've had no official word that he's a wanted man."

"What're you goin' to do about him?"

"I don't know yet."

Troubled, Len said, "You could get yourself in hot water all the way to your chin."

"I've been there before."

Andy took the lead going into Junction. It was a small ranching town, its mostly lumber and stone houses scattered along the North Llano River. Nearing Geneva's frame home, he stopped and told her, "There's a chance he's got here ahead of us. I'll walk through the house and make sure he's not there. You stay out here with Nathan and Joshua."

Len went around to the back in case Bannister should slip out that way.

Nathan dismounted. He said to Geneva, "Might be better if you get down and stand behind me on this side of the buggy." He helped her to the ground and held to her arm. He said, "Nobody's goin' to hurt you

337

if I can help it."

"I know." She leaned against his shoulder, borrowing from his strength.

She noticed two men seated on the edge of a porch across the dirt street and two houses down from her own. Recognition brought a surge of apprehension. She said, "One of them is Vince Slocum. The other is Willy Pegg. Where the Slocums go, Pegg follows like a lost puppy."

Nathan said, "Your husband shot a Slocum, didn't he?"

"Cletus. Vince and Judd are worse than Cletus was, and Finis is the worst of the lot. They must be watching for Donley."

"Did they threaten you in any way after he left here?"

"They knew I had friends who wouldn't tolerate them hurting me. They just watched everything I did, and tried to trail me when I left. I'm sure they expected me to lead them to Donley."

"I almost wish you had." Nathan immediately apologized. "That was an awful thing for me to say. It's just that I can't help hatin' your husband a little. He put you in a bad fix."

Tight-lipped, she said, "It's better if neither of us says anything more. I'm afraid we may have said too much already."

Andy emerged from the house. He said, "I went all the way through it. The bed's been slept in, and the kitchen's been used, but I didn't see Bannister."

Geneva did not have to guess. She said, "Donley's already been here. That's why the Slocums are hovering around like buzzards. They're waiting for him to show himself."

Andy said, "Buzzards just watch for somethin' to die naturally. The Slocums are lookin' for a chance to kill somebody."

Len returned from behind the house, pistol in his hand. Judd Slocum walked ahead of him, his hands raised. Len said, "He was watchin' the rear door. I figured he wasn't up to any good."

Andy said, "Neither are the others." He strode up to them, his rifle across his arm. "I'm puttin' you-all under arrest."

"What for?" Vince demanded. "We ain't done nothin'. We're just sittin' here."

"Is this your house?"

Vince glanced at the two men who flanked him. "Nope."

"Did you ask anybody's permission to sit there?"

"Never saw no need."

"Then you're under arrest for trespassin'. Throw your guns back onto that porch and step out here into the street."

Grumbling, the two brothers and Pegg complied.

Andy said, "There's one of you missin'. Where's Finis?"

"Ain't seen him," Vince said, giving the other two a sharp look that told them to keep quiet.

With these three neutralized, Andy decided one Slocum should not be too much to handle. He told Geneva, "I think it's safe for you to go in the house. If we see your husband coming, we'll stop him before he can reach you."

She cautioned, "I don't want him hurt."

Nathan argued, "But if he intends harm to you . . ."

"He *is* still my husband."

With heartbeat quickening, Geneva stepped up onto the porch, then through the door into the house. She paused, looking around, remembering. Life with Donley Bannister had not been easy. True, there had been good times here when he was at home, but there had been painfully lonely times during periods when he would be gone. Some of his absences were so long that she began to wonder if something had happened to him, or if he might even have abandoned her. His homecomings had brought her brief joy, increasingly tempered by the realization that soon he would be gone again to Lord knew where.

Now, to her regret, she knew where he had been going and what he had been doing. Some things it would have been better not to know.

She smelled tobacco smoke. The Ranger had not been smoking. The scent told her that Bannister had been here, and not long ago. She looked into the bedroom they had shared, often for too short a time. She had made the bed before she left. Now the blankets had been thrown back carelessly. She walked into the kitchen. A dirty plate sat on the table, an empty cup beside it. She felt faint warmth from the stove and found a cooling coffeepot on top. It had not been long since Bannister had cooked and eaten a meal here.

She felt a prickling sensation at the back of her neck. She heard the creak of hinges and froze, a chill traveling down her spine. For a moment she was afraid to turn around. When she did, she saw a pantry door slowly opening. Donley Bannister stepped out into the kitchen.

A startled cry lodged in her throat.

He rushed forward and covered her mouth

with a big, rough hand. He said, "Don't holler. They might come in here shootin'." He lowered his hand, and she gasped for breath. He said, "Yes, It's me. I'm alive. It'll take a better man than Curly to kill me. He wasn't no man at all." He brought his hands up to her cheeks. She shrank back, fearing he was about to choke her. Instead, he kissed her, warmly.

She gasped for breath. "They told me . . ." She could not finish.

"That I figured on killin' you?" He leaned back and stared at her, his face remorseful. He said, "I was like a wild man at first. I told myself I had to kill Curly, and I had to kill the woman he ruined, like I'd shoot a crippled horse. But when I saw him layin' in his own blood like a sheep-killin' dog, I realized what a worthless piece of nothin' he was."

He bent forward and kissed her again. "You're a beautiful woman, Geneva. Nothin' Curly did could change that. I kept closin' my eyes and seein' your face. I knew I could never hurt you. But I got to worryin' that the Slocums might. I had to get back home and see that they didn't."

She tried to speak but had difficulty controlling her voice. Tears burned her eyes. "They must've known you were here."

He said, "I tried not to let anybody see me come in last night, but somebody did. When I got up this mornin' I saw the Slocums, bidin' their time. They didn't have the guts to rush the house, but they knew sooner or later I'd have to come out."

Geneva strained to speak. "There are two Rangers. They'll protect you and take you to the sheriff."

"It's a good ways to the jailhouse. All a Slocum needs is one lucky shot."

"Perhaps you should never have come home."

"I had to. I had to see you again even if it meant takin' a stand against the whole Slocum family."

A shadow came up behind Bannister. She recognized the young Ranger's voice: "Back off, Bannister. I don't want to shoot you."

Geneva said, "It's all right. He's not going to hurt me."

Jess Nathan rushed into the house. He demanded, "Geneva, are you all right?" Anxiously he placed both hands on her shoulders.

She said, "I'm fine." She looked quickly at Bannister, knowing he had to have noticed.

Gravely the Ranger asked Bannister, "Are you sure you've gotten over those notions you had?"

Bannister said, "I didn't have them very long. Look at her. She's still as pretty as she ever was. I could no more kill her than I could cut off my arms and legs. She's part of me."

In spite of what he was saying, she knew she was not the same woman as before. She never would be again.

Bannister asked, "Geneva, do you think we can ever get back to where we were?"

She could not give him the positive answer he wanted. She said, "We can try."

Bannister turned to Nathan. He asked, "Are you a Ranger too?"

Nathan said, "No, just a friend."

"Right now I need all the friends I can get."

"I'm not sure I'm your friend, but I'm hers."

Bannister grimaced and turned his attention to Andy. "Think you can get me to the sheriff's office without the Slocums shootin' me?"

"We're sittin' on all of them but Finis. We don't know where he's at."

"Finis, eh? Could I keep my pistol till we get there?"

Andy shook his head. "I'm afraid not. It would bust hell out of forty-'leven regulations." He reached out to receive the weapon.

Bannister shrugged. "I never thought I'd be glad for a Ranger escort. When do you want to start?"

Andy said, "I don't see anything wrong with right now." He frowned. "I looked through the house before I let her come in. Where were you hidin'?"

Bannister pointed with his thumb. "The pantry."

"I never saw it, but I'll never miss another one."

Bannister said, "You told me everybody thinks I'll be acquitted for shootin' Cletus Slocum."

"That seems to've been the general opinion around here."

"What about the horse business?"

Andy cast a glance at Geneva as he thought about it. "You didn't steal any around here, did you?"

Bannister said, "Even a bird knows to keep its nest clean." He extended his hands. "Goin' to handcuff me?"

"I don't see that as necessary." Andy went to the door for a careful look outside. He said, "Wish I knew where Finis was."

Bannister said, "He's hidin' somewhere. Probably hopin' for a clear shot."

Andy grunted. "That does cloud the picture." He stepped out onto the porch and beckoned for Bannister to follow. "Stay close behind me."

"He wouldn't mind shootin' you to get to me."

"He may think about it some. Everybody knows you don't live long when you kill a Ranger."

Len's face fell as Bannister walked out onto the porch. "He was in the house with his wife all that time? He could've killed her."

Andy said, "But he didn't."

Bannister and the two Slocum brothers exchanged heated glances. Vince hissed, "You better be thinkin' about your last words, Donley, because you ain't got much time."

Andy said impatiently, "I want you Slocums to walk two paces ahead of us. You'd better hope your brother Finis doesn't try anything, because one of you might get in the way of a bullet."

Vince protested, "You've got no right to treat us thisaway."

Andy said, "Sue me." He turned to say to Geneva, "Stay in the house till it's over."

She started to argue. "But . . ."

Nathan said urgently, "Please, Geneva. Do

what he says."

Bannister cut a glance toward Nathan but said nothing.

Geneva retreated to the porch and stood at the door, watching.

Joshua was unarmed. Because of his fugitive status, Andy thought it best to leave him that way. He said, "You stay behind us. Walk alongside Bannister."

Len said, "I was afraid you were fixin' to give him a gun."

"I considered it." Andy said to the Slocums and Pegg, "Now, you three, start walkin' toward the jailhouse." He poked Vince in the back with the muzzle of his rifle to emphasize that he was serious.

Vince grumbled, "Damned high-handed Rangers, you think you're the kings of the world. We've got a right to even the score with Donley. An eye for an eye, that's what the book says."

Andy retorted, "Somebody must've told you that. I'll bet you never read it yourself."

"Our old daddy taught us to not let any man walk over us."

"Everybody has told me it was a fair fight."

"Everybody wasn't there."

They reached the end of the block. Andy said, "Now stop." The street took a slight turn to the right. He doubted that anyone purposely laid the town out like that. This was probably the way the original wagon trail came in, so the trail gradually became a street as houses went up along its length.

Andy said, "Len, I don't like the looks of it. How about you goin' ahead of us and watchin' out for boogers?"

"Just what I was about to suggest."

Andy was in a heightened state of alert, his gaze searching along the street for sign of ambush. He saw Len pause and give serious study to a white church with a bell tower extending well above its roof. Anyone waiting in its top would have a wide-open view of the street. After a minute Len continued up the street almost to the courthouse. He turned and started back, giving Andy a come-on signal.

Andy said, "We're goin' ahead. You Slocums stick close together."

They had gone only a short way when something struck the bell and made it clang. The two Slocums and Pegg suddenly cut to the left and broke into a run, leaving Andy and the others in the open.

Instinctively Andy swung the rifle in their direction, then realized he had no reason to fire on them. He also realized that the striking of the bell had been a prearranged signal. He turned quickly, bringing the rifle's muzzle back toward the bell tower. He saw a movement there. Before he could draw a bead, he saw a flash and felt a sharp burn along his extended right arm. The arm went numb. The rifle fell from his hands.

A second shot came from the tower, its echo lost amid pistol fire from Len and Nathan. Joshua dropped to one knee and picked up Andy's fallen rifle. He fired once. The man in the tower fell backward against the bell, causing it to ring. Joshua fired a second time. Andy caught a glimpse of a bloodied face before the man fell inside the tower, out of sight.

Nathan said, "Good shootin'. You must've been some soldier."

Joshua said, "The army gave me a sharp-shooter medal."

The Slocums stopped running. Vince turned and shook his fist, crying, "Murder! Everybody come see. It's murder!"

Len fired, the bullet kicking up dust near Vince's feet. Vince set out running again. Judd Slocum raced after him. Pegg knelt in the street, sobbing in helpless fright, begging that nobody shoot him.

Len said, "I can catch them if you think I ought to."

Andy said, "It was Finis did the shootin'. The others will get theirs one of these days."

He grasped his burning arm. Blood trickled warm between his fingers.

Andy turned and saw for the first time that Bannister was on the ground. He asked urgently, "Are you all right?"

Bannister grunted and raised up partway to his knees. His face was going sallow. "Hell, no. That damned Finis got me square in the gut. And no pocket watch this time." Blood spilled around the hand he held pressed against his stomach.

Andy said, "We'll get you to a doctor."

Bannister wheezed, "Better call a preacher instead. There ain't no doctor goin' to fix a hole this big."

Townspeople were starting to converge from all directions. Bannister tried to hold a sitting position but could not. He sank to the ground on his back. Voice fading, he asked, "Where's Geneva?"

Geneva came running up the dirt street and pushed her way through the gathering crowd. Trembling, she dropped to her knees beside Bannister and took his limp hand.

He seemed to have trouble seeing her. He whispered, "Geneva, I'm sorry."

She cried, "I'm sorry, too. I wish you hadn't come home."

"Had to. Had to see you." He struggled for breath. "Don't cry over me. I lied to you.

I shot Cletus Slocum like Pegg said. Never gave him a chance." His eyes dulled. His breathing slowed, then stopped.

Geneva wept. Nathan waited a little, then gently helped her to her feet. "I'll walk you home," he said.

She whispered, "I wish you would."

"I'll take you to my place if you'd like."

"Sometime. Not yet a while."

Andy watched them as they walked away, Nathan's arm around her shoulder. He closed Bannister's eyes and placed the man's hat over his face. He stood up, gripping the burning arm.

Len said, "I swear, you got yourself bloodied again."

"I've had a dog bite me worse. I wish you and Joshua would go over to the church tower and make sure about Finis." He looked around. "Where *is* Joshua?"

Len had a false innocent look that usually gave him away. "Well, I'll swun. After the shootin' stopped, he must've took it in his head to leave. I'll go lookin' for him in a day or two, when I get time. Right now I've got to get you patched up and take you back to Bethel."

Bethel. Andy spoke the name aloud. It was like music.

Len said, "I'll turn in the report on this.

351

I'll say you shot Finis. No use stirrin' up a lot of questions about how that soldier boy came to be here."

Andy nodded. "That's best." A white lie, well considered, could sometimes serve justice better than the raw truth.

Len complained, "Bethel's goin' to be real peeved with me, lettin' you get shot again after I promised I'd look after you. I swear, boy, you're an awful burden to us."

Andy and Len rode toward the frame house at the edge of Fort McKavett. Len had talked all the way up from Junction, his subjects ranging from the changing weather ("It seems to get hotter nowadays than it used to") to horses ("Seems to me they was better in the old days before so much mustang was bred out of them") to Geneva Bannister's future.

Len said, "She's a mighty good-lookin' widow. Maybe I ought to go callin' on her myself, after a respectable time."

Andy thought about Jess Nathan. "I suspect her future is already taken care of."

Len shrugged. "My skirt-chasin' days are over with anyhow. I'm too set in my ways. Any woman I married would probably wind up shootin' me, and no jury would convict her."

"What'll you do when you get too old for Rangerin'?"

"By that time you and Bethel will have a houseful of kids. I'll take my pension, settle down next to your place, and help you-all raise them."

"You've got no guarantee that they'll ever give you a pension."

"Then I'll just bum off of you. I don't eat much." Len reined up. "This is far enough. I don't need another lecture from Bethel about me lettin' you get yourself hurt. I'll tell the sergeant not to look for you today. Right now you'd best report to a higher authority."

"Are you sure you won't stay? She'll probably fix us a good dinner."

"Like I said, I don't eat much. There's times when two are just right, and three are one too many." He rode off in the direction of the Ranger camp.

Bethel walked out onto the little porch, excitedly waving her hand. Andy put his horse into a trot and was glad Len had ridden on.

ABOUT THE AUTHOR

Elmer Kelton of San Angelo, Texas is a native Texan and author of fifty Western novels. He has won many awards for his work and has been recognized as the Greatest Western Writer of all time by the Western Writers of America, Inc.